ROCK CREEK

C. J. PETIT

Printed in the United States of America

First Printing, 2017

ASIN: 9781091766525

TABLE OF CONTENTS

PROLOGUE

August 14, 1885
Rock Creek, Wyoming

Otto Krueger was mad, a seething, fuming, ready-to-start-trouble mad. He was tired of the railroad and he was tired of the Chinks.

Whenever the railroad needed money, they cut wages and raised prices at the company store, and it had been fourteen years since the big strike that was supposed to set things right. *But what did these bastards at Union Pacific do back then? Did they negotiate with the miners?* They didn't even bother coming out to Wyoming to talk to them. They just sat in their fancy offices in Omaha, fired all the workers and imported hordes of Squareheads to do the job for less. Four years later, after another strike, they brought in more Chinks to work for damn near nothing. Now there were over six hundred of the slanty-eyed usurpers working right alongside the whites, and they worked for so little, it kept the white miners from making a living.

Over the past few weeks, there had been scuffles in the mines, but they had been nothing more than a pin prick and didn't even draw a glance from the powers that be. Otto wanted the Chinese out, and if the company wouldn't do it, the union would.

Otto was the Sergeant at Arms for the miners' union, the Knights of Labor, but it wasn't much of a union. Wages were stagnant, the hours grew longer, and they couldn't do a damned thing about the housing either, but the union was all they had. It was the white miners' weapon more than a negotiating group because they knew that they'd never get their way by talking.

They knew the only way to make things happen was with a bunch of riled up miners all in one place and that was Otto's specialty. In any other town or settlement, he would have been called a thug, but in Rock Creek, he was respected by the white miners and feared by the Chinese. He was respected as a man who got things done and didn't care a lick about his methods.

He knew that something had to happen, something impressive that would catch the eyes of those potbellied, suit-wearing, smug moneygrubbers in Omaha. He envisioned a massive attack on Chinatown, the enclave across the tracks where all the Chinks lived. They didn't even try to speak English for God's sake! They were nothing more than ignorant savages with their long hair, just like them damned Injuns, and just like the Injuns, Otto thought that the only good Chinaman was a dead Chinaman.

The attack would be easy, but the key was to convince the company to accept their demands and get rid of those Orientals. The Union Pacific would probably send in the usual lower level executive muckety-mucks at first to try to get them to behave themselves and to get everyone back to work, but Otto couldn't let that happen.

He needed to keep them out of Carbon County, away from Rock Creek and the other Union Pacific mining towns. When that first effort failed to calm things down, the company would be forced to call in the Federals like they did after the other two strikes. His question now was how to avoid the army from reaching Rock Creek in the first place. It was the biggest obstacle in his plan to get rid of the Chinese and make things right.

Otto leaned back in his homemade chair still deliberating on how to prevent the army from arriving. The troops were always the big issue and once the Federal government got involved, he knew they had no chance to carry their plan to their desired conclusion.

He heard the door open, glanced up and saw John Jameson enter and close the door behind him. Jameson hadn't been there long, but Otto knew the man would do anything he asked, up to and including murder. He'd drygulch someone without a thought which is what he needed now. Otto didn't trust him, but he had his uses.

"Otto," Jameson said as he approached Krueger, "I heard that the U.P. is sending some vice president to investigate what's happening here. The guy's name is Wilson."

Otto shook his head and slapped his right hand on the table as he cursed, "Damn it all to hell! Already? We haven't done anything that bad yet. Why would they send him now?"

John grinned and said, "Maybe that foreman who stopped the last beating sent them a wire. You oughta be better friends with the telegraph operators."

Otto glared at Jameson but held his temper. He needed him now and couldn't afford to have him as an enemy.

"Maybe so, but this might screw up our plans before they even got started."

"Want me to take him out?" Jameson asked casually.

Otto took a few seconds to ponder the question, but the timing wasn't right yet. He needed to come up with a fix to the Federal issue.

"Not yet," he replied, "But I do need him delayed for a while. We need to make things too hot around here for them to send him in and then I need to figure out a way to keep out the army. I'll tell you what we can do. Let's stir the pot a bit. Beat up a few more Chinks and give them notice to leave town. Then I want you to report to the sheriff that a lot more violence is on the way."

"What good does that do us?" Jameson asked.

"The sheriff won't want some big wig killed while he's supposed to be keeping the peace. He'll warn Wilson and anyone else they send to stay away, and then when we're ready, we'll give him a reason to send for the big boys from Omaha."

"Sounds good to me."

"But I want you to do something else for me. I need you to find out where that Wilson character is staying. My guess would be Cheyenne. You track him down and keep an eye on him. If it looks like he's fixing on coming down here even if the sheriff says he shouldn't, then you kill him, but not before. If you play your cards right, you could even pump some information out of him."

"When do you want me to set out for Cheyenne?"

"Take the train the day after tomorrow. I'll front you some union cash to keep you going for a couple of weeks. It shouldn't take longer than that."

"I'll pack some things and be on my way," Jameson replied.

He hoped that the Union Pacific man ignored the sheriff's warning and still tried to leave Cheyenne. He didn't like just sitting around watching. John Jameson was a man of action.

———

Tom Wilson and his wife Emily stepped off the afternoon train onto the main platform at the Pine Bluffs station. They had planned on going through to Cheyenne, but Tom had been directed at the last minute to check on some bottlenecks at the large cattle shipping pens in Pine Bluffs.

As they walked down the main street toward the hotel at the end of the roadway, Emily spied a large house with a placard reading: Mathias Boarding House.

"Tom, why don't we try here instead of the hotel. It looks homey, and we wouldn't have to go out to eat."

Tom simply nodded, knowing better than to challenge his wife on all matters not involving tracks or anything that used them. So, they turned toward the house and because his hands were full of their travel bags, Emily swung the whitewashed picket fence gate open to allow her husband to enter then closed it behind them.

They soon stepped up onto the wide porch where Emily knocked on the door and then they waited. A few seconds later, a fairly tall young woman with a tired look in her eyes came to the door. Tom guessed her age to be in the mid-twenties, but she looked older because of her fatigued appearance.

"We just arrived from Omaha on the train and we're interested in renting a room," Emily said with a smile.

"Why, of course," she replied returning Emily's smile, "come right in. I'm Barb Mathias."

As they followed her through the foyer into the large house's parlor, Emily said, "My name is Emily, and this is my husband Tom Wilson."

"It's nice to meet you both," Barb replied.

They walked past the parlor down the hallway into the well-kept house where Mrs. Mathias pointed out the sitting room and the dining room. They then retraced their steps through the parlor before she led them upstairs to their room. It wasn't luxuriously appointed by any means, but it was clean and suited their needs.

Mrs. Mathias then said, "The bathroom is at the end of the hallway. If the door is open, it's unoccupied. You're my only guests for the moment, so there won't be a line at the door. Rent is a dollar a day or five dollars per week including all meals, of course. In fact, if you'd like, I can fix something for you now. I imagine you're ravenous after that train ride."

"Thank you," said Emily, "That would be wonderful."

The Wilsons' trunk was delivered onto the porch while Mrs. Mathias was showing them their room, so Tom had to trot down to the first floor to lug it upstairs.

Barb told them that if they'd like, they could store the large trunk in an adjoining spare room as theirs was the only one occupied of the six bedrooms upstairs.

Tom Wilson accepted her offer and deposited the trunk in room four while they would sleep in room two.

Barb then let the Wilsons unpack as she returned to the kitchen to prepare a quick light meal. She had baked biscuits earlier that morning for her and her daughter Beth, so she set some on a plate then she went into the cold room, took out the ham, some boiled potatoes and a crock of butter.

She put on a fresh pot for coffee then scooped some butter into a frypan, chopped up the potatoes and added some chopped onion. She put a smaller frypan next to the bigger one and placed two thick slices of ham onto its already hot surface then sprinkled some salt and pepper on the potatoes before using the spatula to mix the hash browns.

By the time the Wilsons finished putting away their things and returned to the first floor, the ham was already on plates, and the hash browns were almost ready for her only guests.

Emily and Tom Wilson entered the kitchen, and Barb turned, saying, "If you'll have a seat in the dining room, I'll be right in with your food."

Emily gave Tom a mild shove toward the kitchen table and replied, "Nonsense. If you don't mind, we'll eat here and hope you'll join us. It's been ages since I've talked to a normal woman."

Barb couldn't help but smile at the comment, wondering what made her a 'normal' woman.

After placing all the food, flatware and coffee on the table, Barb took a cup of coffee and joined them.

Emily took a sip of coffee and asked, "So, Mrs. Mathias, I'm sure you're wondering why I called you a normal woman, or am I wrong?"

Barb laughed lightly and replied, "I was a bit intrigued, to be honest."

Emily pointed her index finger at her husband and said, "That embarrassed gentleman sitting over there pretending to be eating but is really wishing I'd behave myself, is a vice president with the Union Pacific Railroad. Ever since he achieved that lofty position, it seems that the only women I get to meet are 'proper' women who only wish to speak of the latest fashions or the opera or other concerns of Omaha society. For a woman who grew up on a farm outside of Council Bluffs, Iowa it's enough to drive me mad. If I hear about the benefits of bustles once more, I swear I'll scream."

Tom Wilson rolled his eyes as he took a bite of his hash browns. This was expected and appreciated behavior from his wife, and he still enjoyed everything about his Emily. His faux embarrassment was just his part to play in her enjoyment.

Emily saw the eye roll and laughed before saying, "See what I mean? I'm an eternal embarrassment to my poor husband."

Then she asked, "What about your husband, Mrs. Matthias? Surely, you don't embarrass him."

Barb Mathias calmly replied, "I'm a widow, Mrs. Wilson."

Emily's smile evaporated before she said, "Oh, I'm sorry. I've exceeded my usual rudeness."

"No," Barb replied, "it's perfectly fine, Mrs. Wilson. It's been quite some time now."

"Please call me Emily. Do you mind if I call you Barb?" she asked.

Barb smiled and answered, "Not at all. Everyone does. Thank you, Emily."

Before either of them could add to the conversation, they heard the front door open, close, and was then followed by the sound of small feet pattering down the hallway accompanied with, "Mama! I'm home!"

Emily and Tom turned to the hallway as a small girl shot into the kitchen and suddenly stopped, her eyes growing wide as she stared at the Wilsons.

"Oh!" said the girl, "Excuse me. Who are you?"

Emily was charmed immediately and replied, "My name is Emily. What's your name?"

"I'm Beth, and I live here with my mama," she answered as Barb's face split into a mother's warm smile.

Barb set her coffee cup on the table and asked, "So, how was your first day, Beth?"

Beth stepped slowly towards her mother still glancing at Emily who hadn't lost her smile and replied, "School wasn't so bad. Some of the other children were bad, though."

Barb looked up at Emily and explained, "It's Beth's first day of school. She was worried from the moment she awakened this morning until I watched her enter the schoolroom."

Emily grinned at Beth and said, "I remember my first day at school and had to face our teacher, Miss Ward. Of course, we all thought she was a witch in disguise and called her Miss Wart."

Beth giggled and said, "Miss Clancy doesn't have a wart, but I don't think she likes children very much."

As much as Emily wished she could stay and talk to the charming little girl, she was tired from the trip and knew that Barb would want to spend some time with her daughter, so she thanked Barb for the food and ushered her husband up to their room.

After the Wilsons were gone, Beth asked, "She's a nice lady. Is she going to be here very long?"

Barb picked up Beth and set her on her lap as she replied, "I don't know, sweetheart. I hope so. We could use the money."

Beth kissed her mother on the cheek and said with a child's enthusiasm, "Don't worry, Mama. It will be all right."

Barb gave her precious daughter a hug and replied, "I hope so, Beth. I hope so."

———

The next morning, right after breakfast, Tom Wilson went down to the stockyards to find out why he'd been diverted in his trip to Rock Creek.

There had been delays in the cattle shipments and he needed to find out the cause and get it fixed. He hadn't been surprised at all when Emily had insisted on walking Beth to school that morning, ostensibly to give Barb extra time for cleaning up after breakfast. He knew how badly she had wanted a child but had never even conceived, leading her to believe she was barren. They were talking about adopting but simply hadn't gotten around to it.

When they had returned to their room after their brief introduction, Emily had talked extensively about Beth and that had led to the subject of adoption again. He promised Emily that they'd start the process when they returned to Omaha because he would do anything to keep Emily happy but still held out the hope that they would still have their own child.

————

While Tom Wilson was inspecting the books in the stockyard office the afternoon's westbound train arrived, and John Jameson stepped off the platform in Pine Bluffs.

He had been frustrated by the time he had spent in Cheyenne looking for that Union Pacific trouble maker and had finally realized he wasn't there and had taken the train to Pine Bluffs, the only other town of any size before Rock Creek. He stepped down onto the dirt street and walked toward the only hotel in town still in a foul mood.

He passed the Mathias Boarding House without a glance as he marched quickly along reaching the Pine Bluffs Hotel ten minutes after leaving the train.

As he crossed the hotel's threshold, he noticed a young woman standing behind the desk sorting mail and stepped loudly toward the desk to announce his presence.

She stopped with an envelope still in her left hand then turned to greet him.

"Good morning, sir. How can I help you?"

Jameson wasn't in the mood for cheerful, so he thought he'd balance that out with a little extra surliness.

"I just got in on the train and don't need no kid pretendin' to be nice to me. What I need is to find a friend of mine who might be in this hotel. His name's Thomas Wilson. Is he here or not?"

He was pleased to see her smile vanish.

"No, sir. We don't have anyone by that name registered here."

"Damn it! Are you sure? If you're tryin' to steer me wrong, I'll be mighty upset, and you don't want me upset; do you?"

"No, sir," she replied, confused and fearful of his hostility.

"There any other hotels in town?" he asked as he glared at her.

"No sir. And I'm positive that no one is registered here by that name. You might want to try Mrs. Mathias' boarding house at the other end of town. She rents out rooms, so your friend could be there."

"Yeah, I'm sure it's a wonderful place, too. Well, you were no help at all, so why don't you go back to do what you're doin' and forget I was here."

She didn't reply but simply watched as Jameson turned on his heels and marched out the door then released a long breath of relief that the nasty man was gone.

Jameson figured that even if Wilson wasn't at the boarding house, he'd stay there because it would be cheaper, and he didn't fancy this hotel anyway.

He maintained his bad humor as he stomped down the boardwalk until it ended and then kept up his stride until he reached a white house with a sign out front that read Mathias Boarding House then pushed open the gate and left it open as he headed for the porch.

After crossing the porch, he knocked on the door and just a few seconds later, Barb Mathias swung it wide.

"Yes?" she asked.

"I need a room, maybe for a few days."

"Please come in," she replied already feeling uncomfortable having the sinister-appearing man walking behind her as she entered the parlor.

He entered the house glancing around to see if Wilson was in the house but not finding anyone.

"Rooms are a dollar a day and five dollars for a week," Barb said as she turned to face him.

"Alright," he said as he handed her a silver dollar.

She pocketed the coin then led him upstairs and showed him to his room, pointed out the washroom at the end of the hall and told him that meals were at seven, noon and six o'clock in the dining room. There was also a sitting room if he wished to socialize with the other guests which she didn't think likely. Barb then hustled down the hallway, stepped quickly down the stairs and returned to the kitchen.

When she returned, Emily set down her coffee cup and asked, "New guest?"

Barb nodded, "If you could call him that. He's one of those men that just gives me the creeps. You know the type, I'm sure."

"Too well," Emily replied.

After Barb had made her hasty retreat, Jameson began unpacking his travel bag.

"Socialize," he muttered to himself. *Who talks like that?*

But just before she had gone, he had asked, "You said you had other guests. How many are there?"

"Just the Wilsons, a couple from Omaha."

"Bulls-eye," he thought.

But then she had said he was here with his wife. *What the hell for?* This might make his job tougher, but it really didn't matter that much to him. If he had to kill the woman too, it wouldn't bother him a bit. He'd done it before. Granted, she was just a whore and the local law didn't even bother investigating her death, but it had bumped his death count to four. He expected that number would reach six before he left Pine Bluffs.

———

Just before the evening meal, Jameson woke up from a nap, rubbed his eyes and sat on the bed trying to reorient himself. Then he stood, stretched, pulled on his jacket and tapped the pistol in his right pocket. He wished he had the go-ahead from Krueger and just end this today. He still smiled knowing it wouldn't be long and he was close to his victim or victims, if necessary.

He walked downstairs to the dining room to meet the damned Union Pacific man and found the Wilsons already there. Not surprisingly, he didn't like the looks of them from the moment he laid eyes on them. It was bad enough that he worked for that damned railroad, but he looked like one of those all-superior types that thought he was better than anyone else. He sat smiling at his pretty wife making sure he was using the right fork and even had a napkin spread across his lap. What a fancy gentleman! John Jameson didn't like him one bit.

"I'm going to enjoy this job," he thought as he walked into the dining room.

Tom Wilson looked up as he entered and said, "Good evening. Just get here?"

"Yeah. Figured that out all by yourself, did ya?"

Tom knew the type, so he just shrugged and went back to eating as Emily looked at Jameson and concurred with Barb's assessment of the man. He gave her the creeps as well.

Barb delivered their food and smiled at the Wilsons as she did but left after leaving the dishes and would wait until Jameson left the table before cleaning up.

————

After dinner, Jameson left the house and did some exploring around Pine Bluff. His first priority was to find an escape route after shooting the railroad man and probably his wife. He didn't have a horse, so he was limited to where and how far he could go.

He scowled when he thought about it, annoyed that he hadn't asked Krueger about a horse before he left Rock Creek. He didn't have a horse there either, but he should have been able to pry some more treasure out of Krueger to buy one, but it was too late now.

He walked the main street and then the lone side street which joined the primary road at the western end and turned north. It was a lot shorter than the main thoroughfare, if the dusty byway deserved the name and ended at a whitewashed church. He noted that there was a forest of oak, elm and cottonwood that ran along the back edge of the town and snickered. There was not a single pine tree to be seen. *Pine Bluffs. Ha!*

The opposite side of town had no trees at all. It just backed up to some low hills covered in prairie grass, so there were no good escape routes in that direction, but that forest would be worth checking out. He took the alley behind the boarding house and passed by his temporary residence before walking behind several more houses, two of them made of brick. He had a passing thought of robbing their obviously well-to-do occupants, but quickly discarded the idea. He had a real mission this time.

The alley was his best bet to get away after he did the job. He'd shoot the man, go out through his room's window onto the porch then cross the alley and into the woods. *But where would he go after that?* He wouldn't be able to take the train because they'd be watching for that. He needed a horse and a hideout.

He returned to the boarding house and gave Mrs. Mathias another four dollars for the rest of the week and went upstairs to his room. He was getting restless already and wished that Krueger would launch his plan sooner rather than later.

———

The next day, Jameson walked east from the town along the alleyway. The land swelled as it followed the contours of a gentle hill. He then noticed that the forest turned to the north shortly after the last building. In front of him after the alley ended was nothing but prairie grass divided by the ribbon of rails heading northwest.

If he looked to the south following the tracks, he could see the railroad station and the large stockyards on the other side of the tracks. Some were empty, but he could make out a few scattered drovers pushing a mewling herd of cattle into the pens. Mining may be hell, he thought, but it beats having to deal with those filthy beasts.

He turned and walked downhill toward the main street. It was close to lunchtime and he wasn't about to miss a meal and was determined to make the most of his union money.

CHAPTER 1

Carl Ritter sat on his tired roan gelding on the crest of a hill just south of Pine Bluffs. It had been a short drive and probably his last. Although he had made use of the remuda during the drive, he had ridden his own horse, Jules, more than he should have. Maybe he should have given Jules more breaks, but he felt more at home on Jules than the temporary nags supplied by the trail boss. *Where had he found such sorry horseflesh?* At least he and Jules were free of that outfit, perhaps free of all outfits now. Carl believed it was time to finally do what he was trained to do.

Carl scanned the southeastern Wyoming landscape, the wide, barren expanse, and he smiled. When he studied these flatlands, he imagined what the Easterners would think of him now, riding across Wyoming. *Could they even imagine it?* They'd think of cloud-piercing, snow-capped mountains cut by wild, churning rivers bubbling with giant trout. Those lands existed elsewhere in Wyoming, but not here. This was just a continuation of the plains of Nebraska and the Dakotas.

Carl didn't mind. He was used to the flatlands as he'd been riding across them in summer heat and in biting winter cold for the past five years. He'd crossed the plains on three major cattle drives and quite a few smaller ones. The last one wasn't very big at all; nothing more than a roundup and drive of six hundred head to the rail head just two hundred and eighty miles away. He knew that with the expansion of the railroad, the days of the long drives were long gone and that the cowboy way of life wasn't going to last much longer either. It gave him a touch of melancholy, but no sentimentality. That was the way of the world and he'd have to adapt to the change as would all of the others who called it home. Unlike most of them though, Carl knew he was very well equipped to handle the change.

Pine Bluffs, which had become a central shipping point for cattle, had accepted the small herd into its holding pens and he'd already been paid off. He had neglected his usual habit of wiring his pay to the bank in Kansas City and now he had more than three hundred dollars in the money belt under his shirt. He'd have to get over to the Western Union office and unload most of it when he got the chance.

Now it was time to make the decision. He thought about heading to Cheyenne but when he pulled out his watch, he noted that it was after five o'clock and he really needed a bath. He had bathed in a shallow stream the day before yesterday, but the thought of a warm bath made his decision for him. He'd spend the night in Pine Bluffs and figure out which direction he'd go tomorrow or maybe the day after.

"C'mon, Jules," he said to the roan as he patted its neck, "Let's head into town."

He could see the Pine Bluffs Hotel at the end of the main street and was surprised to note that it was a substantial brick building. He looked forward to spending the night under a roof after a drive. Some of the older hands preferred sleeping out in the open and Carl hoped he never developed the habit himself. But his first task at hand would be to pick up some new shirts and maybe some pants, underwear and socks then after he got a haircut and that much needed bath, he'd finally get a room at the hotel.

He was almost twenty-seven now but still wore a boyish face. By most standards, he was considered a handsome young man, just shy of six feet and weighing in at a well-disguised two-hundred pounds that looked more like a hundred and seventy. His light brown hair and dark blue eyes attracted many young ladies' eyes but just not the right ones.

Jules trotted to the edge of Pine Bluffs, churning up small clouds of dust as his hooves struck the dirt street when Carl spotted a large mercantile as the third building on his right and headed that way. As he did, he noticed a loud printed poster on the side of a vacant shack, so he walked Jules over and read:

CHINESE GET OUT OF WYOMING!
WE DON'T WANT YOU HERE.
GO BACK WHERE YOU CAME FROM.
YOU STAY HERE, YOU DIE!

The message took him aback. He hadn't seen many Chinese in the years he had been on the trail but then, he hadn't seen much of anyone else either. The few Chinese he had met had come off as being friendly enough, but he knew that many folks resented them because they worked so cheaply. He'd have to check on the local state of things when he got the chance.

He turned Jules toward the general store and stepped down from the horse. He decided to leave his Winchester '73 carbine in its scabbard before he removed his Stetson and used it to brush off the worst of the dust that he'd picked up from getting those cattle into the pens.

When he was reasonably satisfied with his level of dust, he popped the hat back in place, stepped into the store and let his eyes adjust to the darkened room. The place was still dark despite its windows to the outside world.

As he walked up to the counter, he knew he'd have to give in to his biggest weakness...his sweet tooth. As he examined the shelves, the storekeeper smiled at the cowboy looking avariciously at the children's treats.

Before Carl could announce his choices though, he noticed a waist-high tussle of brown curls approach the counter. Carl smiled as he watched the little girl scan the same wooden boxes full of penny candy behind the glass-windowed counter that he had just perused.

Carl slid his Stetson to the back of his head and crouched down on his heels until he was eye-level with the girl.

"Do you have any recommendations?" he asked.

She hadn't even noticed him until he spoke then she turned her head, saw the smile on his face and giggled.

"I like licorice a lot," she said as she pointed at the boxful of black candy.

"Well," Carl said, "I'm partial to lemon drops, myself, but let's see what kind of deal we can get."

He stood, set a nickel on the counter and asked, "Sir, do you think you could give me two cents worth of lemon drops and three of licorice?"

The storekeeper grinned and replied, "I suppose I can try accommodate your order."

He filled two small bags, one with black candy and one with yellow.

"How much is that chocolate bar?" Carl asked as he spotted the rare English-made confection.

"Now, that's right expensive," he replied, "Never tried it myself because it'd probably run me into bankruptcy if I developed a taste for it. It runs fifty cents."

Carl hesitated but then glanced over at the wide eyes of the little girl, smiled and set a pair of quarters on the counter.

"I believe I'll gamble that it's worth every penny."

The clerk nodded and handed him the chocolate bar and the two bags of candy.

Carl handed the licorice bag to the little girl who beamed at him.

"Wait," Carl said as she reached into her bag to retrieve her first licorice, "before you go tossing that licorice into your mouth, how about if we share some of this chocolate?"

Her eyes grew even wider as Carl unwrapped the bar, snapped off a piece and handed it to her. She took a large bite off the piece then began chewing with a growing look of ecstasy.

He snapped off another piece and handed it to the storekeeper as he said, "No use avoiding the inevitable."

The storekeeper chuckled and took a bite and made a face similar to the little girl's look of pure pleasure.

As Carl was preparing to break off a piece for himself, he heard a gruff voice behind him snarl, "Well, Mister Candyman, you fixing to share with me, too?"

Carl ignored the man for the time being but glanced to his left to see a woman examining some fabrics.

Carl said to the little girl, "Why don't you go share your candy with your mama, sweetie?"

She glanced up at him and then walked toward the woman down the aisle still clutching her bag of licorice.

Carl turned to face the large, unclean man standing behind him and knew the type. He'd crossed paths with at least one of them in just about every town as he'd wound his way across the West. They rarely worked but got along by bullying people and stealing whatever wasn't tied down. They wouldn't take anything big that could get him sent away for a few years, just small stuff that would inconvenience folks and keep money in their pockets.

"Do you really want some chocolate?" Carl asked as he smiled at him and offered him the open bag, "Or would you prefer some lemon drops?"

The big guy simply stared back at him. It wasn't the answer he was expecting.

"Why would I want any damned candy?" he asked harshly.

"Well, for one reason, you asked me for some. Then it tastes really good, too. It's my big weakness, really. I've got this big ol' sweet tooth. How about you?"

Now the big guy was really confused. *Just who was this idiot who couldn't understand a challenge when he heard it?*

The befuddled man then asked, "What's the matter with you. Are you an idjet or sumpin'?"

"I don't believe so. You specifically came in and asked me to share my candy and I offered you a choice. How can you question my intellectual capacity based on such a completely straightforward proposal?"

The big guy was totally perplexed now. *What the hell was going on?* He saw a seemingly ordinary cowpoke wearing a Colt on his hip, so this wasn't a sodbuster, but he wasn't making any sense at all either. Adding to his confusion were the shortcomings in his own vocabulary so he barely understood the man.

"You talk funny, too," he finally said as he tried to insult his way out of his confusion.

"I'll tell you what," Carl said, "I just got into town and I'm in sore need of a shave, a haircut and a bath. Now that should run me about sixty cents across the street. How about if I give you a lemon drop, and I'll even cover the cost of a bath, shave and haircut for you? How's that sound?"

"I don't need no bath!" he shouted, "The hell with you!"

He gave Carl one last glare before he turned and stomped out of the store, slamming the door behind him as he left.

The echoes of the slamming door had barely died when Carl heard hearty laughter and giggling from behind him.

He turned then shrugged and said, "Well, it was a genuine offer."

"Mister, that was the darndest thing I've ever seen," the clerk said between bouts of laughter, "That was Fred Jenkins. He's kind of a local thug that gets his way around here. I don't think I've ever seen nobody make him back off without getting the hell beat out of him, or worse."

"Well, I'm not one to get into a down and nasty fight if I don't have to and most of the time I don't have to," Carl replied.

The clerk stuck out his hand and said, "I'm Hank Jensen. Me and my missus own this place."

Carl shook his hand saying, "Glad to meet you, Hank."

Then he heard a soft voice from his left, "My momma said I forgot to say thank you for my licorice."

Carl turned and looked into those pretty blue eyes and said, "You're entirely welcome, ma'am, just make sure you don't go spoiling your dinner."

He tipped his hat as she giggled again, and Carl almost giggled himself as he looked down at the cute little girl.

As he brought his eyes level, he was struck by another pair of bright blue eyes belonging to an uncommonly tall woman just a couple of inches shorter than he was. She was wearing a plain homemade blue-checked dress, the fabric worn and frayed. Like her daughter, she had brown hair and just as her daughter, she was well beyond cute. Her handsome face was enhanced with a broad smile.

"That was a rather remarkable performance," she said in an almost musical voice.

Carl was at a loss for words as he caught his breath.

"Didn't mean it to be, ma'am," he finally said, "I was just trying to defuse a situation that could have gotten ugly in front of folks who shouldn't witness such ugliness."

"I heard you say that you just arrived. Are you staying in town or just passing through?" she asked.

"I planned on staying until I came to a decision as to what I would do next, but as you may have overheard a moment ago, I am in dire need of some serious cleaning up. So, my immediate plans were to head across the street and remedy that situation before heading over to the hotel."

"The reason I ask is that I run a boarding house at the end of the street and have some vacant rooms at the moment."

Carl instantly forgot about the hotel as he replied, "That would suit me fine, ma'am. I find that the food in most cafés tends to be questionable at times, but rooming houses usually offer much better quality. I'm sure that yours is even better than most."

"Why would you think that?" she asked, the edges of her mouth turned up into an almost-smile.

Now he was caught. He didn't want it to seem like the poor attempt at flattery that it was, so he improvised.

"I noticed that your daughter seemed to be very well nourished and happy. That's a good indication of a well-run household."

"Good recovery," she said as she laughed, "It's the large white house with green shutters, on the same side of the street as the barber shop and there's a sign out front."

"Then I'll stop by after I have my bath."

"We'll see you later, then," Barb replied with a smile.

The little girl gave him a wave, then took her mother's hand and walked out the door.

Carl watched them leave and eventually turned to the storekeeper.

"I almost forgot what I came in here to buy for some reason," Carl said to Hank.

"I kinda noticed that," he replied, a smile still plastered on his face.

Then he said, "That was Mrs. Barbara Mathias and her daughter Beth. Arrived in town about seven years ago with her husband. He opened a hardware store and had it doin' pretty well, too. Seemed like a nice feller. Wasn't even year before he died of pneumonia and never even got to see his little girl, either. She sold the store right off, because she knew she couldn't run it. Bought the house and had it made into a rooming house. Never has much money to speak of, but she's a fine lady."

"That was my impression, too. Sometimes it seems like all the good folk have bad things happen to them these days."

"Had any bad things happen to you?" Hank asked.

"Surprisingly, no. I've been more fortunate than almost everyone I know. My parents are alive and well, my brother and sister are both happily married, and my brother has two healthy boys and my sister is pregnant. She's going to have her baby in a month or so. Heck, I haven't even had a cold in the past two years."

"I guess that means you ain't good folk," said the storekeeper before he chuckled.

"I must be the exception to that rule. Either that, or I'm just too stupid to know the rule's out there," Carl said with a grin as Hank snickered.

Hank filled his order for a couple of boxes of cartridges for his Colt and his Winchester, two new shirts, another pair of jeans, a pair of slacks, and three pairs of socks and some underwear. Carl then grabbed a copy of the Cheyenne Daily Leader from the counter. It was two days old, but it would update him on what was going on, and maybe even explain that poster about the Chinese.

After paying for his supplies, Carl walked out the door, stuffed his purchases into his nearly empty saddlebags, mounted, and walked Jules down the street toward the livery.

The livery could've used a coat of whitewash and a new roof altogether, but when he dismounted and saw the interior, the floors were clean and there was plenty of fresh hay in the stalls and oats in the feed bins.

As he entered the building, he called out, "Howdy, anybody in?"

The liveryman replied in a deep, gravelly voice from the back of one of the right-hand stalls, "Back here!"

Carl just dropped Jules' reins, then wandered back to where he could make out the liveryman's broad back as he mucked out the stall. The man turned to face him, and Carl stood face to face with one of the largest men he had ever seen in his life, but his broad smile's flashing bright white teeth marked him immediately as a friendly giant.

"Evening," he said as he set the broad-faced shove aside, "The name's Ethan. Ethan Green,"

Ethan reached between the stall's side slats with a paw that was almost too big to make it through and Carl took his offered hand despite his immediate concerns for the geometry of the bones in his own right hand.

But the handshake was surprisingly gentle as Carl replied, "Carl Ritter. I need to stable my horse for a few days."

"No problem. It'll run ya thirty cents a day, including some oats once a day."

"That'll be fine. He'll need his shoes checked and replaced if you think it's necessary."

"I'll check them first thing in the morning, but if I have to get shoes made, it may take a few days."

"No problem, do what you think is necessary."

Carl paid the man for the next week, then removed his saddlebags and repeater before he gave Ethan a short wave before he left the barn to get that bath and haircut.

When he opened the barbershop's door, he made eye contact with the only man in the shop, who had to be the hair cutter, unless a customer would have to sweep his own trimmed locks from the floor. He was a middle-aged man with graying sideburns that accentuated his rather prominent nose. If it wasn't for that very impressive nose, Carl supposed he would look like an average, unremarkable man. But that that proboscis surely did mark him as noticeable as it dominated his thin face.

He slowed his sweeping as he looked at Carl and asked, "Need a haircut?"

"That and a bath and a shave. I just got off the trail and need the works."

The beaky barber nodded, then replied, "Let's do the haircut first and then the shave. It'll give me time to heat up the water."

Carl held out his hand and said, "Carl Ritter."

The Nose took his hand and replied, "Elrod Lydon."

Carl smiled at him, appreciating the perfect marriage between the barber's name and face and wondered if his parents chose that name before or after they saw their newborn son.

He sat down in the barber's chair while Elrod went in the back to fire up his boiler to heat the water. As he sat on the bright red leather upholstered cushions, he thought about those bright blue eyes of Barbara Mathias. He grinned when he found himself already wondering if his mother hadn't been right all along. It was a bit silly, after all, he'd only talked to her for a couple of minutes.

The un-silly part of the concept was that he'd never had the urge to talk to another woman as he had after that brief conversation. Granted, he hadn't had many conversations with young women since leaving college and taking to the cattle trail, but still, he'd had more than a few lengthy talks with girls in his school years.

Elrod re-entered the front of the shop, and wordlessly flew his cotton apron around Carl's neck. After it settled on his torso, the barber started snipping and trimming his dark hair.

———

Forty minutes later, as he stepped out of the barber shop, he felt like a new man, as he usually did after his first genuine bath in two seeks. It was rare that he went two days without some form of bathing but taking one in hot water was always better than stepping into a pond with unknown critters lurking beneath the brown surface. Most of the other cowhands thought he was crazy, but none of them had his mother's constant refrain as they grew.

He walked along the boardwalk until he reached its end then stepped back into the street and pulled out his watch. It had been a graduation gift when he left his home to attend Baylor College in Waco, Texas, but he kept this horrible secret to himself, as there was no need for anyone to know, especially some of his rougher companions on the trail. He had studied engineering at Baylor, and should be building railroad bridges or steam engines, but after matriculation, the cowpoke trail had called his name instead. The world of the cowhand had been his classroom now for five years now, and for Carl, it was five years well spent. But with that classroom door slowly closing, it was time for him to move on to something different, it was time to start doing what he had been trained to do.

It was almost seven-thirty already, and his stomach reminded him of his neglect with a loud, rumbling growl. The cook on this drive wasn't that good, yet he rarely missed a meal.

He arrived at the boarding house, then after walking down the short walk, stepped onto the large, wraparound porch of the well-maintained house and knocked on the front door and waited.

The door opened but nobody was there until Carl glanced down to see Beth grinning up at him.

"Did you eat all of your lemon drops?" she asked.

"Yup. Every last one. Then I bought another big bagful, and I ate all of them, too. So, if I start turning yellow, run away unless you want to watch me change into a giant lemon."

Beth really started giggling as she opened the door to let him enter.

As he stepped inside, Carl removed his hat and waited for Beth to close the door.

Beth smiled up at him and said, "Mama's in the kitchen cleaning up. She said when you got here to come into the kitchen and see her."

She took his hand, then led him through the parlor and down the hallway to the back of the house and soon reached the large kitchen.

Mrs. Mathias was standing by the sink wearing a daisy print apron as she scrubbed a large pot while a lock of hair hung loosely across her forehead.

"Mama, the cowboy is here," Beth announced as she released Carl's hand.

Barb stopped scrubbing and turned, drying her hands on the front of her apron.

"My, aren't you all spiffed up and shining," she said as she smiled.

Carl was only mildly dumbstruck this time as he looked at her and managed to smile back.

"I'll admit to having a less gruff and dull appearance, ma'am," he replied, matching her smile with his own.

Barb asked, "Did you get to eat anything on your way here?"

"Just a piece of chocolate and a big, imaginary bag of lemon drops," he answered as he smiled at Beth.

Beth giggled again.

"Lord, that little girl is cute!" he thought.

"I saved you some stew from tonight's dinner. Is that okay?" Beth asked.

"That sounds perfect, ma'am."

"Go ahead and pull up a chair."

Carl sat down at the kitchen table as Mrs. Mathias took out a large bowl and spooned in a heaping portion of savory beef stew with lots of potatoes. It wasn't piping hot, but the aroma created a welcoming grown from his stomach that created more giggles in Beth.

After she set the full bowl of stew on the table before him, Carl bowed his head for a short while and silently said grace.

Barbara Mathias noticed, but didn't say anything because it wasn't the place of a landlady to talk about religion or politics with her guests.

When he glanced back up, he asked, "Aren't you going to eat?"

"Beth and I have already eaten," she replied, "You go right ahead."

As Carl started in on the stew, she left the table and soon returned with a steaming cup of coffee and some light, fluffy biscuits. There was sugar and cream on the table, but Carl preferred his coffee black.

"I never did get your name," she said as she finally took a seat.

"I apologize, ma'am. I should have offered it right away. I had other things on my mind, I suppose. My name is Carl Ritter."

"No need for an apology. My name is Barbara Mathias. Folks call me Barb, and this little troublemaker is my daughter, Beth."

"It's nice to meet you, and I don't think Beth is much of a troublemaker. If she is, then I believe she's worth putting up with the trouble. As for me, it may come as a shock, but everyone calls me Carl: even my parents."

Barbara laughed then as he smiled, he asked, "May I ask you a question?"

"You may."

"Everyone calls you Barb, but what do you prefer to be called?" he asked before taking a sip of the coffee.

She gave him a curious look before she smiled and replied, "That's the first time anyone has ever asked me that, but to be honest, I've always preferred to be called Barbara."

"Then if it's all right with you, I'll call you Barbara, and before you ask, I prefer to be called Carl, even if I've never had much of a choice in the matter, although I've been hoping for something more grandiose like 'your highness', 'your worship', or 'o' exalted one'."

Barbara laughed lightly as the tiredness that seemed to be ever present evaporated and Carl was stunned by the remarkable change.

After a few seconds of recovery, Carl turned to Beth and asked, "Now, Miss Mathias, I'll ask you the same question. What do you want me to call you?"

She scrunched up her face in deep thought before replying, "Well, everybody calls me Beth, 'cause it's easy. But my real name is Bethany. Can you call me that? That way I'll know you're talking to me."

C. J. PETIT

Carl nodded and said, "Of course, I can. Bethany, it is. It's a very pretty name, too. Your mother must have known what a pretty girl you'd grow up to be."

Bethany's bright blue eyes sparkled as she smiled, then skipped out of the kitchen and disappeared down the hallway.

"I think you have a new friend," Barbara said, "I neglected the business part of our conversation. Room and board will be five dollars per week or a dollar a day. Is that acceptable?"

Carl made a very quick, but not unexpected decision as he replied, "Very reasonable. In fact, why don't I pay for a couple of weeks in advance? I'm still unsure of my plans, so it's likely I'll be around for a while."

With that, he reached into his new denim britches, pulled out a ten-dollar gold piece and handed it to her.

"That's really not necessary, Carl," she said as she accepted and stared at the coin in her palm.

"It's not a problem. I'd just hate to forget the rent and have to run as you chased me down with a frying pan to collect payment."

She laughed again as she slid the money into her apron pocket, then said, "Thank you. I'll show you to your room when you're finished eating. You're my fourth guest in the house right now, so you can have your choice of four rooms."

"I'm sure any one of them will be fine," Carl answered as he ate more of the satisfying stew that had finally quieted his protesting stomach.

———

Twenty minutes later, after she had shown him his room and the location of the washroom, he set his saddlebags and Winchester in the corner and hooked his gun belt over the bedpost. He then opened his saddlebag and retrieved the folded newspaper and stretched out on the bed and began reading.

The lead story was about all the labor trouble just west of Pine Bluffs. It seems that the coal mines were in turmoil, with white miners fighting both the Chinese miners and the railroad that had brought them in at lower wages. There had been strikes and a few beatings of Chinese in Laramie and Cheyenne, which would explain the poster. He could almost feel the tension as he read the article. Things were bad, and it didn't seem to be getting any better, but at least it wasn't his problem.

He was still trying to decide where he should start his new life as an engineer. The most obvious choice would be with a railroad. They were expanding so quickly across the West that the need for qualified engineers far outstripped the supply. The Union Pacific was the biggest by far, but they'd been named in the newspaper story, so he wasn't sure that he'd want to head into that hotbed.

Yet even as he thought about where he might find work as an engineer, thoughts of Barbara Mathias were never far from the center of his mind. His logical, engineer's mind still found it hard to explain how he'd become so intrigued with her so quickly, but he could still hear his mother's constant refrain about finding the right woman.

It was only a little past nine, but he was tired from the day's work and needed some shuteye, so he stripped down to his union suit and crawled under the quilts and was out before he knew it.

———

He thought he'd just napped after a dreamless sleep and was momentarily confused by his location and the time as sunlight blasted through his window.

After his brain caught up with his eyes, Carl hunted for his watch in the morning light and noted the time was 5:25. It was summer and at the latitude, sun would arrive early. On the trail, he'd be up and dressed by now, so maybe he was getting used to town life already after just one day.

He rolled out of bed and pulled on his britches, donned his shirt then sat down and pulled on a clean pair of socks that he'd set out the night before. Next, he turned his boots upside down to shake them clear of any unwanted critters before he yanked them on. It was a necessary habit on the trail, but then he thought that maybe he wasn't quite as accustomed to town living as he believed.

He took a few minutes to make his bed, although he knew it wasn't his job as a paying guest, then walked down to the washroom at the end of the hallway. The door was open, so he went in, washed and shaved.

After combing his newly cut hair, he turned to leave the washroom, and as he opened the door, he almost ran into a man just a couple of inches shorter than he was and a few years older.

"Excuse me, sir," Carl said as he stepped aside to let the man pass.

"Sorry. Didn't see you there," Tom Wilson replied.

Each gave a courtesy smile before passing.

Carl took the stairs as quietly as it was possible while wearing a pair of heavy heeled Western boots, and headed for the kitchen, where Barbara was already up and in the process of making more biscuits which seemed to disappear quickly, no matter how many she baked.

"Good morning, Barbara," Carl said cheerfully as he entered the kitchen.

She turned, smiled at him, and replied, "Well, good morning to you, Carl. Did you sleep well?"

"Better than I have in quite some time. It was a nice room and there were no obnoxious critters nearby making obscene noises to keep me awake."

She laughed and replied, "Well, we haven't hosted any cows here in quite some time. They have a bad habit of not paying before they leave, and what they do leave isn't accepted as payment by any merchants in town."

Carl joined her laughter and asked if there was any coffee. She indicated the coffeepot on the corner of the stove and continued rolling her biscuit dough.

He walked to the big cookstove and poured himself a cup, then stood for a moment and watched as she began punching biscuits and then laying them on a baking sheet. Before she set the full pan in the oven and closed the oven door, Carl poured a second cup.

When she turned, she was surprised to find Carl holding a steaming cup of coffee out to her which she gratefully accepted with a smile.

"Thank you," she said, "I need to add a bit of sugar."

They both stepped to the kitchen table and took seats before Barbara added a teaspoon of sugar and stirred it while she looked back at him. Her blue eyes had an unsettling but not unpleasant effect on Carl, but he quickly adjusted to the expected impact.

"I'll have breakfast ready by seven o'clock," she said, "The other guests should be downstairs by then. We have a couple staying with us, Mister and Mrs. Thomas Wilson. He's an executive with Union Pacific, and we also have a man by the name of John Jameson. I'm not sure what he does for a living and have no desire to find out, but he's been here three days and tends to keep to himself."

Carl nodded and replied, "I believe I've met Mister Wilson already, and I'm sure I'll meet his wife and Mister Jameson at breakfast. Before then, I'll head over to the livery stable and check on my horse, Jules. I give him a treat every morning and he gets cranky when I don't."

"That's an unusual name for a horse. I thought they all were named 'Blackie' or 'Winnie' or something."

Carl smiled and said, "You'd be a bit surprised what some of those cowpokes name their horses. Some of them are quite imaginative, just not fit for women's ears. Jules is short for Julius. I named him after Julius Caesar because I bought him on March 15th."

"Ah," she said as she smiled, "the Ides of March."

Carl returned her smile and said, "Yes, ma'am. I'm impressed because not too many folks around these parts would make the connection. Not many make the connection in other places, either. I'll be off, but I'll return by seven to enjoy your breakfast."

She gave him another smile as he stood, took the cup to the sink, washed it and then set it on the drying rack.

As she watched him walk down the hallway, Barbara wondered why a cowhand would even know who Julius Caesar was, much less when he'd been assassinated in the Roman forum. Carl Ritter was a remarkable man, and her bigger question was why he wasn't married. She knew that it wasn't remotely possible that he would even look at her as anyone more than a widowed landlady with a child.

Barbara had never really had her girlhood dreams of finding true love and from the first moment she'd met Carl in front of the penny candy counter, she'd instantly had a flash of those teenaged fantasies. With each word that passed between them, those dreams exploded and became even more vivid, but she had to push them away. She'd been disappointed before and she was too old now. It wouldn't be possible that he would find her interesting. Besides, he'd be leaving Pine Bluffs shortly to return with the other cowhands and disappear from her life forever.

That thought sent the normally cheerful Barbara Mathias into a funk, but even as she sipped her sugared coffee, she knew that she'd have to get past the feeling and get back to her job as a landlady and mother.

She finished her coffee, stood and took it to the sink where she rinsed it and set it in the drying rack next to the cup that Carl had used.

Barbara stared at his cup, sighed, then resumed preparation for breakfast before she'd have to wake Beth for her second day of school.

———

After leaving the house, Carl wandered the small town, taking note of the different shops and businesses. He was surprised to see a doctor's office with a shingle announcing, Peter

McNamara, M.D. Usually small towns only supported an uneducated pseudo-medic who could fix stab wounds, gunshots, and the occasional stomach ache. They'd have a couple of midwives, of course, but then he figured that since Pine Bluffs had become a cattle shipping hub, the transient population alone would probably keep Dr. McNamara's hands full and his fees rolling in with injuries sustained on the cattle drives and the saloon brawls when the paid off cowboys began spending their loot on cards, whiskey and women.

He took a stroll down the town's lone side street with the church at its end, but with no sign, written or symbolic, to indicate its denomination. He looped around the church, noting the forest that seemed to mark the northern boundary of Pine Bluffs, then headed back to the boarding house. As pleasant as the town seemed to be, Carl couldn't imagine living in Pine Bluffs. There was no place for an engineer to practice his skills in the town.

As soon as he had made that conclusion, a random thought popped into his consciousness: *I guess I'll just have to uproot Barbara and Beth from Pine Bluffs.*

That unexpected thought froze him in his tracks. *Now where did that come from?*

They had only passed a few words between them, *now he was worried about where they would live?* Lordy, it was almost as bad as expecting your horse to answer you back. But at the same time, he knew it wasn't the same thing at all.

He'd been thinking a lot about Barbara Mathias since meeting her, but still, the leap from thinking about her to already planning on taking her and Beth away from town was a shock.

On his return walk, he headed toward the livery stable and noticed that the owner was awake and shoveling hay into the stalls. Jules occupied the last stall on the leftmost row, so he headed to that way to give his gelding his treat.

"Morning, Ethan!" Carl exclaimed loudly, but not reaching the level of a shout, so he didn't startle the liveryman.

Ethan kept shoveling but replied with the same volume, "Good morning to you, Carl."

Carl joined Jules in his stall, rubbed the horse's nose and offered him his expected cube of sugar.

As Jules inhaled the cube, he said, "Guess I'm not the only one with a sweet tooth," luckily with no reply from his four-footed friend.

Ethan walked up to Carl, wiping his huge hands on a grubby cloth that was probably adding to the dirt on his hands rather than subtracting from it.

"I'll be putting on a new set of shoes later. That front right one is loose and the others are pretty worn out. It'll depend on when I can fetch 'em from the smithy."

"Thanks, Ethan. Let me know the cost and I'll take care of it."

"Not a problem."

He checked his watch. It was almost seven and time for breakfast, so he waved to Ethan, then trotted across the street to share breakfast with the Wilsons and the mysterious Mister Jameson, but most importantly, to see Barbara and Beth.

———

The other boarders were already gathered in the dining room when he arrived, and Carl recognized the man he'd almost bumped into was indeed the Union Pacific executive. He was seated next to an attractive woman with dark blonde hair and laughing eyes. Mister Wilson appeared to be in his mid-thirties, and his wife a few years younger.

The man he assumed was Mister Jameson, was sitting two seats away from the couple and was a different type altogether and seemed to bring an air of antagonism to the scene. He was of medium build, somewhere between his and Mister Wilson in age, was prematurely balding and sported a short mustache. It was his eyes that marked him as a man of questionable character. There was no warmth in them as they almost reeked of suspicion and mistrust, and they were looking up into Carl's eyes as the man evaluated him.

Carl quickly broke eye contact, then took a seat at the table as Barbara entered the dining room.

"Mister and Mrs. Wilson, Mister Jameson, I'd like you to meet Carl Ritter, our newest guest," said Barbara as she set dishes out on the table.

Carl reached across the table to shake hands with the other guests, but Mister Jameson's handshake was less than cordial.

On the table was a stack of flapjacks and a mound of biscuits, complete with butter, syrup, and a plateful of bacon. The Wilsons and Jameson already had short stacks on their plates, so Carl took three for himself and set them on his plate.

After he sat down, he bowed his head and silently said grace, but as soon as he finished, he glanced up in time to catch Jameson with an unmistakable sneer on his face that Carl pretended not to notice.

———

As they ate, Carl struck up conversation with the seemingly affable Mister Wilson.

"Barbara tells me that you work for Union Pacific. What brings you to Pine Bluffs?"

Tom Wilson replied, "They sent me here to investigate the delay in the stock trains. Stockyards were piling up cattle for shipment and the trains were waiting too long to load them. That problem's been cleaned up, but now they want me to go out to Rock Creek. We have a lot of labor problems out west in the company's mines and I was supposed to go out there last week, but the sheriff said I'd better not. It had gotten so bad that even the sheriff had to leave."

John Jameson stopped eating as he listened closely as the Union Pacific man talked about the situation in Rock Creek. Krueger had kept him in the dark since he'd arrived, and his frustration had been growing with each passing day. Maybe having that cowboy show up wasn't such a bad thing after all.

Tom Wilson continued, saying, "I told the president of the railroad that he was going to have issues when he tried to ride herd on a bunch of disgruntled miners. You can't have two groups doing the same job and getting paid different wages and not expect conflict. We've been bringing in Chinese workers to replace the white workers because they work cheaper, and the more they bring in, the worse it gets. He just told me that the cost savings outweighed the potential risk and if the white miners objected, they could all go to hell as far as he was concerned. But now I have a feeling that they won't be going to hell so much as bringing it to Rock Creek, and it may take more authority than I have to solve when I finally get there. We may have to go to the governor or even bring in the army."

"Is it that bad?" Carl asked, "I read about it in the paper, but they didn't go into specifics."

"It's that bad."

Carl had the advantage of sitting across the table from Mister Wilson and noticed out of the corner of his eye that Jameson was paying rapt attention to what the Union Pacific man was saying, so as soon as Tom Wilson stopped talking, he turned to Mister Jameson.

"What do you do for a living, Mister Jameson?" he asked.

Jameson quickly answered, "Nothing that concerns you."

He seemed content to leave it there, but Carl wasn't about to let that happen. If nothing else, it was his natural curiosity that almost demanded that he ask more to see what kind of reaction he'd get from the openly hostile man on the other side of the table.

"What do you think about what Mister Wilson has been saying? It sounds like a dangerous situation. Have you ever been out that way?"

He noted that his question irritated Mister Jameson considerably, as he dropped his forkful of food back to the plate and glared at Carl.

"What are you, a Pinkerton? You sure ask a lot of questions for someone who just got into town."

Carl smiled innocently as he replied, "It's just because I'm new here. I don't know anyone around these parts, so I thought I'd try to be nice and make some new friends."

"Well, I'm not about to be no friend of yours, so you can save your questions for other folks," Jameson snapped.

Jameson's opinion that having the cowhand in the boarding house was a good thing vanished as he went back to eating, his eyes downcast to preclude any further questioning by the upstart.

Mister Wilson asked, "What do you do for a living, Carl? It seems that you've spent some time on the trail."

"I have done just that. For the past five years, I've been riding herd to congregations of cows that we persuaded to travel with us to locations that they might not have otherwise wanted to go. They can be pretty stubborn critters, and it is good, hard work, but I can already see that there isn't much future in that line of business with the railroads having stockyards in most towns. Nowadays cattle can be brought in with little outside help and I have no intention of being tied down to any particular brand, so I'm here deciding what direction I'll be taking in the future."

"You certainly don't sound like a typical cow hand. Do you have any skills other than roping and driving cattle?"

Carl smiled and replied, "Yes, sir. I'm an engineer."

This seemed to startle everyone around the table, especially Barbara, who stood just to his right with a pot of hot coffee in her hand.

"That's surprising," Tom said, "I know most of the engineers with the railroads in these parts, and you seem to be a bit young to be an engineer anyway."

Carl laughed and said, "No, sir. I'm the other kind of engineer, one of those folks who use pencils and paper and a slide rule to build things. I received my degree from Baylor in civil and structural engineering five years ago."

Everyone, even Jameson gaped at him, the notion that Carl was a college-educated professional was even more stunning than the idea that he knew how to handle a locomotive.

"Now I am genuinely bewildered," Wilson said, "If you're a structural engineer, why on earth are you driving cattle?"

Carl was still smiling as he replied, "I wasn't sure that I was cut out for a structured life, so after I graduated from college, I wanted to go a different route and see if I was missing something. I learned a lot about life out there on the range, and a lot about men, too, so it was five years well spent. Now I have to change directions again."

"Well, good luck to you. If you ever decide to put your engineering skills to use, give me a call in Omaha. We're always looking for good engineers. They're hard to come by with so many railroads and construction companies vying for their talents, and most make do with self-taught engineers, which shows in their work."

He then handed Carl a business card, which Carl slipped into his shirt pocket.

"Well," said Carl, "I've got a few errands to run, so I'll be seeing you folks later in the day."

With that he stood, pushed his chair back into place, and turned to Barbara, who was reaching for his empty plate. He smiled at her and was rewarded with a dazzling smile in return that sent a warm flush coursing through him, and he hoped he hadn't blushed as he left the dining room.

Carl really didn't have any errands to run, but this gave him an excuse to continue his exploring. He was pulling on his Texas-made genuine Stetson as he headed out the door and by the time that he reached the porch, he had decided that he'd do some shopping rather than just simple exploring, so he headed toward the mercantile.

He found Mister Jensen behind the counter as he crossed the store's threshold and said, "Morning, Hank."

"Good morning back at ya, young fella. What will you be needing today? You didn't eat all of that candy already, did you?"

Carl smiled as he answered, "No, sir, but I'm thinking of expanding my wardrobe a bit. I'm looking for a vest, and maybe a jacket that's not too fancy."

"I think I can accommodate you," Hank said before he stepped around the counter.

He led Carl toward the back of the store, and as they passed the fabric table, Carl smiled and thought of Barbara again. He was having a hard time keeping her out of his head but didn't object to her presence at all.

Hank led Carl to the very back of the store and went behind the back counter in front of shelves filled with shoe boxes, a few cowboy hats, even a wide, black sombrero. To the left were stacks of trousers, canvas britches and jeans, but Hank rummaged through a different pile and soon produced a dark blue vest with silver metal buttons and handed it to Carl, who tried it on. It was a bit tight, but considering the selection, it wasn't bad at all.

Carl nodded and said, "This will work."

The jackets Hank offered him ran the gamut from Plains Indian buckskin to plain old hideous plaid. He settled on a light wool gray jacket that he thought would look good with the blue vest. Hank nodded his approval, as Carl wondered if his sense of fashion was any better than his own non-existent one.

Carl paid for his purchases as Hank put them in boxes and then in a sack, before he asked, "Anything else?"

Carl thought for a few moments and added a box of matches and a box of sugar cubes for Jules.

After paying Hank, Carl took his purchases and walked down the street to the nearby Watering Hole saloon. It was mid-morning when he entered the batwing doors, and there were only two men in the establishment as he walked up to the bar.

The bartender was a heavy man who could barely fit into his own clothes and Carl wondered why bartenders tended to heavy stature as he heard him ask, "What'll it be?"

When he requested a sarsaparilla, he was surprised not to receive any guff from the bartender as he reached under the counter and pulled out a bottle.

"That'll be a nickel."

Carl tossed the coin on the bar and took his bag and his sarsaparilla to the corner table and sat down. The soda wasn't cold, but it was wet and tasted good, so it served its purpose. He had just finished his second swallow when the batwing doors swung open with a loud squeal announcing the arrival of Fred Jenkins, the man Carl had confused in the store just before he'd met Barbara.

He looked right at Carl as he entered, thought about saying something, but evidently thought better of it as he walked up to the bar and ordered a whiskey. When his glass was full, he tossed a dime on the bar, picked up his drink, and headed Carl's way.

"Oh, great!" Carl thought, *"Now what?"*

Jenkins pulled up a chair and sat down across from Carl, set his glass on the table and stared at Carl's dark bottle.

Carl looked at him then took another swig of sarsaparilla.

"Whatcha drinkin'?" Fred finally asked.

"My drink."

"I can see that, you idjet. I want to know what's in the bottle."

"That's a very good question. I know that it's mostly water, but I think they make it by mixing sugar, some crushed plants, and then add carbonated water. It's supposed to be good for you, like a medicine, but I'm not so sure."

"Don't you drink whiskey? It's good for ya."

"Nope. I never developed a taste for it, but you go right ahead. If you like it, good for you."

"You don't rile easy, do ya, mister?" Fred asked with his right eye partially closed.

"Nope. I've only been riled up twice and it wasn't any fun either time."

Fred guffawed then said, "I suppose not. Got your butt whupped, I'll bet."

Carl replied, "No, actually I wound up beating both of the gentlemen quite severely. That's why it wasn't any fun. It didn't fix anything, but those two were laid up for a while."

"You s'pect me to believe that?"

"You should. I've never lied to you before," Carl answered before taking another drink of his sarsaparilla.

"You sure talk funny. I think you're afeared of me."

"Now why would I be afraid of you. You haven't threatened me at all. All we ever do is have nice, cordial conversations. I even thought you were going to be a regular buddy because we get along so well."

Fred replied, "Don't know what gave you that idea. I don't get along with nobody."

"I can understand why that might be that way because of how you come across. You probably make people not want to be around you, but you need friends to make you feel better. Maybe you should try smiling at folks sometimes and they'd like you better."

Fred stared at Carl for almost a minute before he tossed back his whiskey, stood and said, "I still don't know what to make of you yet, but you ain't as bad as I thought."

Fred Jenkins then set the empty glass on the table, turned and walked through the batwing doors leaving Carl alone again.

Carl smiled and shook his head before he finished his sarsaparilla and followed him out of the saloon just three minutes later.

Carl wandered around Pine Bluffs for a while, so by the time he returned, he'd missed lunch, so he headed upstairs to his room and put his bag of new clothes away before stretching out on his bed for short nap.

When he awakened in a bit of a fog, he had to check his watch to make sure he hadn't missed dinner, too, finding it was just after four o'clock, so it hadn't been such a short nap after all. He got up and walked to the washroom, to complete his afternoon awakening, then headed back down the stairs.

As he walked down the main hallway toward the kitchen, he could hear Barbara already preparing the evening meal.

She heard him enter the room, turned and smiled before saying, "Good afternoon, Carl."

"Good afternoon, Barbara," Carl replied as he returned her smile.

"I didn't see you at lunch today. Did you get something at the Mama's Café?" she asked.

"No, I wasn't hungry, so I skipped lunch. Most days on the trail, we only ate twice, so I got used to it."

"Really? That must have been hard to get used to."

"Not as bad as you'd expect, but if you keep feeding me as well as you have, then I know I'll never learn to put up with skipping lunch again."

She laughed and said, "Thank you for the compliment, so I'll make sure you're fed."

"Need any help?"

"No, I'm fine, besides, you're a guest."

"I know, but I feel at home here. At home, I always helped out," he replied.

"Well, Beth and I are both glad you're here. It can get a little boring here sometimes."

"Beth is quite a special young lady, isn't she?"

Barbara nodded and said, "She's everything to me."

Carl said, "I can understand that," then turned back to the hallway, so Barbara could do her work without distraction.

Barbara turned to watch him leave, then sighed and resumed her preparations.

Carl walked to the sitting room, found the Wilsons already there, then waved and sat down in one of the two easy chairs. He picked up a copy of the Cheyenne newspaper and noted that the stories were almost exclusively concerned with the violence in the mining towns to the west.

———

After an uneventful dinner that was filled mainly with forgettable conversation with the Wilsons while Jameson just listened. He thought about offering to help Barbara, but thought he might be starting to become overbearing, so he retired to his room and checked his weapons.

It was a habit he had developed and found it a good distraction in addition to being vital to maintain their accuracy and dependability. When he finished with his guns, he opened his bag and hung his jacket and vest on hangers that were suspended on a pole near the dresser. Once everything was where he wanted it to be, he stretched out on the bed and just stared at the ceiling, letting his mind wander, but none of his thoughts strayed too far from Barbara.

The house was quiet except for the occasional bang of a pot from the kitchen and the noises bothered him. Barbara must be doing the dishes now, and Carl felt guilty. He wasn't doing anything, and Barbara was down there wearing her fingers to the bone. It just didn't seem right. He felt useless and lazy, which annoyed him terribly, and regretted his decision to not offer to help her. Tomorrow, he'd see what he could do to make her life better, at least until he decided what to do with his own.

After a while, he just drifted off to sleep, still thinking about Barbara and Beth.

———

In his room nearby, Jameson was getting even more antsy. This new cowboy was irritating him and seemed to enjoy doing it. To make matters worse, he wasn't getting anywhere. He had finally sent a telegram to Krueger telling him that he had found the railroad man in Pine Bluffs and was keeping an eye on him at a boarding house. He hadn't received a reply, and he still needed a horse.

Whatever plans Krueger was making in Rock Creek had better happen soon or he'd act on his own.

CHAPTER 2

Otto Krueger was still in a foul mood as he sat behind the small table that he used as a desk. He was always in a foul mood, but this was a few notches above his typical ill humor. He had received the telegram from Jameson, and it was good news and bad. He'd found Wilson, which was good, but the Union Pacific big wig had stayed put in Pine Bluffs, not Cheyenne. In Cheyenne, it would have been easier for Jameson to keep out of sight, but now he was staying in the same boarding house with Wilson. *What an idiot!* He felt as if he was surrounded by morons as he stood, then angrily marched from the room and stormed outside hunting for someone who could remedy the situation.

He found Emerson Lydon where he usually was at this time of the evening, sitting in the corner of the saloon playing solitaire and drinking beer. Lydon was an odd sort, even in a community of odd sorts. He wasn't stupid, and he was pretty good with a gun, and Krueger wondered how he got into the mining business in the first place. He seemed more attuned to gambling or gunplay than working the coal shafts. He guessed that Lydon was hiding from the law.

"Emerson, got a minute?" he asked as he approached Lydon's table.

Emerson began sliding the cards of his finished game back into a deck as he waved him over.

Krueger looked around to assure himself of their privacy amid the din of the gambling and drinking miners before he took a seat across from him.

Otto said, "I need you to do something. Don't you have kin in Pine Bluffs?"

"Yeah. I got a useless younger brother. Cuts hair for a livin'. He ain't much, though. Why are you askin'?"

"Well, he may come in handy. I need you to take a train to Cheyenne, buy a couple of horses, and ride down to Pine Bluffs. Contact your brother and ask him to give you information and maybe some help but I don't want you to stay in town. Jameson's there and may need to make a fast getaway, so you need to find some abandoned line shack or something out of the way so you both can get out of there after he's done his job. You tell him that as soon as that Union Pacific man decides to head our way, kill him. You're gonna help him make his escape."

"Is that all, Krueger? You sure you don't want me to assassinate the president of the United States while I'm at it?" he asked in a tone dripping in sarcasm.

"No, that's not all. I'm going to give you some dynamite to take with you. We're going to have some serious trouble here soon, and the railroad's gonna send a some of their bosses to Rock Creek or the Federals to try to stop us. When you find out what they're up to, I want you to take out a bridge or trestle just before the train arrives carryin' the Union Pacific crowd or whoever else they might send our way. That will solve more than one problem."

Lydon looked at him as if he had lost his mind.

"You've got to be kidding. There are too many holes in that plan. It'll never work."

"Yes, it will. Nobody expects us to do anything other than kill Chinks here. We'll catch them all with their pants down."

"I don't know, Krueger. You're askin' a lot."

"I'll give you an extra hundred dollars and you get to keep the horses. How's that?"

Lydon thought about it. It was the best offer he'd had since he had to make his escape from Denver just before the sheriff caught up with him.

He replied, "Throw in the rigs and you got yourself a deal."

Krueger had forgotten that he'd have to cough up cash for the tack for the two horses, but he nodded his agreement anyway.

"Okay. I'll pay you the hundred and give you enough for the horses, but you'll have to buy used saddles."

"Okay. I'll leave on Monday. I should be able to make it to Pine Bluffs by Thursday without a hitch."

They didn't bother shaking on the deal, because neither man really trusted the other anyway.

―――――

That night, after dinner, Carl followed Barbara into the kitchen carrying his own plate and cutlery.

As he set them into the sink of sudsy water, he said, "Barbara, I really wish you'd let me help you with some of the work. I feel useless now that I'm between jobs and I have to do something to keep busy or I'll go crazy. You don't want a nutty cowboy running through your halls looking for invisible cows, do you?"

Barbara laughed then replied, "I still think you should at least pretend to be a guest, but if you insist, I'll let you help."

Carl grinned as he stepped to the sink and as he began washing his first plate, said, "I feel saner already. I don't even hear those cattle mewling in the halls."

Barbara smiled as she accepted his first clean plate, rinsed it and then began to dry it with a towel. She doubted very much that Carl was really going stir crazy but hoped that his offer was much more than just a chance to work his way into her bed. She'd had more than just a few men try various tactics to spend the night with her. Her best defense against those kinds of offers was Beth, and her own high standards she'd set after the death of Beth's father had made her refuse all of the more serious offers of marriage from the others.

As much as she wished that Carl wanted her as a woman, she wished even more that his intentions were much more honorable simply because she already thought so him so highly and didn't want to have him fall from his lofty perch.

But despite his pleasant nature, she still couldn't imagine that he'd even think of marrying a widow with a young child, especially once she knew that he was a college educated engineer and would probably be leaving soon.

All she could do now is to enjoy having Carl around, knowing that it would break her heart to see him leave.

————

In Rock Creek, Otto Krueger was busy marshaling his thugs to begin his planned escalation of violence against the Chinese.

He didn't want to reach the final explosive step until he thought the time was right but knew that it would have to be soon.

───────

The next two days passed without any significant events for Carl or anyone else in either Pine Bluffs or Rock Creek. He got to know the Wilsons better, and thought well of them. He and Barbara spent a good amount of time together as he expanded his work in the boarding house and they engaged in sometimes deep, but more often, light, fun conversation.

It was when they were standing at the sink washing dishes when he gleaned the fact that she had no suitors. It had been a delicate question to ask, and she didn't seem to mind answering, not realizing that asking her the question had flamed the spark of her tiny hope that he wasn't just being pleasant to her because of his kind nature.

When Barbara said that there wasn't a single beau waiting in the wings, it was the best news he'd heard in a long time, and it surprised him. He hadn't met any woman with her combination of intelligence, wit, sense of humor and, he was free to admit, her handsome face and well-formed figure. He hadn't asked any questions beyond the vague query of any boyfriends to delve into the reason why there wasn't a line of them trying to woo her. He hoped that she hadn't decided never to remarry because of Beth or a bad experience. She certainly didn't seem emotionally scarred or even cool in her behavior, so he had no idea why she was still an unmarried widow. Whatever the reason, Carl thanked his lucky stars that he'd stopped at the store.

In addition to his time with Barbara, he also spent a lot of time talking to Beth and was getting very fond the cute little girl. She was like a miniature Barbara in her coloring and her nature, which made her even more adorable. Beth seemed just as happy to spend time with him as well, but between school and homework, Beth didn't have much free time. She didn't seem to have any friends, either and that surprised Carl as well.

———

On his fifth day in Pine Bluffs, things changed dramatically, and it began during breakfast.

Carl and the Wilsons were in their usual seats and on the table were heaps of flapjacks with crock of butter and a pitcher of syrup nearby.

Each male boarder piled three or four flapjacks on his plate, and Mrs. Wilson only took two. After spreading butter on them and pouring coffee, Carl said grace silently and began eating as Barbara entered the room with a plateful of fresh biscuits.

"No bacon today?" Jameson snapped as he scanned the table.

"I'm sorry," said Barbara, "I needed to make a grocery run but was too busy yesterday."

"Well, see that you have some tomorrow. I shouldn't have to go to the café and pay to get a good breakfast," he snarled before ramming a dripping piece of flapjack into his mouth.

"I'll make sure that there's bacon or ham tomorrow," Barbara said as she set the plate of biscuits on the table.

The Wilsons were clearly uncomfortable with the exchange, and Carl said nothing because he knew that Barbara was probably short on funds. He knew that with the limited number of guests, and still having to maintain the house and care for Beth, there wasn't much left each month and she was probably running up her credit at Jensen's General Store.

Carl finished his coffee, stood, looked at Barbara and said, "Thank you, ma'am. That was a delicious breakfast. Those flapjacks were the best I've ever tasted."

Barbara smiled and said, "Thank you, Mister Ritter."

Carl gave her a quick wink, which made her smile even more broadly, then turned and walked out of the dining room. After he left the boarding house, he looked down the street at the sheriff's office and headed that way.

As he opened the door to the sheriff's office, he was greeted by the sight of the soles of a pair of boots propped up on the desk. Before he could say anything, the boots returned to the floor with a bang and their owner quickly stood, brushing some crumbs from the front of his pants.

"Good morning," Carl said.

"Howdy," replied the sheriff.

Carl extended his right hand and said, "My name's Carl Ritter and I just arrived in town last week."

"I know. I've seen you around. I'm Sheriff Luck Schuster. Have a seat."

As Carl sat down, the sheriff asked, "What can I do for you?"

"Not much. I make it a habit to get to know the local lawmen whenever I visit a new town. I know that strangers sometimes make folks nervous and I hate to be the cause of such problems."

"Glad to hear it. I heard about your little run-in at the general store with Fred Jenkins. Hank Jensen told me about it and I just about popped a button laughin'. Usually, when someone runs afoul of Fred, somebody either gets busted up or arrested. It's the first time I've ever heard of someone gettin' the better of Fred, especially over somethin' like candy."

"I'm not one to try to force any issues. Usually there's an easier way out than the traditional methods of resolving disputes out here. It's a lot less messy and usually cheaper, too. In fact, I had another nice little chat with him a couple of days ago in the saloon. I believe he started the conversation with an idea of provoking me again. It may have been the same intent, but it had the same results."

"You don't say," Sheriff Schuster said as he sat back with a grin.

"While I'm here, I do have a question for you."

"What's that?"

"Do you know anything about Mister Jameson, the one staying over at Mrs. Mathias' boarding house?"

"Not much. He showed up a few days earlier than you did, got off the train, headed for the hotel, then must've changed his mind and went to see Mrs. Mathias. Why do you ask?"

"Just a gut feeling. He's hiding something and doesn't seem to fit in, which worries me."

"I'll keep an eye on him if I can, but there's nothin' I can do unless he breaks the law."

"That's fine. I just wanted to see if you knew anything about him."

Carl then stood, shook the sheriff's hand and walked out of the jail. Once outside, he turned left heading for Jensen's

General Store and noticed Hank Jensen out front, sweeping the boardwalk in front of his business.

"Morning, Hank," Carl said as he approached.

"Morning. Need anything today?"

"Yes, sir. I'll need a few things when you get finished," Carl replied.

"I'm as done as I'm gonna be."

Hank leaned the broom against the outer wall and followed Carl into the store.

"What can I get you today? More lemon drops?" he asked followed by a chuckle.

Carl laughed before replying, "Maybe. But first I'll need some things that are a bit more nutritious. How about twenty pounds of flour, five pounds of sugar, five pounds of coffee, a tin of baking powder, a slab of bacon, a box of dried apples, and a nice ham if you have one."

"That's quite an order. You plannin' on leavin' town?"

"Not for a while."

Hank began writing on a chalkboard, then said, "That'll be $9.20."

"Hank, can I ask you something in confidence?"

"Maybe. It depends on the question."

Carl asked, "How is Mrs. Mathias' credit?"

"Well, that's kinda private stuff, Carl. I'm not sure I can tell you."

"The reason I'm asking is that at breakfast this morning, one of the other boarders gave her grief for not serving bacon with our flapjacks. If I had to guess, I imagine that she's short on cash and as hard as she works, that's not right."

"That's the truth of it. That nice lady works from dawn to late at night and sometimes she doesn't have any boarders at all. It's hard on her."

"So, what's her credit?" he asked again.

Hank made a lemon-tart face, opened up a ledger, and said, "Right now, she owes $68.44. It's really hard for me and the missus to keep giving her credit when we know she can't pay."

Carl reached into his pocket and pulled out five double eagles and handed them over to Hank.

"This'll pay off her bill and give her some credit, so she won't have to keep worrying about it. Don't tell her about it, though. Just let her keep buying things on credit, even though it won't be. I think that she has too much pride to accept charity, so this'll have to be our little secret."

"At the risk of being punched in the nose, do you mind if I ask if this is honest money? I'd hate to think otherwise."

"That's okay, Hank. I'm glad you asked because it means you're an honest man, so I'll set your mind at ease. When I left Waco five years ago, I already had a decent stake even after I had set up my rig. Then while I was riding the trail, I'd put most of my pay in the bank and never had a need to buy much, so the money kept building up. Whenever I need money, I just wire my bank in Kansas City and Western Union gives me a voucher, and I've only needed to do that once. Over the years, I never felt a need to spend much, but this time I've got to make an exception."

"I'll be happy to honor your request, Carl, and she'll never know about it unless you tell her."

"Thanks, Hank, but there's one last thing you can do for me."

"What's that?"

Carl grinned and asked, "Do you have any root beer?"

"You'll be surprised to know that I do. Not many folks even know about it."

"I tried some down in Kansas City, and it's pretty tasty stuff. Add three bottles to my order."

Hank grinned and handed him three bottles, "These are on the house. Just return the bottles. I get a penny apiece for 'em."

Hank picked up the heavier bags and put them over his shoulder. The bag with the root beers he lugged in his left hand as he walked out the door as Hank waved.

He arrived at the boarding house and walked up the steps to the porch. After clumsily opening the door, he waddled down the hallway with the awkward load and found Barbara in the kitchen, still cleaning up after breakfast.

She heard him enter and turned with a startled look on her face as she asked, "What's all this?"

"Well," Carl said, "I had planned on making a trip before I got here, so I had all this stuff that I didn't need any longer. I didn't want it going bad, so I thought you could use it."

"Do you really expect me to believe that?" she asked with the corners of her lips turned slightly upward, so he knew she wasn't angry.

"No, but it was the best that I could come up with at the time."

Her small smile evaporated as she replied, "Carl, you're making me feel guilty."

"That's not my intention, Barbara, but I was so angry when Jameson caused a fuss about not having any bacon at breakfast, I felt like I needed to do something. I couldn't smack his smarmy face, but I figured I could at least keep him from saying anything like that again. I'm not blind, Barbara. I know that it must be tough to maintain the house and still keep enough food in the pantry for you and Beth. I'm just trying to take a bit of the burden off your shoulders. You have enough to worry about with Beth and other things."

Carl was unloading the groceries as he made his explanation.

Barbara was speechless as she watched, so Carl said, "Of course, there is one totally unnecessary item among all of this, or should I say three unnecessary items?"

He opened the smaller bag and produced the three bottles of root beer as he asked, "Think Beth would like one?"

Barbara smiled as she replied, "I'm sure she's never had one and I haven't either. She's at school now, but when she gets home, we can surprise her."

Then she said, "But I still don't feel right about you spending your money. I know how hard it is to come by."

"Barbara," he replied softly, "when I was talking to Hank, he was concerned that my money might have been obtained through illegal means and I had to assure him that it wasn't. You, on the other hand, are worried that it will leave me penniless and it won't. Let me explain. I simply never had a need to spend money before. Over the past five years, I've been accumulating pay and only buying what I need, which wasn't much. Now, for the first time in my life, I've discovered a good reason for spending just a tiny part of it. So, please, accept it for what it is."

Barbara didn't care about 'what it is', meant to him, as she looked at him. She suddenly didn't care if he was just trying to take her to his bed or hers any longer. She walked up to him, wrapped her arms around his neck, and started sobbing.

Carl didn't know what to do, so he put his arms around her and whispered, "It's okay. Really."

For a full minute, even after she stopped crying, Barbara and Carl remained in each other's arms.

Finally, Barbara stepped back and began drying her eyes with her apron.

"I'm sorry," she said, "I didn't mean to embarrass you."

"I was hardly embarrassed, Barbara. I understand and I'm just happy to help."

"I guess Mister Jameson won't be complaining about bacon tomorrow," she said as she sniffled despite her smile.

"No, he won't be, but I'm sure he'll find something else to grouse about. By the way, I had a chat with the sheriff about him a little while ago."

Barbara blinked at the sudden change in topic, then tilted her head slightly and asked, "You did? Why?"

"Nothing in particular, it's just a gut feeling. I don't have a problem with someone being unfriendly because a lot of folks just have that in their nature, but he goes beyond that. His eyes are furtive and seem to be hiding something, something evil. I can't put my finger on it, but I just think he's planning on doing something bad."

"I know that the first time I met him he made my skin crawl. Do you think he'd hurt me or Beth?"

"No, I don't think so, but I'd be careful anyway. I don't want to worry you, but at the same time, I couldn't live with myself if something did happen to you or Beth and I didn't at least warn you of the danger."

"What can we do?" she asked.

"Do you have a gun?"

"No, I don't even know how to use one."

"Let me think about that. I don't believe you're in any danger, but I'm trying to figure out what his angle is. I'll probably do a bit more checking around."

"Let me know if you find anything. I'm not going to tell Beth, though. It would only worry her without helping."

"That's a good idea, besides, children tend to repeat things and that could make a bad situation worse."

Barbara then let her blue eyes settle on his as she said, "Carl, you're a very mysterious man. Everyone had you put into a nice little cowboy box and you shock everyone with your admission about being an engineer. You just keep surprising me, and not in a bad way. Could we talk about more of your secrets? I may ask some personal questions. Would you mind?"

71

"Not at all. I tend to keep things to myself most of the time and that can cause surprises when folks get to know me a bit better."

"I'd like to get to know you a bit better myself," she said quietly.

Carl smiled at her, but inside he was melting. He wanted to ask about her reason for not remarrying, and when they began talking about his personal life, she'd open up about hers. But the very fact that she said she wanted to know about him gave him hope that her decision to remain single wasn't set in stone.

"I won't hide anything from you," he said, "But right now I'm going to continue checking around. I'll be back in time for dinner, though. Speaking of dinner, how come you don't join us at mealtime? It would be a good time to talk."

"If it was just you, I'd be happy to, but with other guests, I have to play the landlady."

"Okay. But I'll hold you to that if I'm the only one here."

"Thanks for all of the groceries, Carl. I'll put the root beer in the cellar where they'll get cold and then I'll let you surprise Beth."

"That sounds good, Barbara. I'll see you later today," Carl said as he smiled, then quickly turned to head down the hallway before he said something stupid.

He had only been in town for a few days, and so many changes had already happened, Barbara Mathias being the biggest.

"Lord only knows how it would be in another week," he thought as he passed through the foyer.

Little did he know that as momentous as those past few days had been, the ones in the near future would be much more exciting, dangerous and critical.

Carl strode outside and took a turn toward the main part of the town, aiming in the direction of the Pine Bluffs Hotel. There was something that the sheriff has said that hadn't impressed him at the time, but after he'd told Barbara about his concerns, the sheriff's passing comment had echoed in his mind and a new question now needed answering.

Five minutes later, he walked through the hotel's door and found the lobby of the hotel was as nondescript as it could be. There were two tan couches of unknown fabric with a semblance of a coffee table in between. No one was sitting on either couch, or anywhere else for that matter.

In contrast with the unimpressive décor of the lobby, he noticed that off to the right was a nicely furnished restaurant with an adjoining bar. It was a definite step up from the café and the saloon.

He stepped up to the desk and was met by a young woman who could shed a few pounds. She had a handsome face, though, and seemed cheerful enough.

"Can I help you, sir?" she asked as she smiled.

"Yes, ma'am. My name is Carl Ritter. I arrived a few days ago and was looking for a gentleman by the name of Jameson. He should have arrived last week on the train. Did he check in here?" he asked, then described Jameson for her.

"Well, there was a man who looked like that who arrived last week and came to the desk. He asked me if there was a man named Wilson staying at the hotel and I told him there wasn't anyone by that name here and he got very rude. Actually, he was past being rude and was very threatening. He asked if there was another hotel in town and when I told him there wasn't one, he got even madder. So, I told him that Mrs. Mathias down the street had a boarding house and he may be there. He huffed a bit and then left. I haven't seen him since and I'm very happy about it."

"That sounds like him. He tends to be a bit rude. I apologize for his behavior."

"Thank you, sir. To be honest, I think he should be apologizing, not you."

Carl laughed and said, "You're quite correct. But he never does. I don't think he knows how. Maybe I should teach him."

"Good luck with that," she said.

Carl waved and headed back out of the hotel.

That was one mystery solved. Jameson was on the tail of Mister Wilson of the Union Pacific. *But why?* If he wanted to do him harm, he would have already done so. *What does he want and why is he waiting?*"

With his mind boiling with new questions without answers, Carl headed down the street to the livery.

Carl strolled into the barn and called out, "Ethan?"

Ethan shouted his reply from one of the back stalls, "I'm back here. I just finished shoeing your horse. He's a well-mannered critter."

"He is that. Unless he doesn't get his treat every morning, then he gets downright ornery."

Ethan released a rumbling laugh as he stood with his right hand on Jules' rump.

Carl headed toward the stall, and when he found the roan, he stroked his nose, then let him snatch the offered and anticipated cube of sugar.

Ethan rounded the horse and rubbed Jules' neck as he asked, "Had him long?"

"Six years now. I bought him down in Waco, Texas and we've been through a lot together, including some wild storms and stampedes. We even had a run-in with a tornado once down in Kansas."

"Spend much time talkin' to him?"

"More than I'd be willing to admit to, but at least I was never lonely enough to expect an answer."

Ethan laughed again and shook his head before saying, "Could be worse. He could have done the talkin' and you the listenin'."

"Then I'd know I was gone, but it's time I took Jules out for a bit of a ride. I don't think he's had a day off since we've been together, except on those long drives when I'd have to use some of the remuda rides. I never had one as good as Jules, though. How much do I owe you for the shoes, Ethan?"

"Three dollars will handle it."

Carl reached into his pocket and sorted out three silver dollars and handed them to Ethan.

"Thanks, Ethan. We'll be seeing you in a little while."

Carl then tossed his saddle blanket across Jules and began saddling him for the ride. After he finished, Carl stepped into the stirrups and walked Jules out of the livery, turned him southeast out of town and began following the tracks of the Union Pacific as they disappeared over the horizon of the Great Plains.

After about two hours, he stopped and sat in the saddle scanning the landscape. There was a small creek nearby that miraculously for August, still had some water running, so he set Jules to a slow trot to the creek, then dismounted and led his gelding to the creek and let his reins drop so he could fend for himself. After Jules had pulled his muzzle from the water, he left the creek to munch on some nearby grass while Carl sat down and drifted deep into thought.

He thought about the problems with the Union Pacific coal mines a few hours west by train and what Mister Wilson was going to do about it and wondered what connection Jameson had to the issue. It had to be there or why had Jameson been looking for him. *What was his plan, assuming he had one?*

But most of his time was spent thinking about Barbara. It had only been few days. *How could he feel the way he did about someone in such a short time?* That still didn't make any sense at all. The only thing that made any sense was what his mother had repeatedly told him, but he hadn't believed – until now.

He sat for almost an hour, but he didn't come to any conclusions on either topic. He didn't even come up with any paths to solutions, so it looked like playing it by ear was the only thing he could come up with and that was a lousy play. Just as he started to get a bit down about his lack of answers, he was nudged on his back by a large head.

"Sorry, Jules. I didn't mean to forget you," he said as he smiled at his horse.

He paused, then laughed as he realized he half expected a reply. Maybe he was going daft after all.

Still smiling, he mounted Jules and turned him back to Pine Bluffs.

––––––

He returned shortly after five o'clock and dropped Jules off with Ethan at the livery stable, then crossed the street and headed for the boarding house. As he walked up the steps to the porch, he automatically used his hat to dust off his clothes before opening the door.

As he entered, he was greeted by one of his new favorite sounds.

"Mister Carl! You're back!" Beth shouted as she came running down the hallway to greet him.

"Well, good afternoon to you, Beth. How was school?"

She frowned, "I thought you were going to call me Bethany."

He squatted on his heels and whispered, "That's what I'll call you in private. That's like a secret word. When I call you Bethany, you'll know it's me and no one else. But when there are people around, I'll call you Beth. Okay?"

Beth whispered back, "Okay. That'll be our secret. Do you have a secret name that I can call you?"

Carl thought about it for a second and answered, "Just because I trust you, I'll let you know my secret name. If there's no one else around and you want to talk to me, call me Hans."

"Hans? Is that your real name?"

"No. Carl is my real name. Hans is my middle name. I was named after my grandfather. No one knows my middle name except you."

Beth nodded seriously and said, "Okay. That's a good secret. I won't tell anyone."

"That's how it should be. Now I'll know if anyone calls me Hans, it'll be you."

Beth was beaming when she took his hand and led him back to the kitchen where Barbara was preparing the evening meal.

As they entered the kitchen, she turned and smiled as she asked, "What are you two up to?"

Beth replied seriously, "We're sharing secrets that no one else can know."

"Not even me?" Barbara asked with a hurt expression.

Beth glanced up at Carl who shook his head slowly.

"No, I'm sorry, Mama. It's a real secret."

Barbara laughed and said, "I guess I'll have to try to guess the secret then."

Beth replied quickly, "You could never guess 'cause it's a good one, and only I can call him Hans."

As Beth grabbed her mouth and her eyes popped into discs, she slowly turned to look at Carl, expecting him to be really, really mad, and was relieved as she looked at his laughing eyes.

"Don't worry, Beth. It's still our secret. Your mama only spies for our side. She won't tell anyone."

Beth had no idea who spied for whom, but the fact that Carl wasn't mad at her made it all right.

"Before we have dinner," Carl said, "Your mama and I have something we want you to try. Okay?"

Beth looked at him questioningly, and then turned to her mother with the same expression.

"I'll be right back, Beth. You stay there," she said, then turned and went down the stairs to the cellar.

In less than a minute, she was back in the kitchen with three bottles.

"What's that?" she asked, as she pointed at the three brown bottles.

Carl answered, "It's my favorite drink."

"Is it whiskey?" Beth replied.

Carl laughed and was glad he didn't have a mouth full of root beer which would have sprayed the kitchen floor into a sticky disaster.

"No, I don't like whiskey. It tastes horrible. This is much better. It's root beer. Would you like to try it?"

"If you like it then I should, right?"

"Absolutely."

Barbara was grinning as she pulled the corks out of the three bottles and handed one to Carl and another to Beth.

Beth watched as Carl took a long drink followed by a satisfied, "Ahhh!"

Then she saw her mother take a short drink and smile, which shook her automatic child suspicions that the adults were trying to sneak her some foul-tasting medicine. Satisfied that must taste good, Beth took a short drink, swallowed and her eyes went wide before she put the bottle on the table.

"It's like candy water!" she exclaimed.

Carl smiled and said, "That's pretty close, really. It's a sparkling soda."

Beth took another sip and hurriedly asked, "Can I have this every day?"

"No," answered Barbara, "It's like candy. It's a treat. So, you have to appreciate it when you get it. Okay?"

"Yes, Mama," she said with downcast eyes.

"Besides," Carl said, "if you had it every day, pretty soon you'd get bored with it and not want it anymore."

"I think I'd still want it every day," Beth assured him.

"Most things are like that," Carl explained, "Even the best things in life can get unappreciated if we have them too long."

"Even people?", she asked, finding the hole in his logic.

"Now people are different," Carl said, "Because people are always changing all the time, so they can be different every day. Now root beer, on the other hand, will be root beer every day and taste the same every day. So, it can get boring after a while, but if you wait a long time between root beers, it'll taste even better than the last time."

Beth looked at him and slowly nodded her head before saying, "That sounds true, so maybe I can save this one for later."

"If you'd like to, we can put the cork back in the bottle and put it back down in the cellar, so it stays cold. Would you want to do that?" Carl asked.

"Let me have one more drink, and then we can put the cork back in. Okay?"

Carl nodded and glanced at Barbara, who was already looking at him with a warm smile.

Barbara stood near the stove and watched the conversation between her daughter and this man she had not even known for a week.

Then she closed her eyes and drifted. *How could he fit in so easily into her life?* She felt like she'd known him for years already and wondered how she and Beth had gotten along without him, and how they'd feel when he left. The renewed thought of his possible departure bothered her, but she knew it would still most likely happen even if she shared her bed with him and shuddered at the thought.

Carl noticed Barbara shake and asked, "Are you okay, Barbara?"

She opened her eyes and shook her head as she replied, "Oh. No, I'm fine. I was just thinking."

"Nothing bad, I hope."

"Just uncertainty," she replied as she managed a weak smile.

"Life can be like that. We seldom see the changes that are coming. Some of them are bad, but some are good, and some are extraordinarily good. I always like to hope that they'll be the best of the good ones. The bad ones I deal with as they come and hopefully, they won't be as bad as I expected in the first place."

"Thank you for the thought. I'll remember that in the future but now, I need to get back to cooking."

"You go ahead. I've got to talk to Mister Wilson. Have you seen him?"

"No, he went down to the telegraph office a little while ago. His wife is still in the room, though."

"No, I need to speak to him. Preferably alone. I'll see if I can hunt him down."

Carl left the kitchen and walked down the hallway to the front door. As he swung it open, he almost ran down Mister Wilson, who had a telegram in his hand.

"Excuse me, Carl," he said.

"Mister Wilson, I wonder if I could talk to you for a few minutes in private."

"Sure. How about over there?" he said, pointing to two rockers on the far side of the porch.

"Fine."

They walked to the rockers and sat down before Tom Wilson asked, "So, what can I do for you, Carl?"

"Mister Wilson," he began.

"Please, call me Tom, Carl. I'm not some geezer."

"Okay. Tom. I know that you're not much older than I am, but it's the way I was brought up. Anyway, by nature, I'm not a suspicious man. I find it easier to get along with folks than confront them and it's a philosophy that has served me well. That being said, I have a bad feeling about our fellow roomer, Mister Jameson."

"He struck me as a cold fish myself, but I didn't see him as a threat. He's been here almost a week and hasn't caused me any problems."

"That has me a bit confused as well, but earlier, I went over to the hotel and asked if he had tried to check in there. I knew he hadn't, but I asked anyway. The clerk at the hotel told me that he had shown up and instead of asking for a room, he asked if you were registered. She said that when she answered him that you weren't there, he became very agitated. When he asked if there were any other hotels in town and received a negative reply, he got very angry."

"Then she suggested trying Mrs. Mathias' boarding house. She said he was very rude, but my real concern is why he would be looking for you and wanting to stay in the same place as you. I would have thought that if he wanted to harm you in any way, he would have done it already, but he hasn't. That increased my curiosity about him and his purpose for being here."

Tom sat back and furrowed his brows before replying, "As we've discussed before, there is a serious problem in the Union Pacific mining communities to the west. The worst is at Rock Creek, probably because it is the largest. There is a labor union there called the Knights of Labor. Like most unions, they have their good points and bad. This one has a lot more of the bad ones, I'm afraid. They've been involved in strong arm tactics against both the Chinese workers that the railroad has brought in and against Union Pacific management that has gone in there and tried to stop the violence. Now I'm not saying that the railroad is blameless in all this, far from it. They've been using their power of the purse to control lives and make more profit, but at least they're not killing anyone yet.

"This Knights of Labor group has used many tactics to stop the railroad from either bringing in more Chinese or to get rid of them entirely. I wouldn't be surprised if Mister Jameson was one of their agents, but I just don't know what his plans could be. I am worried for my wife, though."

"That's understandable. I think it's best if we just keep an eye on him to make sure he doesn't try anything. It might be wise to spend a lot of your free time in the sitting room with your wife."

"That's a good idea," he replied, "Just to let you know, I received a telegram that Governor Warren has been notified by the railroad that this violence can't be tolerated, and he needs to take action. I'm not sure it's serious enough to demand his attention yet, but it's coming to that and it won't be long before troops have to be dispatched to Rock Creek."

Carl replied, "Well, that part of the situation is out of our hands, so all we can do is take care of ourselves and keep an eye on Mister Jameson."

Tom Wilson agreed, then they stood and walked back into the house.

After going to his room and changing his shirt, Carl returned downstairs to the sitting room and noticed that Mister and Mrs. Wilson were both already there in conversation.

"Good evening, folks," Carl said as he entered the room.

"Hello, Carl," Tom Wilson answered as if he hadn't seen him all day.

"Good evening, Carl. How was your day?" Mrs. Wilson asked.

"More interesting than I expected," he answered, "but all in all, a good day."

"You'll have to tell us what happened that made your day interesting," she replied.

"Well, this afternoon, I rode out for a few miles and did some exploring, discovered some places that I had never seen before, but then again, I've never been to Pine Bluffs before, so that should have been expected."

She laughed as Barbara entered the room.

She smiled at Carl and said, "Dinner will be ready shortly."

Carl answered, "Thank you, Barbara. We'll be in directly."

Mrs. Wilson smiled and turned to her husband and said in German, "It seems that our landlady may have set her cap for our young friend and he seems to be thinking along similar lines."

Her husband smiled in agreement before Carl stood to go into the dining room, turning a bright shade of red before he even got to his feet.

As he began to sit down at the dining room table, he glanced at Barbara who noticed his flushed look and gave him a curious look. She had heard the comment in German but didn't understand it.

———

Dinner was a delightful pork roast with roasted potatoes, gravy, and corn bread. Even Mister Jameson didn't complain. He didn't praise her, but he didn't complain either. There was an apple pie for dessert that they all enjoyed with their coffee, except for Mister Jameson, whose opinion remained appreciably unheard.

After dinner, Carl stopped by the kitchen sidled up beside Barbara as he plunged his hands into the sudsy water.

Barbara smiled at him as she said, "It's odd enough for a guest to help with the dishes, but even stranger because you're a man. Men don't do dishes, Mister Ritter."

Carl laughed as he replied, "You didn't grow up in my house, ma'am. My father did the dishes probably more than my mother did. He even cooked, usually when he made some of his famous sausages, but he also made some incredible strudel. So, doing work in the kitchen isn't unusual for me. I could use this time to answer some of your deep questions that you asked about earlier."

"Did your father really do dishes?" she asked with a slight smile.

"Yes, ma'am. He really did the dishes. She didn't help him in the smithy, though. She's a petite woman and probably couldn't even lift his hammer."

"Your father was a blacksmith?"

"He still is. He and his older brother run a large smithy outside of San Antonio, Texas. They employ six other smiths and handle jobs from all over central Texas."

As he talked, Carl walked pulled a heavy pot into the sink and began scrubbing.

"Is your mother still alive, then?" she asked.

"My mother is one of the most alive people I've ever known. As small as she is, she dominates the household. No one would dare argue with her, and that includes my older brother and sister, their spouses, children and any other relative that enters the door."

She laughed at the thought then said, "It sounds like you have a nice family."

"That's very true. We all got along and always have. I have been remiss about writing home, though and haven't written in a few months. I'm sure my mother will straighten me out when I get home."

"Were your parents born in Texas?"

"No. They met and were married in Alsace Lorraine in France. He was German and she was French. It's a common thing in that part of the country. They came here at the invitation of my Uncle Heinrich. He had set up the blacksmith shop and needed help and convinced my father and mother to join him."

"Can you speak German, then?"

"Both German and French. I don't talk about it very often, and it rarely comes up. It is an advantage, though, being able to understand what some people say when they don't know you can understand them."

"Is that why you were so embarrassed when you came to dinner? I know Mrs. Wilson said something in German to her husband."

Of course, just having Barbara ask the question triggered the same reaction in Carl that hearing the first comment had created and his cheeks and ears turned pink before he replied.

"Well, yes. It was. If it's okay, I'd rather not repeat it, though. You may turn as red as I did."

Now Barbara slipped into a deep shade of crimson brought about by a vivid imagination that wound up in her bedroom.

Carl noticed her discomfort and began laughing, which was contagious and Barbara soon followed.

"I won't ask, then," she said as she giggled.

"Maybe one of these days I'll tell you," he said, "If nothing else than to hear you laugh again."

He pulled another dirty pan into the dishwater and began scrubbing again as she dried the first one.

"Do you have a girlfriend?", she asked in a somewhat subdued voice.

"No, but that was my parents' fault, mostly my mother's."

She looked at him curiously as she asked, "Now that is probably a story worth hearing."

"Well, unlike a lot of friends I've had, my parents really got along. My mother told me that she knew she would marry my father the first time they met, and my father said the same thing. In all the time I've known them, I've never heard a cross word between them. You can literally see the love they share when they're together.

"It's a wonderful thing and made me want that more than anything else in my life. My mother used to tell me that I'd know for certain when I met the one girl that was meant for me, and I took her at her word, even though I still had my doubts because it seemed so illogical. But she was my mother, so I listened.

"I've met a lot of girls and many of them were quite pretty, and to be honest, several were keen on putting a bridle on me, but there was always something lacking. I guess that makes me too particular, but as I said, I'll blame my parents for my notions."

"There's something to be said for that point of view," she replied softly.

"I think so," he replied, and thought this was the time to bring up his big question, so he quickly asked, "I know you were married, so you must know what it's like to be in love, but I wonder why you haven't married again. You're a very good-looking woman, Barbara, and I would have imagined that you would have been getting proposals almost daily."

She looked at him and replied, "Actually, I didn't feel that way about my husband at all. Sometimes people marry for other reasons, Carl. I was eighteen when we were married. My husband, John, was a good man. He was a good provider and a hard worker, but he wasn't very demonstrative on the romantic side, and there were times I thought he preferred his business to me. After he died, the prospective suitors started showing up within a month. The first was the barber."

Carl was stunned as he asked, *"Elrod Lydon? Really?"*

Obviously. Barbara understood the reason for his response and grinned before she replied, "Yes. He was also the most persistent. Others would show up once or twice, but Elrod kept reappearing until I finally had to be nothing short of abrupt when

I told him to keep away from me. But as I turned them away one after the other, it gave me time to concentrate on raising Beth. She was born after John died. When the suitors finally stopped, I think I had used up all of the eligible bachelors in Pine Bluffs."

"Barbara, that tells me that you rejected all of the suitors, but not why."

Barbara sighed, then said, "They weren't all suitors, Carl. I had many male guests since I bought the house and most of them tried to lure me into their beds and some even offered me money, as if I was a common whore. That happened even before Elrod appeared at the door with a marriage proposal. I had decided after John died that I wouldn't settle for just being content anymore, and those offers strengthened my determination not to allow someone that I didn't love to share my bed or my life."

"I'm sorry that you had to go through all that, Barbara, and I'm ashamed of my sex for that kind of behavior. You deserve to be treated with respect."

Barbara studied his compassionate eyes and whispered, "Thank you, Carl, but you shouldn't apologize for what they did. You've treated me and Beth with nothing but respect and kindness."

Carl found himself sinking into Barbara's blue eyes as he quietly said, "You must have been very lonely."

"Yes. Yes, I was," she whispered under her breath.

Carl softly said, "Being lonely is different for a woman, isn't it? When I was alone over the past five years on the trail, I never felt empty because I was just doing my job. But for a woman, especially one who has an incredible child to care for, the loneliness must have been crushing."

Barbara looked at him, wondering how he could understand the depths of her loneliness and felt the urge to hold him and push that loneliness away forever.

She said, "For a man who professes to know nothing about women, you seem to do pretty well."

"Not all women, just those that I understand," he replied as he continued to gaze into her bright blue eyes.

She stared into his dark blue eyes and asked quietly, "Do you think you understand me then?"

"I can't claim to understand you, because you're a very complex human being, Barbara. It would take a long time to understand even a decent part of you."

"That's one thing no one has ever called me before – complex," she said as a wide smile formed on her lips.

"Maybe it's because they didn't try to understand you in the first place."

She said, "They rarely even talked to me as you have. They just looked me over as if I was for sale."

Carl could feel the conversation sliding into a dangerous area where he may say something stupid and destroy her image of him. After hearing about all of those men who'd tried to seduce her or even pay to have her warm their beds, the last thing he wanted was for her to think that it was on his mind, which it was, but only as one part of the reason he wanted to be with her.

He suddenly smiled, then said in a normal voice, "Well there is some advantage to your rejection of all those suitors, ma'am."

"And what might that be?" she asked with a smile.

"I'm just thinking that how kind it was of you to allow all of those single men to be evenly distributed with the other womenfolk of Wyoming. I mean, with you obviously being the most extraordinary woman in the territory, it could have caused some other distraught female a lot of distress had you stolen her beau by just smiling at him."

Barbara laughed as they continued their chores until all the pots, pans, and dishes were cleaned and put away. Neither spoke after that brief excursion into their private desires.

As he placed the last pot away, Carl asked, "Where's Beth hiding?"

Barbara replied, "She's in our room doing her homework."

"Do you mind if I go talk to her for a while?"

"Of course, not. She likes you a lot and you really like Beth, don't you?"

"Don't tell her, but I think she's stolen my heart. She's a very special little girl."

Barbara beamed and said, "Go ahead. Our room is the first room on right."

Carl smiled at Barbara unsure if she knew that he was well aware of her room's location, then walked down the hallway. When he reached the first room on the right, he knocked lightly on the door and opened it.

Beth was seated at a small table with a book open and a pencil in her hand and looked up as Carl entered the room then smiled at him.

"Hello," she said, unsure of which of his names she should use.

"Good evening, young lady. What are you studying?"

"Letters. It's hard," she replied with a grimace.

"Let's see," he said as he leaned over her open book, then said, "Hmmm. That can be a tough subject. Want some help?"

"Mama said I have to do it by myself."

"Well, she said I could help you a little."

"She did? Really?" Beth asked hopefully.

"No, not really. But I can explain letters in a way that will make it easier to understand."

"You can?"

"Sure. First off, you need to stop looking at letters as if they were just lines on a piece of paper."

"Then what are they?" Beth asked as she stared at the alphabet.

"They're people," Carl answered.

Beth giggled and said, "Really? That's silly."

"Not so. Look at them. They're just differently shaped people lying flat on the paper, and just like people, they have differences in the way they behave. For example, there are girl letters and boy letters."

Beth looked back down at the paper and stared at the shapes, saying, "I can't tell any difference."

"Well, you have to know them first. There are only five girls and twenty boys. One letter doesn't care and likes to confuse everyone by pretending to be a boy in some words and a girl in others. The five girl letters are called vowels, and just like girls, they are soft, and just like girls, they are much more important than the boy letters."

Beth giggled then asked, "They are? Which one are the girl letters and why are they important?"

"The girl letters are called vowels, and are 'A', 'E', 'I', 'O', and 'U'," Carl said as he pointed at each letter in turn.

"When you say them, they have a soft sound. Most of the boy letters, they're called consonants, sound hard just like real boys. The girl letters are more important because every word must have at least one. There are words that don't have any boy letters, but boys can't live without girl letters."

She giggled louder as she stared at the girl letters.

Carl smiled back at Beth and said, "Then, you have to look at each letter and wonder about what makes it different. Let's take a gander at a few and you'll see what I mean."

"Okay," she said getting excited at the prospect.

Carl leaned over and pointed at the letter chart in her reader.

"Let's start with the first letter, 'A'. It's number one and proud of it. She's a girl letter and gets to make a word all by herself. She's also the first letter in the word alphabet, so it makes her even prouder."

"What word does she make by herself?" Beth asked.

"She makes the word 'a'. We use it in a lot of sentences, don't we? It's one of the most used words we have. Like you are *a* pretty girl."

Beth smiled at the concept as well as the compliment and asked, "Oh. What's the next letter?"

"'B' is the first boy letter. He's jealous of 'A' because he wants to go first, like most boys, but he is the first letter in boy, so he's happy about that."

Carl skipped to 'E' and told her that this girl letter was the most popular letter and the next girl letter, 'I', was almost as popular because she made people think of themselves when she was a word by herself. From there they spent almost an hour talking about different letters and how they behaved and how they fit in. When Carl finally finished explaining how 'Z' was upset about being at the end of the alphabet and not being used very often, he sat back.

"So, how do you feel about those letters now, young lady?"

"I think I like 'A' the best," then she giggled and said, "But I just used 'I' twice, so maybe it's my favorite."

"You are doing very, very well, sweetie," Carl replied as he smiled at her.

"Thank you, Hans," she whispered.

"You're welcome, Bethany," he replied, then winked.

As he stood, she put out her arms, and Carl gave her a big hug as she gave him a peck on the cheek. If she hadn't stolen his heart before, she had now.

"Good night, Bethany," he said softly.

"Good night, Hans," she replied as Carl set her back down, then left the room. As he passed over the threshold, he almost bumped into Barbara who had been leaning on the door jamb in the hallway.

"Oh, sorry. Barbara!" he said as he avoided hitting her.

She looked at him and said, "You are an amazing man, Mister Ritter. I was wondering what was taking you so long, so I've been listening for a while. That was the most extraordinary teaching lesson I've ever heard. Beth was mesmerized and I think she learned more in that hour than she has since she started school."

Carl grinned and said, "It's just a way of taking something as abstract as letters and using something that is understandable to make it easier. Besides, it gave me an excuse to spend some time with Beth. She's really an exceptional child, Barbara. Aside from being a real charmer, she's very smart. You must be very proud of her."

"I am. She's been the center of my life for seven years. I'll go and check on her," she said before she gave Carl a giant smile and went into her room, closing the door behind her.

Once inside, she sat with Beth and asked, "Was that fun?"

"Yes, Mama! I know my alphabet now and it was a lot better than Miss Garrison was. She can be mean if we don't do what she says, but Carl makes it so easy. I really like him, Mama."

Barbara kissed her daughter and said, "So, do I, sweetheart, so, do I."

―――

As the door closed, Carl sighed and walked to the sitting room where he again found the Wilsons. Tom was reading a paper as his wife knitted what appeared to be a very colorful scarf and both looked at him when he passed trough the arched doorway.

"Good evening, folks," he said as he entered.

"Hello again, Carl," Tom said.

"*Guten abend, Frau Wilson*," Carl said to Mrs. Wilson with a smile on his face.

After a short, shared glance, both broke into convulsive laughter as they turned back to look at a grinning Carl Ritter.

"So much for my attempt at subterfuge," said Emily Wilson as her laughter slowed, "I hope I didn't cause offense."

"No offense taken. Although, to be honest, I was a trifle embarrassed to be so obvious."

"It's perfectly understandable, Carl," she replied, "And it's only obvious to those of us who understand such things."

"Well, I, for one, am glad that you understand such things. I, on the other hand, am a comparative novice in the subject."

"That is a bit of surprise, but I should have guessed that you understood German immediately after hearing your name. At least it's a subject that you seem to be undertaking with some relish," she answered.

"That I am," Carl replied before he turned to Tom Wilson and said, "Tom, any idea where our other boarder is right now?"

"No. I haven't seen him in a while. After dinner, he left the house. Maybe he went down to the saloon."

"That's probably a good guess. I doubt if he'd be heading to a church meeting."

Tom nodded and went back to reading while Emily looked at her husband and then Carl wondering what secret they obviously shared and it wasn't about Barbara Mathias.

Carl decided to head out to the porch and have a seat where he could see what was going on. *Who knows what he might see out there?* More than likely he'd spot nothing, but one never knows, but as it turned out, on this night at least, it was nothing.

CHAPTER 3

The next three days passed into a normal routine. Carl spent time helping Barbara around the house, but they both knew it was an ill-disguised attempt to get to know each other better.

Barbara didn't complain about Carl's assistance for the secondary, more practical reason either. For the first time that she could remember, she wasn't bone tired when she retired to her room, although part of that might be due to her newfound inner excitement inspired by the man who now had a firm grip on her heart. She had finally tossed aside the notion that he would leave without her and Beth. Each day after she accepted the idea, every minute that they spent together only deepened that belief.

Carl had long since decided that Barbara and Beth were now part of his life, but still hadn't decided where that life should be.

The after-dinner ritual of the sitting room with a casual meeting with the Wilsons continued and Carl grew even more fond of the couple. Tom had repeated his offer of a job in Omaha on more than a couple of occasions, and Carl was beginning to believe that it would be a good choice, but wasn't ready to agree until the whole Rock Creek business was over and he could have a much more meaningful talk with Barbara.

He had also marked Emily as another extraordinary woman and enjoyed talking to her almost as much as he did with Barbara.

John Jameson was in and out, and rarely was seen for periods of more than thirty minutes, even at mealtimes. Where he was going was a bit of a mystery as well, as no one ever saw him in the other locations around Pine Bluffs, including the saloon.

––––––

Early Friday afternoon, Carl entered the house after spending some time with Jules, knowing his horse was feeling neglected, and vowed to take care of that situation on the weekend. As he passed by Barbara's room, he noticed the door was open and saw her busy with needle and thread.

He stopped in the doorway and said, "Good afternoon, Barbara. What are you making?"

Barbara looked up with the now ever-present smile on her face and said "I'm making myself a new dress and one for Beth as well. It's about time, too."

"Now there's a skill I've never mastered and am not inclined to do so. I've repaired some holes from time to time, but they've never been pretty."

"You know," she said as she laid down the fabric, "there was something odd today at the Jensen's earlier."

"How's that?" Carl asked but had a pretty good idea what it was.

"Well," she replied, "I know Mister Jensen well, and I've always liked him and his wife. They've been very nice to me and Beth over the years, but over the past couple of months, I've had to stretch that friendship a bit because of my financial situation. I wish I didn't have to, but it was necessary. Because of that tension, whenever I'd go to the store, as I did when I first met you, there was a strained and distant relationship between me and Hank Jensen. It wasn't as if he was rude or anything. He'd never be that. It's just that he seemed tense and I can't say that I blame him either.

"But today, when I went in to buy some salt, it was like the old, friendly Hank Jensen. He was all smiles, and the tension was gone. He even showed me some new fabric he had just received and suggested that it would make nice dresses. I agreed, and he sold me a few yards as well as some nice lace trimming. I bought some lovely marine blue cotton for me and a nice green for Beth, but it was his attitude that struck me as strange. I'm pleased with the fabric, and happy that I seem to be in his good graces again, but it does have me puzzled."

"Maybe his wife gave him a good talking to. Perhaps she reminded him of his Christianity and to treat others with respect."

"I doubt that. She's the store's bookkeeper. If anything, she'd remind him of her desire to balance the books and that added to the strange sensation, too. She was smiling at me just as much as I made my purchases."

Carl didn't see any way out of this, so he took the coward's way out and changed the subject.

"That is odd, but there's no figuring what goes on in people's minds. So, how long will it take to finish your dresses?"

"I'll have them done after dinner. We'll be able to wear them to services this Sunday. Are you a churchgoer, Carl?"

"Not religiously," he answered with a straight-face as Barbara rolled her eyes, "I've spent so much time on the trail or by myself these past few years that attending church wasn't high on my list of priorities."

"When you do go to church, which church to you attend?"

"That's a good question. My father was a Lutheran and my mother was a devout Catholic. By Catholicism's rules, we had to be brought up as Catholics, and my father didn't mind. He said that there wasn't that much difference in Christian religions and the only ones that said there was a difference were the ones in charge. When I was at Baylor, the Baptists were intent on my conversion but never succeeded. They seemed too serious to me. My parents taught me that religion was in each person's heart and not in some building or in the words spoken at the pulpit. So, I'll attend any church and pray the way I want to when I do go. If the pastor starts spouting words of damnation and the demons of hell, I'll just think of something more peaceful until the service is over."

"Our current minister is Presbyterian. Mister Reed is a very mild preacher, so I think you'd get along."

"Well then, I'd be honored to escort both newly attired Mathias ladies to church on Sunday."

"We'd be delighted to have your company, sir," Barbara said as she bowed her head and smiled.

"Well that's settled, then. I'll leave you to your dressmaking and wander over to Ethan's to check out Jules. He's probably getting a bit cranky from neglect."

Carl then waved, turned and headed out of the house and stopped when he reached the porch. He scanned the street and felt as if something was different, but he couldn't put his finger on it. He looked around more carefully, but nothing struck him directly. Then he finally noticed what was different. There was a strange horse tied to the hitch rail near the barber shop. Normally, he wouldn't have noticed, but it was a tall Appaloosa mare that was still covered in dust after a long ride.

———

Inside the barber shop, Emerson Lydon was confronting his younger brother.

"Listen to me. You always said you wanted to get involved in something big, so now's your chance. You have the easy part. All you need to do is keep buyin' me supplies over the next few days and keep your eyes and ears open. I've been campin' out on the prairie and it's getting downright cold at night. So, I need to find me someplace to hang out away from town. I have another horse out of town, so I'd prefer something with a corral. You know any place like that?"

Elrod was always afraid of his older brother. When they were kids, he was the enforcer. His father didn't care, and his mother was afraid of both his father and Emerson, so she didn't do anything to protect him either. He'd felt bullied from the day he was born and now was no different.

He wasn't looking directly at Emerson as he said, "I don't get out of town much. I don't even have a horse."

Emerson was getting frustrated with his useless younger brother and snapped, "You got a gun at least?"

"Yes. I keep it in the back room in case I need one."

"That's something, I suppose. Now, what I need you to do today is to get a hold of a guy named Jameson. He's staying at the boarding house. Just tell him I'll meet him at the saloon after six. I'm going to do some house hunting."

He tried in vain to catch Elrod's eyes, then shook his head in disgust, turned and marched out of the barber shop.

———

Carl had reached the street and quickly walked to the Appaloosa tethered in front of the barbershop. He was trying to come up with a reason for going into the barber shop but couldn't come up with an excuse and wished he hadn't been doing his own shaving the past few days and maybe if he hadn't taken a bath, but that was out of the question. He wasn't about to start offending Barbara.

As he was pondering his options, a thin, hatchet-faced man around six feet tall exited the barber shop. Carl noticed that he exited the barber's still needing a shave and a haircut, which meant he hadn't stopped there to give Elrod any business.

Carl was sure that he had never met the man before as he'd have remembered that face with his hard eyes and prominent nose. Carl was positive he had never seen him in town before, and although he'd only met a few of the residents, his memory was sharp enough to recognize strangers, and this man was definitely a stranger. Carl approached the man as he began untying the horse's reins.

"Howdy. New in town?" he asked pleasantly.

The man turned toward Carl without a smile but didn't sneer either. He just looked at Carl as if he had no business even to ask such a stupid question.

"I don't see no badge, so it's none of your business."

"Probably not. I'm new here myself and still trying to make friends."

"Well, I won't be one of them, so you may as well go on your way."

"Not a problem. Have a nice day."

The man stepped into the stirrup, swung his leg over the saddle and swung the tired Appaloosa away from Carl and headed down the street toward the boarding house. Carl watched for a while until he passed the boarding house and drifted east out of town.

"Now what's that all about?" he asked himself quietly.

He then turned and continued down the road, entered the sheriff's office and found Luck Schuster standing in front of the bulletin board attaching a wanted poster before he turned as Carl entered the door.

"Afternoon," he said.

"Afternoon, Sheriff," replied Carl, "thought I'd fill you in on a couple of things."

"Go ahead," as Luck continued to hang posters.

"Well, for one, did you notice that stranger that just left the barber shop?"

He replied, "Yup. Of course, you're dang near a stranger yourself, podner."

"True. But I'm getting kind of fond of Pine Bluffs, and I'm a bit friendlier than that cuss. He didn't take kindly to my attempt to become acquainted, either. In fact, he was downright rude."

"Ain't no crime in being rude. If there was, my little hoosegow would be stuffed to overflowing. Heck, I may even have to lock myself up at times."

"Maybe, but with his arrival and the presence of Mister Jameson, I'm beginning to get a bit worried. I found out a few days ago that our Mister Jameson, when he first arrived, had gone to the hotel and was looking for Mister Wilson, who's staying at the boarding house with his wife. Jameson got awfully out of sorts when the clerk told him he wasn't staying there. When she suggested he try Mrs. Mathias' boarding house, he left and then checked in there. I think he's planning on doing something to Mister Wilson, but he hasn't tried anything yet, and that has me wondering why."

"I'll admit that sounds suspicious, but there's nothing that I can act on. I've seen Jameson wander about town, but not doing anything that would set off alarm bells. The only odd thing about his behavior is that he doesn't seem to go anywhere. He hasn't gone into the barber shop, Jensen's store or even the saloon. It's curious, but that's all it is."

"I know. It's the same at the boarding house. He shows up for meals and either leaves or goes to his room, and never spends any time talking to anyone. I just wanted you to know what's going on. I'll keep an eye on him, though."

"You do that. I like things peaceful, and that's the way they are right now. It's more than I can say about all that coal mine territory in Carbon County. Seems like there's all sorts of law breakin' going on over there. I'm just glad that it ain't my jurisdiction. A man could get laid out livin' in a place like that."

"That's what Tom Wilson says. He's supposed to be going over there and checking out the conditions for the Union Pacific when he gets the go ahead from the local sheriff."

"That may be a long time coming, though."

"Well, it's not my call. See you around."

Carl left the sheriff's office, believing that he had done his civic duty. Then he headed for the hotel, finding the same girl standing behind the desk when he entered.

"Good afternoon, miss," Carl said as he approached the desk.

"Good afternoon," she replied with a warm smile.

"Say, a tall skinny gentleman with a thin face didn't try to check in, did he?"

"Another one of your missing friends?" she asked.

"No, ma'am," Carl replied with a grin, "just curious. I ran into him in the street and he was a bit on the nasty side. So, my curiosity got the better of me and I was wondering if he was staying or going."

"Well, if he's staying, it's not here. We haven't had any new guests in two days."

"Thank you, ma'am. Hopefully I won't bother you anymore."

"Oh, you're no bother. Feel free to come by any time," she replied as she smiled broadly at him.

She didn't bat her eyes at him, but she may as well have.

Carl touched the tip of his Stetson, then turned and left the hotel.

So, now a new character has entered the mix. Carl hoped he hadn't circled back and gotten a room at the boarding house, but with that possibility in mind, he quickly strode down the road and marched up the walk to the boarding house.

He crossed the porch, went inside, and walked down the hallway to Barbara's room. The door was closed, so he pressed on to the kitchen, finding her there preparing dinner.

"Barbara," he asked, "Have you had new boarders today?"

She turned and answered, "No. Why?"

"Well, there's a stranger I just met that reminds me of Jameson and he hadn't checked in at the hotel, so I thought he might be heading down here. He has me a bit worried."

"Why?"

"A few days ago, I did some checking on Jameson. I went to the hotel and found out that he had been questioning the clerk about Tom Wilson and when she told him he wasn't there he got angry. Then she suggested your place and he came here and rented a room. It seems he may try to harm Tom Wilson, but his lack of action has me puzzled.

"Now this new guy arrives and doesn't check in anywhere. I talked to Tom Wilson about Jameson and he thinks Jameson may be a member of a labor union out west called the Knights of Labor. They're causing all sorts of trouble out there in the mining camps and probably aren't too anxious to have Tom show up. I would have told you earlier, but I didn't want to get you worried. Now, with this second guy, I'm not so sure anymore. I just don't want you to rent him a room. If he tries, tell him you're all filled up."

"I could use the rent, though."

"If he shows up, turn him away. I'll make up for any lost rent. That's not a problem but I want to keep some measure of control of the situation."

"Carl, you shouldn't be throwing away your money like that."

"It's fine. Money's not a problem. I'm not rich or anything, but I've saved up enough to not have to worry about it."

Barbara had a worried look on her face, but said, "Okay. If he shows, I'll send him to the hotel and let you know. Will that work?"

"Yes, that's fine. Thank you, Barbara. I really hate to put you into this position, but I don't see a way out of it until Jameson leaves and this whole situation blows over or it comes to a head."

"I understand."

Carl took a deep breath, smiled, then said, "I'm going to head up to my room and stretch out for a bit to think, but I'll be back down for dinner."

Barbara smiled back and said, "I'll see you then, Carl."

Carl quickly walked back down the hallway before climbing the stairs to the second floor and entered his room. He pulled off his boots, hung his gunbelt on the bedpost, and stretched out on the bed with his hands behind his head. He knew he wasn't going to nap, but he had to try to get a handle on this whole affair.

After almost an hour of deep thought, he was still getting nowhere and decided to go down to the sitting room and see if the Wilsons were there and maybe Tom could shed some light on his growing concerns.

He sat up, put on his boots without checking for critters, but strapped on his gunbelt before he headed downstairs. He wasn't going anywhere unarmed anymore.

When he arrived in the sitting room, he found the Wilsons in residence and sat down in an easy chair.

"Find anything new?" Tom asked.

"I'm glad you asked, Tom. I just saw a recently arrived stranger at the barber shop, a tall, thin guy with a hawk-like face, and not a very friendly disposition, either. He reminded me a lot of Jameson, at least in his character. He rode a nice Appaloosa mare, which is what first caught my attention. In fact, after I talked to him, he rode that mare east right out of town. It was an odd thing for him to do. There's nothing east of town at all to my knowledge, then when I checked with the hotel, he hadn't checked in there either."

"It sounds like you should have been a Pinkerton agent, Carl."

"No, thanks. I'd rather not have a job where getting shot at is a daily requirement."

"So, what do you think?" Tom asked.

"I wish I knew. My gut tells me that the new guy and Jameson are working together. Their personalities are similar and neither wants to talk about what he's doing."

"I guess all I can do is keep my eyes open."

"We all can keep our eyes open. I'll have your back, Tom."

"Why? You don't have a dog in this hunt."

"Maybe not directly, but I hate to see good folks being put on the defensive by bad actors, and those two are bad actors."

Tom replied, "Well, thanks for your help. It's appreciated."

Tom then took out his watch and said, "It's about time for me to do my daily telegram check. I'll be back in a few minutes."

He rose and left the sitting room and soon exited the house.

After Carl heard the door open and close, he was about to stand when Emily Wilson said, "Carl, please sit down. I'd like to talk to you."

"Yes, ma'am," Carl replied as he returned to his seat.

"And stop calling me ma'am or Mrs. Wilson. I don't know why you're still doing that after all this time. It makes me feel old. I'm barely past thirty. My name is Emily and I'd appreciate it if you'd call me that."

"My apologies, Emily, and I never considered either you or Tom old. In fact, I'd consider you both quite young and handsome."

"Very nice recovery, Carl. Now, what can you tell me about what's going on? Tom has been dancing around the subject every time I try to ask."

Carl began to squirm and felt as if a noose was being tightened around his neck or at the least, an ugly, overly tight necktie.

"Emily, I really think you should hear it from Tom. I've only mentioned some suspicions I've had concerning some men that are in town."

"You mean Jameson, of course."

"He's one of them. The other is the man I just mentioned."

"Are they going to cause my husband harm?" she asked with raised eyebrows.

"I'm not certain. They may just be hunting for information. I just know that Jameson was looking for your husband when he arrived but hasn't done anything since to indicate he's hostile toward Tom. It's just a gut feeling I get when I see him. That's all."

"I have the same feeling, but I'm helpless to do anything."

"Well, there are some steps you can take. First, when you go to sleep at night, make sure your door is locked and the curtains are closed. If there is a knock at the door, ask who it is and make sure you know who it is before you open it. Aside from that, all any of us can do is wait."

"I understand, and we'll do as you suggest. Are you taking any steps?"

"I usually lock the door of any room I'm in and close the curtains out of habit. I also sleep with my Colt loaded and easily accessible."

"Are you any good with that pistol?" she asked.

"I practice with both of my weapons, so I'm proficient, but I've never fired at a man before. I've always been able to avoid any confrontations through other means."

"Good for you, but just knowing you're nearby will help me sleep better."

"That's the idea. I hate the idea of good people coming to harm."

"Especially Barbara Mathias?" she asked with her eyes full of mischief.

"And Beth," he answered honestly, smiling back at her.

"Well, you protect us as best you can."

"I'll do that, Emily."

At precisely that moment, Barbara entered the room, and Carl wasn't sure how much of the last few sentences of the conversation she had heard but noticed there was a definite pink shade in her cheeks. He wasn't the least bit upset that she had heard it, either.

"Dinner will be ready shortly," she said, then smiled at Carl as she left the room.

"Well," said Carl as he rose, "I guess we'll head over to the dining room."

As they were walking down the hallway to the dining room, the front door opened, and Tom Wilson entered, followed closely by John Jameson, and Carl wondered if Jameson had been tailing Tom.

They all entered the dining room as Barbara began bringing in the platters and bowls of food. After they had seated, and Carl had said his silent prayer of grace, each began putting the sliced beef and mashed potatoes on their plates, then as they began to eat, Tom began speaking.

"Well, Carl, looks like I'll be leaving you for a few days."

Carl glanced out of the corner of his eye and noticed that Jameson's head jerked up suddenly.

"Why is that, Tom?"

"The boss has decided for me not to wait on the sheriff and head over to Rock Creek to check out the situation. I'll be taking the morning train and I should be back by Tuesday or Wednesday."

"Are you going alone?" Carl asked.

"It seems that way. The railroad doesn't want a lot of presence there, so they're just having me go there for a quick evaluation."

"It seems like a precarious situation to put you in. Why don't they send one of their railroad agents down there instead?"

"Because the agents are good at finding theft and protecting things, but they wouldn't be able to get a handle on labor problems. I could get a much more accurate picture of what's going on than they could."

"I'm guessing that Emily is staying here until you get back?"

"Yes. I'm sure she'll be safer here. You and Barbara can watch out for her until I get back."

"I don't know, Tom. Are you sure you wouldn't want me to come along? I could serve as a bodyguard. Besides I need to feel useful."

"No. If I needed a bodyguard, I'm sure that Union Pacific would have assigned me one."

"I'd still feel better if I went along, though."

"I appreciate the offer, but I'd sleep better knowing you were here to help Emily if she needs it."

"I noticed neither of you two manly men have asked my opinion," Emily finally said.

Tom turned, looked at his wife and knew this wasn't going to be a light-hearted argument.

"Your opinion is always welcome, dear. It's just that I'm being ordered to go there, and I don't have many options."

"I think having Carl there would be safer," she argued.

"Maybe. But in this case, I don't think it would matter. I'll be staying at the Union Pacific hotel and they have guards there, so I'll be fine."

Emily shook her head, understanding that there would be no victory in this one and had to let it go for once.

She said, "Okay. I'll give in just this once, but you had better get back here as soon as you can, husband."

"Yes, ma'am. I'll do that," Tom replied with a slight smile after the surprisingly swift and bloodless victory.

The subject was finished, and the rest of the dinner was spent eating and talking about useless topics that everyone recognized as little more than time fillers.

When they finished, Carl continued his tradition of helping Barbara in the kitchen while Beth went to her room to do homework.

Carl and Barbara worked side-by-side doing the dishes and pots and pans with little conversation as each was lost in thought.

Suddenly, Carl stopped in the middle of scrubbing a particularly food-encrusted pot, then put it back down and looked straight ahead.

"What's wrong?" Barbara asked, alarmed by his expression.

"I don't know. I suddenly had this bad feeling that something is going to happen. I have no reason for it, it just exploded inside me."

Barbara just looked at him, waiting for him to explain more, which he did.

"I've had this nagging feeling most of the day, but until a few moments ago, it was just that. Now it feels like impending disaster and I can't shake it."

Barbara put her hand on his shoulder, but was so overcome by his feeling of dread, he almost didn't notice it – almost.

"Maybe it's just a buildup of all the tension over the past week," she suggested.

"Maybe. I just don't think so. But I guess all I can do is keep a watch out and see what happens. It's probably nothing. I'm sorry I brought it up."

"That's alright. Sometimes we need to get things like that out."

Carl nodded and went back to washing the grimy pot as Barbara removed her hand from his shoulder. He wished that her touch would have made that ominous feeling vanish, but it hadn't even faded, and that made it more relevant.

After they'd finished with the dishes, Carl smiled at Barbara then walked past her bedroom where Beth was doing her homework and entered the sitting room but found it empty. It surprised him until he realized that Emily probably felt that maybe some private time with Tom would get him to change his mind, or maybe they just needed some private time. That thought did diminish his premonition enough to allow him to chuckle under his breath.

There was no reason to stay in the sitting room and talk to himself, so he reversed course and headed back to Barbara and

Beth's room, stopped at the door and rapped on the pine surface.

From inside the room, Beth called, "Come in, Carl," so, he turned the knob and entered, leaving the door open.

Beth had her read spread before her and a pencil in her hand as she smiled up at him.

"Writing those letters?" he asked.

"I'm trying to, but some look goofy."

"Now that puts me into a real dilemma."

"What's a dilemma?"

"It's a time when you have to decide something that's very hard."

"Oh. Why does this make a dilemma?"

"Well, ma'am, here I was expecting to find you all finished so I could see if I could talk your mama into take you down to the drug store for some ice cream, but you're still studying. I guess I'll have to wait for some other day."

"But…but I'm almost all done, Carl!" she exclaimed with big eyes.

Carl looked up, scratched the side of his neck and said, "I don't know, Beth. Homework is really important."

"Please, Carl? Can you ask mama?"

Carl kept a poker face, which was getting more difficult to hold as he looked across at the Christmas morning expression on Beth's face.

"I suppose I could do that, but you might have to convince her to let you go before you're done."

"I can do it, Carl!" she quickly replied before slamming her reader closed, tossing her pencil on her bed and bouncing from her chair.

It was almost painful to keep the serious expression on his face by the time she grabbed his hand and yanked him toward the kitchen with her small legs churning.

"Mama! Mama! Carl needs to ask you something right now!" she exclaimed as they exited the hallway into the toasty kitchen.

Barbara looked at Beth's wildly expectant face and then at Carl's face which was just beginning to crack, but at least Beth's focus was on her mother now.

"And what is the nature of this critical inquiry?" she asked as she managed a stern mother image, which was much easier for her than Carl as he tried to keep his poker face.

Carl met her blue eyes as he replied, "Well, Barbara, I just told Beth that I was wondering if it would be okay if we postponed Beth's homework, so I could escort her to the drug store for some ice cream."

"Well," Barbara said as she looked at Beth's round eyes, "homework is very important, young lady. Do you think that I would allow you to put it off just to go off with Mister Ritter so you could have a treat?"

Beth's big eyes shriveled as she looked at her mother's stern face as she quietly replied, "No, Mama. I'm sorry. I'll go back to my homework. I guess I know what a dilemma is now anyway."

Before she turned, Barbara said, "Well, Beth, I'm sorry, too. I would have thought that at least you would have asked Carl if I could come along. Then maybe I'd give in to your request."

Beth's head snapped up before she whipped around to look up at Carl as she blurted out, "Can she come too, Carl? It would fix the dilemma! Could you ask her? Please?"

Carl finally smiled, relieving the tense facial muscles that had been holding it back, then looked at Barbara and said, "Mrs. Mathias, I know that Beth has been working very hard on her homework and she's almost done for the evening, so perhaps you would grant her this small boon as a reward for her hard work and excellent progress."

Barbara looked at Carl as if she was making a critical decision, then looked down at Beth's revived expectant face.

"Well, she has been doing all of her homework and I suppose that a break wouldn't hurt. So, as long as I get some ice cream of own, then I guess she can go."

Beth began bouncing on her toes as she looked at Carl, waiting for his answer.

Carl smiled at her, bowed at the waist and said, "Her majesty has spoken, therefore, I, your humble servant, shall patiently wait on the porch whilst she and her princess gown themselves appropriately. Upon exiting the castle, I shall lower the drawbridge and escort her royal personages to yon purveyor of frozen treats."

Beth was giggling as he straightened, gave a quick wink to Barbara, who was close to giggling herself as he turned and majestically marched down the hallway.

Carl soon reached the porch and took a seat in the nearest rocking chair to await the Mathias ladies. As he rocked, he studied the surroundings and assumed it was a typical Friday evening in Pine Bluffs, Wyoming. He could hear the music coming from the big saloon at the far end of the street with the accompaniment of some of the cowboys and local men letting off steam, but it didn't sound like anything getting out of hand, at least not yet. He imagined it would be different later.

Sooner than he expected, Barbara and Beth exited the front door and he rose from his rocking chair.

"Your majesties, shall we depart?", he asked as he removed his hat, bowed and swung the Stetson in a graceful arc toward the street.

They both giggled this time, as he plopped it back on his head. Barbara took Beth's right hand and Carl her left as they stepped down from the porch, crossed the short walkway, then strolled down the street. They moved to the boardwalk when it began just a couple of hundred feet away, and Carl could feel Beth's excitement as she gripped his hand. It was just a couple of blocks before they reached at the drug store, and when they swung open the door, a small bell rang announced their arrival.

"Good evening, Mrs. Mathias," said the proprietor from the far end of the counter.

"Good evening, Mister Adams," Barbara replied, "This is Carl Ritter, Mister Adams. He's a guest at my boarding house and has graciously offered to buy Beth and me some ice cream."

"Well, it's a perfect night for it. What flavor would you like?"

Beth asked the obvious question, "How many do you have?"

"I have chocolate, vanilla, and strawberry. I also have some orange sherbet."

Beth's face scrunched up in indecision, so Carl said, "I'll tell you what, why not give Beth one scoop of each and I'll have a scoop of the sherbet."

Then he looked over the top of Beth's head and asked, "Barbara?"

"I'd like some vanilla, please."

Carl turned back to Mister Adams and said, "There you go, sir."

Ben Adams smiled as he nodded then said, "Coming right up, folks," and turned to scoop out their order.

Two minutes later, they were seated at one of the three small tables in the shop and Carl watched as Beth assaulted her ice cream with her metal tool. As he watched Barbara's more reserved spooning of her vanilla, he assumed that neither had ever even had ice cream before, and he thought that was a sin.

He was polishing off his sherbet and probably wouldn't have noticed if it was steaming mashed potatoes and gravy as he looked at Barbara. She worked so hard to provide for her and Beth and never had the opportunity to enjoy even the simplest of earthly pleasures. He took his last bite of his rapidly melting orange sherbet and silently vowed to change that if she let him.

Barbara hadn't looked across at Carl but knew that his eyes were focused on her. She wasn't in the least annoyed or even remotely uncomfortable. With each passing hour they shared, she became more convinced that their time together would never end.

After they had finished, and Carl paid for the treats, they left the drug store heading back to the boarding house with Beth in the middle again and Carl on the street side.

Beth was almost dancing as she held onto Carl's and her mother's hands when she exclaimed, "Thank you, Carl! I've never had ice cream before! It's even better than root beer!"

"You're entirely welcome, Milady," Carl replied.

"I enjoyed it as well, Carl. Thank you for the wonderful evening," Barbara added.

"You both deserve much more than ice cream, Barbara," Carl replied as he looked at her in the dim light.

Barbara just smiled, but inside, she danced more than Beth.

Just as they arrived at the end of the house's walkway, Carl picked up the sound of hoofbeats, then turned and spotted the stranger atop his Appaloosa trotting behind them.

The rider passed and gave them a quick glance before heading toward the saloon.

Carl just followed him with his eyes as they turned down the walkway to the house, but soon stopped.

"Is that the man you told me about?" Barbara asked as she looked at the fading rider.

"That's him. At least he's going somewhere," he replied before they resumed walking.

As they were walking up the porch steps, Jameson exited the front door, nodded at them without a word, and quickly stepped down the walkway and headed down the street following the path of the unknown Appaloosa rider.

"You go inside," Carl said, "I'm going to have a seat on the porch for a few minutes."

Beth asked, "Why? Does your tummy hurt from the ice cream?"

Despite the tension of seeing the stranger and Jameson, he still smiled. Only a seven-year-old cutie could break up a potentially dangerous situation.

He replied, "No, sweetie, I'm feeling fine. I just want to watch the street for a minute or two."

Barbara glanced at Carl before she herded Beth into the house. His earlier premonition about impending danger replaced the simple joy she'd been feeling since he'd asked her and Beth to share the evening treat. She hoped that his feeling was wrong, but knew he needed to be alone and would want her and Beth away from any danger.

After they had gone inside, Carl sat in the nearest rocker and mimicked a casual guest enjoying the evening after dinner. He scanned the street, paying particular attention to the disappearing shadow of Jameson. *Where was he headed? What were they up to?*

His first question was answered a minute later when he watched Jameson enter the saloon and Carl guessed it was to meet with the Appaloosa rider when he spotted his horse tied up at the saloon's hitching rail. He'd love to find out what they were talking about but knew that would only cause trouble as soon as he passed through the batwing doors, trouble that may not even be necessary. He'd have to wait to see how this played out, but just knowing that the two men were in cahoots was an advantage. It was why there were in cahoots that still bothered him. Whatever it was, he was convinced that it involved Tom Wilson, the Union Pacific, and the increasing violence in Rock Creek.

———

In the saloon, Emerson Lydon saw Jameson enter and just watched him until they made eye contact.

Jameson then headed in his direction, nodded at the bartender, held up a finger and said, "Beer."

The bartender acknowledged his order as Jameson pulled out a chair and sat. Neither man spoke until his beer was delivered a minute later, then they watched the bartender leave.

As soon as the bartender was back to his place behind the bar, Emerson looked at Jameson and said in a low voice, "Krueger has added a bit of a twist to our job."

Jameson had just taken a long drink of his beer, finishing half of the glass, then set the glass back onto the scarred, stained tabletop, wiped the foam from his mouth with the back of his sleeve and belched.

Then he stared at Lydon and asked, "What are you talkin' about? What kind of twist?"

Emerson grinned and replied, "After you do your job here, we're gonna head west and blow up a bridge."

"What?" Jameson asked too loudly, startled by the news.

"Quiet down," Emerson snapped, "It ain't that bad."

John Jameson was still stunned as he listened as Emerson Lydon explained what and why Otto Krueger wanted the bridge or trestle destroyed and when they had to get it done.

Jameson wasn't happy at all that Krueger had just sent this messenger to give him orders and he thought the whole plan was too complex and required more information than they'd be able to get, but was most made him angrier was that he was sure that he wasn't getting paid any extra for doing it and was sure that Emerson was making more for the job.

When he finished his explanation, Lydon asked, "Are you ready to do your job before we take on the bigger one?"

Jameson nodded and replied, "Yeah, it won't be too hard, but it's gotta be tonight 'cause that railroad man is supposed to be leavin' on the train tomorrow."

"I didn't hear about that, so it looks like I got here just in time. I'm all set up anyway, so I'll be ready. I'll be waitin' out in back of that boardin' house tonight with some horses for our escape and then to get on with the next job, the one Krueger sent me here to do.

"You just need to get your ass along the porch after you kill him, then then climb down one of those porch posts. I've got to borrow a horse for my useless brother, Elrod, too. He's gonna help us to get out of here but that's all. I found an abandoned line shack about five miles north of town and a path to get there that will hide our tracks, unless they got some Indian to come lookin'."

Emerson snickered before continuing, "Elrod will come along only far enough to cause some confusion, then I'll send him back. I don't want my idiot brother givin' us up. He's a weak bastard and I'm ashamed that we share the same name."

Jameson laughed and said, "I met your brother, and I reckon he's not exactly happy to have you for as kin, either."

Lydon just glared at Jameson for a few seconds, but asked, "You figure you can do what I just told ya?"

"Yeah, it's not a problem. Let's go over what we gotta do after we leave this nothin' town. Krueger's gonna have to ante up some more money for me, too. He didn't pay me for two jobs."

"That's between you two, Jameson," Emerson replied.

With the first part of their mission settled, they began discussing the follow-up job in a hushed, conspiratorial volume as more patrons entered the saloon. Despite his reservations about the second half of the job, Jameson found himself growing more enthusiastic with the idea.

Blowing up a railroad bridge and killing a train loaded with railroad folks was going to be an exciting thing to watch, even more than pumping a few slugs into that bastard back at the boarding house. He could already visualize the train hurtling off of the tracks and flying into the chasm before crashing into the rock. Jameson was soon smiling as he listened to Lydon.

————

Just a few hundred yards east from where they were plotting, Carl continued to scan the saloon, but after about a half hour, he realized that they weren't coming out soon and it would be too dark to see them when they did, so he headed into the house. He walked down the hallway to check if the Wilsons were in the sitting room, but they weren't, so after noticing an empty kitchen and Barbara's closed bedroom door, he sighed and walked upstairs to his room. He took a seat on his bed to try and understand what was happening down in that saloon, and although his earlier feeling of pending disaster was gone, it had made him more anxious. With Tom leaving in the morning to catch the train west to Rock Creek and those two getting together, he could feel the converging paths about to crash together, but made the critical mistake of believing that whatever they were planning, it would be on board the train after it left Pine Bluffs.

A short time later, as he was still deep in thought, he heard the sound of footsteps in the hallway followed by a door opening and closing. He knew that Tom and Emily were in their room, so that left only one other possibility. Jameson had returned from his meeting, and Carl momentarily considered making up some excuse for going to his room and having a late-night chat, but couldn't see any advantage to letting him know that he was suspicious, so he just continued to think.

———

In Jameson's room, John Jameson sat on the stiff wooden chair and ran his part of the plan through his head. It wasn't a difficult or really a very dangerous task, but he still spent another forty minutes reviewing what he was going to do.

He'd wait until everything was quiet and everyone had been asleep for a couple of hours, then he would quietly walk up to the Wilson's door. He wouldn't even try the doorknob because he suspected the door was locked. He'd checked the workmanship on the doors and found them to be second rate, so he could just throw a shoulder into the door and blast it open.

Once he was in the room, he'd empty his revolver at the Wilsons and put them both out of their misery. He took a few seconds to almost inhale the image of the bloody mess he'd leave behind and had an almost beatific smile on his face before he let his mind continue to his escape when the killing was done.

Before he left to do the shooting, he'd open his room's window then, after shooting the Wilsons, run back to his room, crawl out onto the wraparound porch roof, head to the back of the boarding house and climb down one of the roof support posts and just ride away with the Lydon brothers. They'd ride to the line shack and after that, it was up to Emerson Lydon.

It was going to be a noisy, but exciting night. He had his revolver in his hand and made sure it was loaded before setting it on his bed. He blew out the only lamp in the room and waited impatiently in the dark. He was as excited as most men would get when they were about to meet an attractive and willing young woman. To John Jameson, this was much better and would leave an even bigger mess.

————

As he sat in his room, despite his conclusion that Jameson and the Appaloosa rider wouldn't act until they got Tom alone on the train, he hoped that Emily remembered the advice he had given to her and that she had locked their door. He still didn't believe that Barbara or Beth were in any danger, but would feel better in the morning when he was sure that Jameson would be gone.

He checked his Colt, making sure there were five cartridges in the chambers, then removed his gunbelt and hung it over the corner bed post. His Winchester still sat unused in the corner with his saddlebags, so he didn't go check on his repeater's load.

He didn't even take off his boots, before he stretched out on the bed, planning on just resting for a few minutes before he got up and did some reading and could provide some measure of protection for the Wilsons if he was wrong about Jameson's plans. He just couldn't believe that Jameson, or any other man, could shoot an innocent woman.

His plan may have been just to relax and do some more thinking, but he didn't execute it well.

Carl soon drifted into a deep sleep that was suddenly broken when something startled him to an instant state of alert. He didn't know what had awakened him or even what time of the night it was, so he stayed on his bed and listened carefully but heard nothing. *What woke him up?*

It wasn't a bad dream, because he'd remember that. Out in the prairie a lot of things would wake him suddenly and sounds that didn't belong there were the most common reason. *So, what sound didn't belong here?*

———

In the dark hallway, Jameson walked as quietly as he could. He had his pistol drawn, the hammer back and ready to fire. His heart was pounding with excited anticipation as he leaned back on the opposite side of the hallway, took a deep breath, then launched himself at the Wilsons' door. Even though he expected the hinges to give way, he was surprised how easily the screws surrendered. He was also surprised by the noise, which threw him into the start of a panic, knowing that he needed to get the job done quickly if he wanted to make his escape.

In the subdued moonlight coming in the room's window, he spotted his victim bolt into a sitting position then watched his eyes grow wide at the sight of Jameson's pistol.

Instead of lunging at the shooter, Tom turned and flung his body over Emily as Jameson fired once, then cocked his hammer and fired again. But as he pulled back on the hammer for the third shot, the hammer stuck. *A jam!*

Jameson swore loudly after taking a few precious seconds to free the frozen piece of steel, then gave up, knowing that his first two shots had hit Wilson, and ran down the hallway to his room, snatched his travel bag as he passed by his bed, and slipped through the window into the porch.

It was wet with dew and he almost slipped but quickly regained his footing and headed for the back end of the porch. As he reached the rear, he noticed the shadowy figures of the Lydon brothers on horses leading a spare.

He tossed his travel bag to the ground, then slid down the porch roof and rather than bother with the support column, simply dropped off the edge, rolling as he hit the dirt. As he mounted the horse with the only empty saddle, he noticed Elrod's worn-out horse.

"Is that the best you could do?" he asked Emerson with a grin.

He snickered, replied, "It was the best he deserved," then asked, "did you kill him?"

"Him and that bitch of a wife," Jameson answered with pride.

"Good. Let's get out of here," Emerson said before he wheeled his horse around and headed east.

John Jameson gave one more quick look at the boarding house as he nudged his horse and set off behind the brothers at a reasonable pace.

———

Even as Jameson was sliding along the porch roof, chaos had arrived in the boarding house. Carl had been shocked by the loud crushing crash from the hallway, and as he started to stand, he heard a pistol shot followed by a second.

There was a pause followed by a loud curse and the sound of running as Carl stood, snatched his Colt out of his holster, cocked the hammer and headed for the door, then cursed himself when he realized that he had locked the door.

He quickly released the lock and stuck his head out into the corridor, making sure the shooter was gone. Once he knew it was clear, Carl rapidly exited his room and turned left in the hallway, already knowing who had been shot and who had pulled the trigger. He had to help Tom Wilson before he went after Jameson, who he was sure was already making a planned escape. If he'd thought that the creepy bastard was going to do some harm to Barbara or Beth, he would have been in a real dilemma, but dismissed that idea. Jameson had wanted to stop Tom Wilson.

As he headed for the Wilsons' room, Carl glanced into Jameson's empty room with its open window before he turned back and saw that the Wilsons' door had been smashed off its hinges, so he rushed into the room and found Tom Wilson on top of Emily, who was sobbing and holding onto her husband.

Carl scanned the room to make sure it was empty, quickly released his pistol's hammer, thrust his Colt into the waist of his britches, stepped to the edge of the bed and the bloody scene.

Emily's shocked reaction prevented him from being able to help Tom, so he tugged on her arm and shouted, "Emily! Let him go! I need to check on him. This is Carl! The shooter is gone! Let him go!"

Emily acted as if she hadn't heard him and continued to cling to Tom as blood spread over his back and head and onto the bedding. Carl pulled on her arms to free them, but she was fighting him.

"Emily! Let go! Now!", he screamed at her just three feet from her ears, and she finally seemed to notice that he was there.

"Carl! He shot Tom!", she yelled, but she finally began to relax her vice-like grip on her husband.

Carl replied more quietly, "I know, Emily. The shooter is gone, but we need to get Tom to the doctor now. Let him go and I'll take care of him."

Emily finally opened her arms to let Carl roll Tom onto the bed where Carl quickly examined his injuries in the poor light. He quickly realized that one of the shots had creased the right side of his head and the second had hit him somewhere on his back, but where it had struck or how much damage it had caused wasn't apparent. There was a lot of blood, there wasn't much light, and Tom was wearing dark pajamas making it difficult to pinpoint the wound's location.

"I'll take him to the doctor, Emily," Carl said.

Suddenly, the hallway was bathed in light as Barbara arrived in her nightdress carrying a lamp.

"What happened?" she asked.

"Tom's been shot. I've got to get him to the doctor," Carl said loudly without looking up at Barbara.

Barbara replied, "He's probably at home right now. His house is three houses down the street. I'll take you there."

Carl slipped his arms under Tom and gently lifted him from the bed and rolled him close to his chest. Carl was lucky that Tom wasn't a very big man and probably weighed less than a hundred and seventy pounds. That being said, Tom still was awkward to carry as Carl lugged him down the hallway and carefully stepped down the stairs. By the time he reached the first floor with his unconscious load, Barbara had grabbed a coat and led Carl out the door.

Emily followed, but didn't put anything on over her blood-covered nightdress.

Carl carried Tom down the empty street as quickly as he dared. No one was outside as it was either very late at night or early in the morning.

After walking for what seemed much longer than it probably was, Barbara turned and opened a gate to a large brick house, trotted down the long, paved walkway, then stepped up the porch stairs and began pounding on the door before Carl arrived at the bottom of the porch steps.

A few seconds after Carl arrived at the door with Tom, a light illuminated the front window and the door opened to reveal a short man in a nightshirt.

"Doctor McNamara, we have a man who's been shot and needs help!" Barbara exclaimed.

The doctor looked at the entourage on his porch and waved them in and wordlessly waved them inside.

Once Carl entered, the doctor said, "Take him into the first room on the right. I have an examination table there."

Carl turned into the examining room, saw the table and slowly lowered Tom onto its surface.

The doctor looked at his patient, turned and said, "Okay, I need you all to please wait across the hall in my sitting room."

As they slowly crossed the hall, the doctor's wife was already heading to the kitchen to boil the water she knew her husband would need. After she put the water on the stove, she walked down the hallway to the examination room, entered and closed the door behind her.

After they'd taken seats in the sitting room, Carl turned to Barbara and said, "Barbara, can you go back to your house and bring Emily some clothes and shoes? And it would probably be a good idea to bring Beth back here for her safety. I'm sure that Jameson is gone, so you'll be safe."

Barbara looked at Emily's distraught face and nodded, realizing that Emily's needs were greater than her own, then rose and left the house.

Carl sat down next to Emily and asked, "Are you okay, Emily?"

She nodded and sniffed but didn't reply.

"Stay here, okay. Barbara went to get you your clothes and shoes. I need to go and get the sheriff. Will you be all right?"

"Yes," she whispered.

The examination room door opened, and Emily's head jerked up to see if she was going to be given horrible news, but it was Mrs. McNamara, who was just returning to the kitchen to retrieve the warming water.

Carl patted Emily on the shoulder, wishing he could tell her that her husband would be all right, but that was the doctor's call, so he hurriedly walked outside. As he reached the porch, he noticed the sheriff trotting down the road toward him. He was only half dressed but was wearing his Colt at his hip and carrying a shotgun, so Carl stayed put and awaited his arrival.

As soon as the sheriff spotted him, he pointed his shotgun in his direction as he continued to walk and said loudly, "Carl, stay there and put your hands in the air!"

Carl was puzzled at first and then he grew angry as he exclaimed, "Dammit, Luck! What the hell are you talking about?"

"Don't give me any guff. Just do it!"

Carl was still seething as he raised his hands before Luck reached over and removed the Colt from Carl's britches. He then gave the barrel a quick sniff and then handed the revolver back to Carl, who slipped it back under his pants' waist.

"Sorry, Carl. But there's been a shooting and you were there with a gun. I had to make sure."

Carl sighed a breath of relief and said, "I understand, Luck. You were just doing your job."

"So, what do we have here? I talked to Mrs. Mathias when she was on her way back to her house and she gave me the basics that Mister Wilson had been shot and not much else."

"I was in my room and out like a light when something woke me. I listened for a while but didn't hear anything until I heard a door being crashed open followed almost immediately by two shots. After the second shot, I heard the shooter cuss and start running. I stuck my head out and didn't see anyone, so I ran down to the Wilson's room and saw it broken off its hinges, then I went inside and found Tom shot. Two wounds that I could see, a crease on the right side of the head and another in the back. Then I grabbed him and brought him to the doctor. That's where we are now."

"Let's go inside," he said.

After entering, they spotted Mrs. McNamara as she toted a pan of hot water into the examination room. She nodded at them, then entered the room, closing the door behind her again.

Carl and Luck walked into the house and entered the sitting room where they found Emily sitting on the couch with her head down still crying, as Carl walked to the couch and sat down next to her.

"Emily, the sheriff is here. Do you think you can talk to him?"

Emily nodded but didn't look up.

The sheriff sat down in the chair across from the couch and asked, "Mrs. Wilson, can you tell me what happened?"

She raised her head and looked at the sheriff with red rimmed, tear-filled eyes.

"We were sleeping. Suddenly we heard a loud noise and realized that the door was broken open. There was a man standing there with a gun. I couldn't see who it was. He was just a shadow. Then Tom realized what was happening and he rolled over me to protect me. He didn't want me to get hurt! He took two bullets, so I wouldn't be hurt! I heard the two gunshots and felt Tom jerk, but he never said anything. Then the man with the gun began swearing. I think his gun jammed or something, so he ran away and the next thing I knew Carl arrived and picked up Tom and took him here."

"Thank you, ma'am. We'll get him. Don't you worry about that."

"Thank you," she whispered before she rested her head on Carl's shoulder.

The sheriff stood, looked at Carl and said, "We won't be able to find anything until we get some light. My deputy is pretty worthless for anything more than cleaning out the jail. Can you track at all?"

"Fairly well, but I'm no Kit Carson."

"But will you help?"

"Count on it," Carl answered.

"See you at first light," said the sheriff, who took one last glance at Emily before he turned and left the doctor's house.

Shortly after the sheriff had gone, a fully dressed Barbara entered the room leading a very sleepy Beth and holding Emily's clothes as she approached Emily and touched her shoulder.

"Emily, I have your clothes if you'd like to get dressed. I'll see about making some tea, too. Come with me."

Emily took her head from Carl's shoulder and slowly stood, looked down and asked, "Can I wash my feet first?"

"Of course, you can," Barbara replied before guiding Emily from the sitting room as Beth crawled into a big cushioned chair, where she curled up and closed her eyes.

Carl was still sitting on the couch when Mrs. McNamara left the examination room, closed the door behind her then entered the sitting room and searched for Emily.

"How's Tom?" Carl asked.

"He'll be fine. He's lucky he got here so quickly. He didn't lose as much blood as he could have. The wounds themselves weren't as serious as you probably expected. They appeared to be smaller caliber bullets and one shot barely grazed his skull and the second glanced off the rib rather than penetrating the chest. The bullet didn't even break the rib. My husband finished cleaning the wounds and is suturing them now and should be done in about another thirty minutes. Mister Wilson shouldn't even be laid up that long. He was very lucky, or the shooter was a horrible shot."

"Thank you, ma'am. Barbara and Emily are in the kitchen, I believe. Emily is getting cleaned up and dressed and I think Barbara's making some tea as well. But to be honest, I'm sure your news will be a lot better medicine than a cup of tea."

Mrs. McNamara smiled and said, "I imagine that's true. I'll go tell her."

Carl noticed that Beth had was already sound asleep in the chair recently occupied by the sheriff. Carl smiled as he looked at her, knowing that only a child could find peace on a night like this.

Carl sat on the couch wondering if he could have done anything more to prevent the shooting. He was angry that he'd fallen asleep and been so wrong in his belief that Jameson was going to wait until he got Tom alone, but in the end, he knew that it was pointless to spend time worrying about what should have happened. It still bothered him, though, and felt an overwhelming sense of relief knowing that Jameson had failed. If he'd succeeded, then he'd be questioning his failures for the rest of his life. Now, he'd have to avoid making more mistakes if he was going to help the sheriff, Tom and Emily.

While he was lost in his reverie about the shooting, Barbara entered the sitting room and took a seat beside Carl.

ROCK CREEK

He looked up into those marvelous blue eyes, obviously saddened by what had happened in her boarding house.

"Did Mrs. McNamara tell you and Emily about Tom's condition?" he asked.

"Yes. Emily started crying again, only this time it was from relief. She gave us both hugs and finally sat down to have her tea."

"I'm glad to hear that because she needed some good news. I'm glad you brought Beth with you, I was worried about her," he said, then paused and added, "this still bothers me, Barbara. I feel as if I should have done more to protect Tom. I thought I could stay awake after I heard Jameson return, but I drifted off to sleep. This shouldn't have happened."

"Carl, you know you couldn't have prevented this, even if you'd stayed awake. All we can do now is make sure that the shooter is caught and punished."

"There's more to this than just that, Barbara. I'm sure that this shooting was just a piece of a much larger problem that is on the horizon. It all revolves around that damned coal mine in Rock Creek."

Barbara's eyebrows rose as she asked, "Is it because of what you said about the union?"

Carl nodded, then replied, "Tom was supposed to go there when he first arrived in Pine Bluffs, but he was held up because the sheriff in Carbon County said it was too dangerous. Then Jameson arrives, looks for Tom and Tom thinks he's a member of that thug union in Rock Creek, but Jameson doesn't do anything. Then Tom is given orders to go to Rock Creek and he gets shot, probably by Jameson. What do they hope to accomplish by assassinating a Union Pacific executive? What is their strategy? There must be one, but I can't figure it out. If they keep this up, it'll just bring the wrath of the Federal government down on their heads and the army at their door. I just don't get it and it's making me crazy."

"Whatever it is, it's nothing that we can solve tonight, and I think it's the railroad's problem now anyway. Let's check on Emily."

Carl nodded before they both rose and after Barbara checked on her sleeping daughter, they walked down the hallway to the kitchen finding Emily seated at a table sharing tea with Mrs. McNamara. They both looked up as Carl and Barbara entered the room.

"How are you, Emily?" Barbara asked.

"Much better. I'll be able to see Tom shortly."

"That's good. Did you want us to stay here with you?"

"No. You both go home. I'll be back after a while. And Carl, thank you so much for taking care of Tom. I know I wasn't much help."

Carl smiled at Emily and said, "I wish I could have done more, but it looks like he's going to be okay. If you need anything, don't hesitate to ask."

Emily gave him a weak smile and nodded, before Carl and Barbara turned, then headed back to sitting room. After passing over the threshold, they looked down on the sleeping Beth.

"Don't wake her," Carl said, "I'll carry her back."

Barbara smiled and answered, "Okay."

Carl gathered Beth, who never opened her eyes, and hugged her close. She automatically put her arm around his shoulder and sighed making Carl smile before he followed Barbara out of the sitting room, then the front door and into the night.

The return walk carrying Beth was a lot easier for Carl than the one to the doctor's house carrying Tom, and much more pleasant for many reasons, Tom would be all right, he was holding the precious Bethany in his arms, and Barbara was walking beside him, almost shoulder to shoulder.

They arrived at the house, climbed the steps to the porch, then Barbara trotted past and opened the door. After quietly going inside, she went ahead to open their room as he carried Beth into the house, nudged the front door closed behind him with his boot heel, then carried his bundle into the bedroom and gently lowered her into the small bed near the window. The blankets were already pulled back when Barbara had taken her from the room, so Barbara quietly removed Beth's shoes, then pulled the blankets up over Beth before she and Carl stepped out into the hallway.

In the dim light of the hallway, Carl softly said, "Barbara, I need you to go into your room with Beth and lock the door. I'm going to do a walk through the house to do a thorough inspection to make sure everything is safe. I'm almost positive that Jameson is gone, but when I'm completely sure, I'll tap four times on your door to let you know it's okay. I'll lock both front and back doors and stay in the sitting room until the sheriff arrives so we can track Jameson. Okay?"

Barbara nodded and said, "Alright. Good night, Carl. And thank you for everything."

Carl gazed into those incredible blue eyes, wanting to kiss her in the worst way, but thought the timing was terrible, so he simply said, "You're welcome."

Barbara smiled, then turned, entered her room, closed the door and Carl waited until he heard the lock click.

He then walked to the kitchen, lit a lamp, made sure the kitchen door was locked then took the added precaution of putting a chair under the doorknob before beginning his inspection. All the other downstairs rooms were empty, including every closet and hidden space he could find, so he went upstairs for the first time since the shooting.

He checked out his room to make sure his Winchester was still there. It was, as were his saddlebags, then he slid his Colt into the holster hanging from the bedpost, strapped on the gunbelt and left his room to resume his search.

Next, he passed through the shattered doorway and checked the Wilsons' room. Blood was splattered over the bed and the wall, but except for that despicable mess and the door broken from its hinges, there was nothing notable.

Then he checked the three vacant rooms finding them untouched and even checked under the beds, but saved Jameson's room for last. The door was still open, and he could see the open window, but there was just a minute chance that Jameson was off to the side with his pistol, waiting for the law to arrive, so Carl took a deep breath and just took one step into the room, then stepped back.

There weren't any shots, so he entered the room and except for the open window, there was nothing remarkable about the room. The bed was still made and there were no personal belongings anywhere. It looked just like the vacant rooms, with the exception of the open window. He went to the window and looked outside, hoping that Jameson wasn't waiting for a head to appear, but thought it very unlikely, and given his poor marksmanship earlier, it was even less likely that he'd get a hit even if he did try a shot.

ROCK CREEK

There was enough light to see the roof of the wraparound porch and could even make out some darkened areas where the early morning dew had been disrupted, making it obvious that Jameson was the assassin and he had planned his escape through his room's window.

Carl closed the window, left the room, quietly tiptoed down the stairs, then went out the front door one more time and scanned the outside. It had returned to a normal quiet night, even though it was close to the predawn.

He closed and locked the door, then as he passed Barbara's door on his way to the kitchen, he tapped four times lightly, then went to the back of the house.

After he arrived in the kitchen, took some kindling and started a fire in the stove. Soon he had a good fire going and closed the firebox door, pumped some water into the coffee pot and put it on the hot plate. A few minutes later, he made a full pot of hot coffee to pass the time until the sun rose and use the time to think about Jameson.

He sat down at the kitchen table and looked over at the chair under the doorknob, realized that wasn't necessary if he was there, so he walked over and returned it to its normal duties at the kitchen table. Finally, he remembered that he didn't know what time it was, so he pulled out his watch and looked at the hands which told him it was 4:15 in the morning. He knew the sheriff would be arriving shortly to begin his investigation, so he opened the pantry and took out some bacon, then went to the larder and took out six eggs and some bread.

He had just put the frying pan on the fire when he heard noise behind him, and with the doors all locked, he knew it had to be Barbara and that the best thing he could do was to try to return the house to an atmosphere of normalcy.

Without turning around, he said, "Good morning, Mrs. Mathias. How are you this fine late summer Saturday morning?"

He heard her light laugh before she replied, "Well, just fine, Mister Ritter. I didn't know you could cook."

"Well, there's cooking and then there's cooking, ma'am. I can handle bacon and eggs, and even a steak now and then but that's about it. I surely can't create the delightful food that you prepare. Your cooking is the best I've had since I left home, and that's not an empty compliment."

Carl saw no reason to expand on his own culinary talents that had been passed onto him by his parents, as it would sound like so much bragging.

"Well, thank you for the compliment, empty or not. Would you like me to take over now?"

"No, ma'am. I want you to sit down and let me serve you for a change."

"If you insist," she replied with a smile as she took a seat.

"I do. Besides, you'll have to cook Beth's breakfast when she wakes up."

"Oatmeal isn't cooking. It's pretty easy."

"I actually still like oatmeal. Of course, I add honey and cream to make it less bland and tasteless."

"I'll remember that."

By then the bacon was sizzling and Carl had added a few slices for Barbara.

"How do you like your eggs?" he asked.

"Over easy, if you can manage it."

"I can. Did you want to go unlock the front door in case Emily or the sheriff arrives? I don't think we have anything to worry about with the sun ready to come up."

"Okay," Barbara answered before she rose, then left the kitchen as Carl pulled the bacon from the pan, then after cracking open the eggs into a bowl, slid them onto the hot frypan.

They were popping in the bacon grease when Barbara returned then retrieved some plates, cups and cutlery and set the table. Carl picked up one of the plates, dropped some bacon and two eggs, over easy, onto the plate and handed it to Barbara. He loaded another plate with bacon and four eggs, also over easy, then sat down across the table from her. He bowed his head and a few seconds later began demolishing his breakfast as Barbara ate hers, but in a more dignified, ladylike manner.

"Hungry?", she asked as she smiled.

"I have no idea what could have given you that impression," he replied with a grin.

She looked at him more seriously and asked, "So, what are you going to do now?"

He sat back and looked into her eyes and didn't answer for a few seconds.

Finally, he said, "Well, first, I'll help the sheriff track the shooter, but I'm sure it's Jameson, and I'm just as sure everyone else does as well. His room was empty, and the window was wide open. When I looked at the porch, I could see where he slipped down to the porch's roof and went around back. After that I have a few things I need to take care of."

"Will you be staying around?" she asked expectantly.

Carl misinterpreted her question entirely, and replied, "It depends on what I learn after I talk to Tom. I'm going to offer to go to Rock Creek in his stead to look the place over."

Barbara couldn't hide her shock at his unexpected answer, and quickly exclaimed, "Carl, you can't do that. You could get killed!"

"Barbara, Jameson shot Tom and would probably have killed him and probably Emily as well if his gun hadn't jammed or he'd been a better shot. I feel like I owe him for that mistake."

"That's the silliest reason I've ever heard, Carl. You don't owe him a thing! If anything, we all owe you. You came here ten days ago and all you've done is help people, including me and Beth. You've warned Tom and the sheriff about Jameson and did everything you could do to prevent what happened. Going to that Godforsaken place would serve no purpose except to ruin other people's lives. You're too good a man to throw all that away for some misguided sense of obligation."

Carl didn't say anything for thirty seconds as he looked at the concern and strength in her eyes.

Finally, he exhaled and replied, "You may be right, Barbara. I may be tilting at windmills and there may be no useful purpose for my going to Rock Creek, so let me talk to Tom. If he convinces me that there's nothing to be gained by heading there, I'll stay. Okay?"

"Well, if that's the best I can hope for, it'll have to do."

Any further conversation was interrupted by a knock on the front door.

"Come in, Luck," shouted Carl.

He figured if it was Emily, she would have just walked in and was proven right when the sheriff walked into the kitchen thirty seconds later.

Barbara stood, then nodded to the sheriff as she passed him before heading back to her room.

Carl watched her leave, then looked at the sheriff and asked, "Need some coffee or breakfast, Luck?"

"Coffee's fine. Already had breakfast at home."

Carl rose, poured a cup of coffee and began filling in the sheriff on his discoveries about Jameson's room before handing him the cup.

After they were seated, Luck said, "Looks like we have our shooter."

"It's not really a big surprise to anyone, is it?"

The sheriff shook his head, almost in embarrassment, but didn't reply.

Carl noticed and said, "If it makes you feel any better, Luck, I heard him pass by and go into his room, but then fell asleep which gave him his opportunity. At least he failed in his attempt, so all we can do is find the bastard."

Luck nodded, then replied, "We gotta get goin', Carl."

They quickly finished their coffee, then walked down the hallway to the front door. As they passed by Barbara's closed door, Carl wondered if she went back to get some more shuteye but doubted it. He guessed that she was simply watching Beth and waiting for her to awaken.

Luck and Carl stepped down from the porch, turned to the left, then cut across the front of the yard and walked to the area that faced Jameson's room. Carl pointed out the correct window and Luck began searching the ground near the porch.

"There doesn't seem to be any tracks at all."

"I wouldn't expect there to be any," said Carl, "I noticed that the dew on the roof was disturbed and there was a darker path leading to the back porch that Jameson had left behind. I'm guessing he had someone waiting for him. Probably that guy on the Appaloosa."

"That makes sense," the sheriff replied as they walked to the back of the house.

When they approached the back alley, it was obvious to both of them how Jameson had made his escape. There were multiple sets of hoofprints along the back of the porch roof, and judging by the amount of manure, it appeared that the horses had stayed near the porch for a while. The hoofprints showed agitation as the horses were upset by something, probably the gunshots and the startling arrival of Jameson. The animals wanted to leave, and their riders had to keep them in position.

"Looks like Jameson had help getting' outta here," Luck commented unnecessarily.

Carl just nodded but noticed that there were more than two sets of hoofprints before he began walking eastward following the escape route with his head down watching the hoofprints as Luck walked alongside doing the same. After they had gone almost hundred feet, Carl stopped and bent down.

"Looks like there were three of them," he said, "They must have waited in those trees just over there for even longer than they did behind the house."

He pointed to a stand of elms just to the north of the property, and continued, saying "Then, when they saw Jameson open his window, he must have signaled them from his room, and two of them came out mounted and trailed the third horse. You can see the hoof prints are deeper on two of them when they headed toward the house, but all three were the same when they left."

Then Carl walked into the elms and searched their waiting spot, finding manure piles and a good number of cigarette butts.

"They had to wait for a few hours. I'm guessing they were here before midnight."

"Can you trail them out of here?"

"I'm not exactly an Apache scout, but I'll see what I can do."

Carl and Luck began tracking the three horses on foot for almost a mile before they stopped.

"Well," Carl said, "I think it's time to start riding rather than hoofing it ourselves."

Luck agreed, so they reversed course to get their horses before they resumed the search.

Luck headed back to get his horse and some provisions, not knowing how long they'd be out.

On his way back to the house, Carl turned and headed to the Western Union office next to the train station.

After entering, he approached the telegrapher and said, "You received a telegram for Tom Wilson yesterday. I'm guessing it was from the president of Union Pacific. Is that right?"

The clerk looked at him with suspicious eyes and replied, "I'm sorry, sir, but I'm not allowed to divulge any information regarding telegraphic messages."

"It doesn't matter, really. I'll need to send a telegram. I'll write it out and if it's not the same address, don't sent it. Okay?"

The telegrapher didn't commit one way or the other, so Carl wrote out his message and handed it to the clerk. As he read the message his suspicious eyes faded and were replaced with a look of incredulity as he asked, "Is this correct?"

"Yes. If it wasn't, I wouldn't be sending it."

The telegrapher read the message:

PRESIDENT UNION PACIFIC RR OMAHA NEB

**THOMAS WILSON SHOT THIS MORNING IN HIS ROOM
WOUNDS NOT LIFE THREATENING
SHOULD MAKE FULL RECOVERY
HE BELIEVES SHOOTER A KNIGHTS OF LABOR MAN
SUSPECT STILL AT LARGE WITH TWO PARTNERS**

CARL RITTER PINE BLUFFS WYOMING

He counted the words and said, "That'll be sixty cents, sir."

Carl handed him the change, then said, "If you get a reply, I'll be over at Mrs. Mathias' boarding house."

"Yes, sir," the operator said before turning and sitting at his set where he began quickly tapping the key.

Carl left the office and headed back to the house to check on Barbara and maybe Emily if she'd returned.

After he entered, he found Barbara in the kitchen and told her that he was going to grab some bread and a canteen of water and hopefully he and the sheriff would find where the three riders had gone.

"Wait a few minutes and I'll fry up some bacon for you," she said.

While he waited on the bacon, Carl went to his room and picked up his saddlebags and his Winchester, then checked the repeater, making sure the action was still smooth and it was fully loaded. After he checked the saddlebags to make sure they still contained enough ammunition, he left his room and went back downstairs.

Barbara had his bacon cooked and had even sliced some bread and made a bacon sandwich that she wrapped in butcher paper. She looked up at him when he entered the room and smiled.

"This should keep you fed during your trip. Hopefully you won't be gone long."

"Thank you, Barbara. I expect we'll be back quicker than Luck might expect. My guess is that these guys knew where they were going and picked a route that would be difficult to track. They sure have had their time to do it. My real question now is, who is the third man?"

"There were three?" she asked in surprise.

"Yes, ma'am. There were two men waiting in that stand of elms behind your house and must have been waiting there three or four hours. When Jameson finished his job, he slid along the porch roof and then they had a horse waiting for him, so they could get off quickly."

"That's going to make things worse, isn't it?"

"Maybe."

She handed him his sandwich, which he slid into his saddlebags, then he filled his canteen at the pump, threw the saddlebags over one shoulder and the canteen over the other and began to leave the kitchen.

Barbara said, "Be careful, Carl."

Carl glanced into her blue eyes and replied, "Always."

Then he turned and headed out the back door and crossed the street to Ethan's livery to retrieve Jules. As he entered the stable, he overheard a string of vile language that would put a Boston longshoreman to shame.

"What's up, Ethan?" he asked loudly as he crossed the barn floor.

From deep in the livery, Ethan replied gruffly, "Some bastard stole one of my horses!"

Carl stepped back to Jules' stall, grateful that they hadn't taken his mount, rubbed his horse's nose, fed him his treat and then turned to Ethan.

"As it turns out, Ethan, I bet I know who took your horse."

"You do?" he asked with raised eyebrows.

"Yup. Somebody shot Mister Wilson in his room at the boarding house early this morning and got away by sliding along the roof. He had two accomplices waiting for him and I'll bet that one of the horses was yours, and I'd further guess that you're missing a full rig as well."

"That, too. I wonder why they didn't take the buckskin, though. The one they took was one of my older horses. I don't have any respect for a damned horse thief, but this one was just plain stupid."

"This bunch seems to be doing stupid things left and right. The sheriff and I are going to be tracking these hombres shortly and I'll let him know about your horse. Personally, I think they're just going to use him for a while and set him loose. Don't be surprised if your missing horse comes wandering back to you, but let me or the sheriff know if he does, will you?"

"I'll let you know, and I'm obliged for you tryin' to find him," Ethan said as Carl quickly began saddling Jules.

He soon walked his gelding out of the livery and wasn't surprised when he spotted Luck riding his way. The surprise was to see the sheriff riding a mangy old horse that didn't look like it had too many miles left before it just flopped over and expired.

"Good God, Luck! That horse may not make it out of Pine Bluffs!" he exclaimed when the sheriff was close.

"Ain't meant to. It's a rare day that we have to travel more than a mile or two."

"As it turns out, I don't think we'll have to travel that far today anyway. I have a feeling that these three already planned their exit and picked a path that won't leave much sign, but I may be wrong. One other thing, Luck. Ethan found that someone had stolen one of his nags, but they didn't even take that nice buckskin he has. They took one of the old ones and took a full rig, too. I told him we'd be tracking the horse thief today, but I have a feeling that his animal will be turned loose and come back on its own. It would be too easy to spot them if they were seen on Ethan's horse. The Appaloosa is bad enough."

"You're probably right. Let's go find that trail."

They picked up the trail where they had left off, and by now the sun was high in the sky and the tracks were easy to pick up and it didn't look like the escapees had made any effort to disguise their tracks, which surprised them both.

After an hour of plodding, they left the soft ground behind, began running into rocks and shale, and the trail became much harder to follow.

Then it entered a stream, and Carl knew that they would soon lose the trail altogether. He knew the tendency of tracked men to follow water upstream and then exit on the same side as they entered, so he kept Jules at a walk on the entry side while the sheriff walked his tired critter on the other bank, but after a few minutes neither had found where they the three riders had left the stream. They continued for another mile before they gave up hope of picking up the rail again, so Carl crossed to the other side and pulled up before the sheriff.

"Do you reckon there's any point on goin' further?" the sheriff asked.

"Nope. But it's not like I expected to find anything. The ground is hard, and I was looking for any sign of passage. An upturned stone or some mud that didn't belong or a scratch on a rock, but I found nothing."

"Might as well head back, then."

Carl was angry with his own lack of ability. He knew he was in over his head, but that didn't mean he had to like it.

They got back into town just around noon, but before they separated, Carl told the sheriff, "By the way, if you hear a bunch of shooting this morning, that'll be me taking some target practice."

"Glad you mentioned it. I'd hate to get old Wizzie here out for a second ride in one day."

Carl laughed, then asked, "Wizzie? Really?"

"His name used to be Wizard, but he's only worth a Wizzie these days."

Carl was still laughing when they separated, and Luck headed for his office while Carl continued to the end of the street, then pulled up before R.M. Topper's Firearms. He dismounted, flipped his reins over the hitching post, then entered the gun shop.

He hadn't even noticed the tucked away small shop for the first two days he had been in Pine Bluffs, then we did notice the place, he'd been surprised that the owner had set up his business in the town, but then put it in the same category as the doctor. He'd be busy just repairing the passing cowhands' weapons and selling them new and better ones, not to mention the ammunition that went with them.

After entering, he found the shop to be empty, so he let out a middling loud, "Hello, anyone here?"

"Just a minute," R.M. replied from his workroom.

A few seconds later, the diminutive man exited the curtained room and stepped up to his counter.

"I haven't met you before, son. You come in with that last cattle drive?"

"Yes, sir. They've headed back, but I think I'm going to leave the cow business."

"What can I do for you?"

"I'm looking for a couple of smaller caliber revolvers that a woman can handle. Something on the order of the Colt Pocket Navy. Got anything that fits the bill?"

"I have more than I should. They're not as popular as the six-shooters and don't use cartridges, so I'll make you a good deal."

"Do they have the four-and-a-half-inch or the five-and-a-half-inch barrel?"

"These all have the shorter barrel. It's probably another reason why I still have them."

He turned, re-entered his back room, then returned with six boxes, placed them on the counter and opened the topmost box.

Carl picked up the revolver, pulled the hammer and after pointing it at the back wall, squeezed the trigger. After the hammer snapped back, he set it on the counter.

"This one seems pretty tight. Let me check the others."

After looking at the first four, he selected the two with smoothest action and the lightest hammer pull.

He set aside his two chosen pistols, then said, "I'll need some ammunition and percussion caps, too."

The gunsmith didn't have to leave as he dropped to his heels and pulled the correct size ball and paper pouches of powder for the Colt.

When they were all stacked next to the pistols, Carl asked, "Do you mind if I put a couple of rounds through each pistol?"

"Not at all. I have a range set up out back. I hope you're not expecting much in the way of accuracy. I wouldn't say more than twenty yards with those short barrels."

"That sounds about right," said Carl.

He took the two revolvers, and some of the ammunition and percussion caps, then headed out the back door to the range with R.M. following. The shop owner didn't expect Carl to walk off with the pistols and wouldn't even have cared if he did. He just was curious to see how good he was with the small Colts.

After loading the first pistol with three rounds, Carl took aim at the target which was set at about fifty yards as he wanted to see how close he could get at that range. Anything within a foot would be impressive. He quickly settled the sights on the target, cocked the pistol and fired. It wasn't as much kickback as he expected and noticed that his first shot caught the outer edge of the target.

"Better than I expected," said the shop owner.

Carl looked at him and replied, "So, am I. I didn't think that .36 would come close."

Carl took his last two shots with the first revolver and hit the target with the last two. The second pistol also shot well, so it was a satisfied Carl Ritter who returned to the shop with a very impressed gunsmith.

Once they were back in the shop, Carl set his two new pistols on the counter and asked, "How much for both guns and the ammunition?"

"Twenty-six dollars."

"Do they come with cleaning kits?"

"Yes, sir."

Carl paid for his purchase as R.M. returned the pistols back into their boxes, then put the ammunition and percussion caps into a cloth bag.

"Come back and visit some time," R.M. said as Carl picked up his order.

"I should have stopped by the first day I was in town," Carl replied before he turned and headed out of the shop.

He returned to Jules, slid the boxes and bag into his saddlebag, then mounted and set his roan to a walk and headed for Ethan's livery.

He stopped outside, dismounted, then led Jules inside where he saw Ethan still forking hay up to the loft.

Before Carl could announce his presence, Ethan spotted him, waved, then set down his pitchfork and strode toward him.

"Find anything?" Ethan asked.

"Nope. The trail petered a couple of miles out, and even though I kind of expected we'd lose it, I'm still a bit annoyed."

"I can understand that," Ethan replied, then asked, "What exactly happened. You didn't tell me much. I've been hearin' all sorts of stories."

As Ethan listened, Carl began explaining while he unsaddled Jules and was still talking as he gave the gelding a good rub down then finally finished and led him to his stall.

"Give him some extra oats today, could you Ethan? He's earned it."

"Not a problem."

Carl hung his overloaded saddlebags over his left shoulder, then picked up his repeater and headed for the boarding house.

After entering, he walked through the foyer and headed for the kitchen, but as he passed the sitting room, he spotted Emily reading a thick tome, so he turned into the room.

"How are you, Emily?" he asked when she looked up from her book.

She wore a tired smile but didn't look nearly as upset as she had earlier, even after learning that her husband's wounds weren't serious.

"I'm much better. Tom was awake and eating when I left. He's still sore but should be able to come back tomorrow. Did you find anything?"

"We lost the trail about three miles out of town in some rocks and a stream. It still makes me mad that I couldn't find it."

"You did all you could."

"If you have a minute, I'd like to talk to you and Barbara at the same time."

"Okay. I think Barbara's in the kitchen."

Emily put down her book and followed Carl into the kitchen where he found Barbara slicing a large ham.

Upon hearing them enter, Barbara turned, visibly relieved to see Carl walking in with Emily.

"You're back," she said with a smile.

Carl smiled back as he leaned the Winchester against the kitchen wall and replied, "Yes, ma'am. We lost the trail, but that was expected. When you can take a minute, I'd like to talk to you and Emily."

As Carl and Emily took seats at the kitchen table, Barbara put down her knife, stepped across the room to join them as she wiped her hands on her apron.

After she sat down, Carl set his saddlebags on the table, then flipped open the flap, reached inside and shook his head as he pulled out the bacon sandwich.

"I guess you weren't hungry after all," Barbara laughed.

Carl grinned, said, "Wrong saddlebag," then slid the sandwich back into its temporary leather home.

He then flipped the saddlebags over, stuck his hand into the right saddlebag and extracted the two boxes. The women glanced at each other after they read the brand name.

"Are those what I think they are?" asked Barbara.

"Yes, ma'am. These are Colt Pocket Navy revolvers and I'd like each of you to keep one with you until this is all settled. Tom or I may not be around when trouble arrives, and I'd feel a whole lot better if you each had one in your purse, or anywhere else you'd feel comfortable carrying them. They aren't heavy, and they don't have much of a kick, but because of their short barrels, they're effective only at short range, about fifty feet or so."

"Carl, I've never fired a gun before," said Emily before Barbara echoed her own lack of experience with firearms.

"I suspected that might be true, which is why I picked these. I'd like to spend a little time showing you how to use them but won't bother showing you how to reload or clean them. In fact, my greatest hope is that you'll never even need to use them at all. It's just that I'm very concerned for your safety, and these weapons are a last resort, but one that might become necessary."

"I think that we could handle them," said Barbara.

"If you think so, Carl," Emily added.

"We'll try it out later. I just wanted to let you know about it first, but there's something else I need to ask both of you."

Barbara and Emily exchanged a second wary glance. *If the first request involved shooting people, what might the second entail?*

"I know that Tom is laid up until tomorrow, and we've lost Barbara's other boarder, hopefully for good. So, with the house as empty as it's been for a while, I'd like to invite both of you, along with that other little lady, to a nice dinner at the hotel restaurant tonight. My treat."

"Carl, that's not necessary," said Barbara.

"No, it's really not," Emily chimed in.

"I know that. But when was the last time you had a night off, Barbara? I'll bet it's been years. And Emily, you need to relax after today's ordeal. Besides, this would be a rare chance to escort the three prettiest ladies in the whole territory to dinner. It might be a bit selfish on my part, so are you really going to deny my selfish desires?"

"If you put it that way," said Barbara with a small smile, "how could we fail to grant you one night to indulge in such a fantasy?"

Carl extended his arms and said, "Tada! Thank you, ladies. I'll pick you up at six and escort you to dinner."

Amid much laughter from the ladies, Carl stood, bowed, collected his saddlebags and Winchester, then headed back to his room. As he passed Barbara's room, Beth plowed into him as she exploded out of the doorway.

"What is happening?" she asked.

"I just invited your mama and Mrs. Wilson to dinner tonight at the hotel restaurant."

"Oh," she said, with a tinge of disappointment.

"Of course," he continued, "this is bad news for you, you know."

"I suppose," as she slipped deeper into the depths of sadness that only a seven-year-old can know.

"That's because when you come with us to the restaurant, you'll have to wear that brand-new dress your mama made for you, and you won't be able to spill any food on it because it has to stay clean for church tomorrow."

She couldn't wait for him to finish his sentence when she squealed and threw her arms into the air.

Carl pulled her from the floor and gave her a hug as he said, "You didn't think we'd really go anywhere without you, now did you?"

Without a word, Beth hung on tight and Carl let her stay where she was for a few more seconds before he lowered her to the floor. As he did, he saw her glance down the hallway, then turned and saw her mother and Emily watching with moist eyes from the end of the hall.

Carl smiled, then wiggled his fingers rather than wave, feeling it was more appropriate, then tapped a happy Beth on the head before he continued down the hall to the stairs.

Once in his room, he shucked his hat, boots, and saddlebags, propped his rifle in the corner, then removed his gunbelt and hung it over the bedpost before he stretched out on the bed. He took a deep breath, then remembered the forgotten and uneaten food in his saddlebags. He didn't want to let it go to waste, especially because Barbara had made it for him.

As he munched on the sandwich, Carl ran the day's events through his mind and found a mixed bag of answers and many more questions.

By the time he'd popped the last of the sandwich into his mouth, he hadn't come up with any conclusions, but at least he'd be having a very enjoyable supper in a little while. He'd talk to Tom as soon as he could to explain what had happened after he'd been shot and maybe he'd be able to shine more light on what lay ahead.

The long, adrenalin-filled night and lack of sleep caught up with him and Carl drifted into a good nap to recover some of the lost rest. Even before he lost awareness of the outside world, he suspected that he'd need all the sleep he could get over the next few days.

———

An hour and a half later, Carl awakened, unsure of the time yet again and wondering what had happened to his internal clock. He pulled out his watch, hoping he hadn't overslept, and found it was only four-thirty. He smiled when he reminded himself that either one of the adult women or the young lady would have probably tapped on his door shortly anyway. Now he needed to get cleaned up and ready to escort the ladies to dinner.

He popped out of bed, headed for the washroom, shaved and washed what needed washing, then brushed his hair and returned to his room where he changed into his Sunday best and went downstairs. All was quiet, and for a minute, he debated about going back and getting his gunbelt, but decided that it wasn't necessary, at least hoped it wouldn't be necessary.

He scouted out the house but couldn't find anyone anywhere. *Where were the women? Where was Beth?* He noticed that the door to Barbara's room was closed and thought she was taking a short nap with Beth, so he decided to walk down the street to see how Tom was doing before they went to the hotel restaurant.

Carl quietly shut the front door behind him, crossed the front porch and trotted down the steps and was soon heading east. Three blocks later, he turned onto the doctor's walkway and soon knocked on the door. After thirty seconds or so, the door opened, and Mrs. McNamara smiled at him.

"Good afternoon. Carl, isn't it?"

"Yes, ma'am. I just thought I'd check on Tom."

"Join the crowd," she said as she opened the door to admit him, "they're all gathered in his room. It's down the hall and the last door on the left."

The mystery of the missing ladies solved, Carl pulled off his hat and followed the doctor's wife, and after she continued onto the kitchen, he stopped and entered Tom's sick room. He found all three missing females in the small room, fussing over poor Tom. Well, the two adult females were fussing, but Beth seemed a bit bored.

Carl cleared his throat to announce his arrival, and everyone turned to face him, including the grateful eyes of the patient.

"It's about time you showed up!" Tom said from his bed, "I'm getting mothered to death in here. I keep telling them that I'm not on my deathbed. I'm just sore."

Carl grinned as he replied, "I'm sorry, Tom. You deserve the attention. All I wanted to tell you is that you might want to lose a pound or two."

"About that, Carl. Emily told me what you did, and the doctor said if you hadn't gotten me down here as quickly as you did, that I might have lost too much blood. I know that Emily or Barbara couldn't have carried me here. I'll never be able to thank you enough."

Carl opened his mouth to confess his mistakes, when Tom put up a finger before blunting anything he would say.

"And don't you dare start telling me how you should have stopped it, either. Barb told me how you believed you screwed it up, but I don't want to hear it. Only that bastard Jameson is to blame for what happened. I don't want to hear another word about your noble attempt to place any fault on yourself. It's downright silly."

Carl smiled, then shrugged and said, "I suppose that you think that my offer to take the ladies to a nice dinner at the hotel restaurant is silly, too."

"I heard about that. I don't think it's silly, but you have no idea what you're getting yourself into. If they get together like this, it's only a matter of time before you're corrected and scolded like you're a troublemaking eight-year-old boy."

"Now you're beginning to scare me, Tom. I thought it was a great idea until now," Carl said before asking, "How are you really doing, Tom?"

"Like I said, I'm sore where the bullet nicked my side, and I still get a little dizzy when I try to stand up from that new part in my hair, but it's already clearing. I can't do any heavy lifting for a while even if I wanted to try. My chest will remind me that it's a bad idea before I even think about it."

"It could be worse, Tom. I'm sure that the doc mentioned that if either of those bullets had been an inch closer, you wouldn't be sitting there being pampered by the ladies. Of course, the opposite is true as well, Jameson could have missed entirely. I still find it hard to believe that he was as ill-prepared as he was."

"We'll talk about all that when I get out of here."

Carl nodded, then replied, "I needed to talk to you about other things, too. By the way, I sent a telegram to your boss letting him know what happened because he'd sent you that telegram telling you to go to Rock Creek. I thought it'd be best that he knew. Was that okay?"

"Absolutely. I wish I'd thought about it myself as soon as I woke up. Carl, Barb tells me that you're thinking of going to Rock Creek in my place to scout the town and I strongly advise you not do that. You may be able to find trouble spots, but it's the labor issues that has the railroad worried. I can address those more easily than you could. It would be a personal favor to me if you'd stay in Pine Bluffs. I probably won't be able to make it for a week or so, and by then, it may have blown over or blown up anyway."

"After reflection, I'm leaning toward staying. I've been reading about the situation in the paper, and it seems like it's getting pretty bad."

"That's a wise decision, Carl. I should be back to the boarding house tomorrow, so enjoy your dinner with the ladies."

"I'm sure I will. I'll try to behave myself, so I'm not lectured on my poor decorum. I wouldn't want the ladies to think I'm a bad boy. I suppose I'll have to leave my slingshot in my room, too."

Barbara and Emily smiled, and Beth giggled as Carl asked, "Barbara, are you all staying here any longer?"

"Beth and I will return with you, but I think Emily wants to stay for a little while."

Beth then stepped over to Carl and took his hand as Barbara wished Tom a speedy recovery before she took Beth's free hand and they left Emily alone with her husband.

The trio left the doctor's house and as they began the walk back to the boarding house, Carl said, "When we get back to the house, I'm going to head upstairs and I'll take a look at the

Wilsons' room to check it out in the daylight and see what repairs are needed to the door."

"Carl, we're going out to dinner in an hour. You can let the handyman fix the door on Monday. I'll just move the Wilsons' things to an empty room and remove the dirty linen. I don't know if they can be salvaged, but I'll see if I can clean them."

"Okay, but I'll still look at the door. It may not be as damaged as it looks. At first glance it looks like the hinges were just ripped out of the doorjamb and if that's the case, it will probably just need longer screws and a touch of paint to fix it."

"I suppose it won't hurt, but don't get yourself all dirty again, Carl," she replied as they neared the boarding house.

Carl looked at Barbara, grinned and said, "Yes, Mama. I promise."

Barbara laughed and shook her head as they turned down the walk and soon entered the house.

After letting Barbara and Beth go to their room to change for the fancy dinner, Carl climbed the stairs, then walked down the hallway and examined the damaged door jamb and leaned over to pick up one of the scattered screws that had failed to do their duty. He was surprised to see that whoever had hung the doors used inch-long screws to hold the hinges in place. No wonder it gave way so easily.

There weren't any big pieces of wood ripped from the door jamb, so the fix should be easy and cheap. He entered the room and examined the wall behind the bed. Now that there was light in the room, he could pick up more details. He noticed the way that Tom's blood had spattered across the wall, took out his pocketknife, and after sliding the bed out of the way, he scraped the wood from around the hole until he could see the back of the bullet.

Pushing the small blade alongside the projectile, he slowly eased the slug out from the wall, then dropped it into his palm and examined it closely. It was a .32 caliber bullet and after traveling just a few feet, ricocheting off of Tom's head or ribs, it had penetrated less than an inch into the dry wood. That didn't make any sense at that range. It should have punched a hole in the wall and continued through into the adjoining room. If he had tried to assassinate someone, he would have used his .44 caliber Colt and there would have been much less chance for anyone to survive. *Why would any self-respecting assassin use such a small-bore weapon?* But the fact that he had used it and it had jammed or misfired also meant that it probably wasn't well-maintained and was most likely a percussion pistol. Cartridge pistols greatly reduced the risk of either a misfire or a jam.

But even a properly loaded .32 caliber percussion pistol should have done more damage. Either he'd loaded the pistol with a flask of powder and used too little or the powder was contaminated. If he used a paper cartridge, then the powder might have been wet before he loaded the cylinders.

Regardless of the reason for the lack of power or reliability of the pistol, the result of the shooting pointed to the work of a real amateur.

Recalling that night and the cussing that followed the jammed pistol, Carl guessed that he had planned on emptying all the chambers into Tom. That would have been foolish as well because it would have left him without a defensive weapon if he'd been caught leaving the scene. He had to have known that Carl was sleeping in a nearby room and was heavily armed. This whole setup looked like a job by rank amateurs.

He pocketed the bullet, returned to his room and still had an hour to kill, so he spent most of the time cleaning his own weapons as well as the two Colt Navy Pocket pistols. The oil should smooth their action enough to make it easy for the women to cock the hammers. After they were cleaned, he loaded all of the cylinders on both weapons.

He put the small pistols into his saddlebags, before he finally changed into his new clothes, then left his room and headed downstairs. He was wearing real slacks, vest, and his new jacket, and as he turned around the bottom bannister, he was greeted with the sight of three well-dressed and remarkably handsome ladies. One of the three happened to be of the diminutive kind, but she was no less charming than the two taller females.

"Why, Carl," Emily commented, "you're quite the handsome escort."

Carl bowed and said, "Ladies, I confess to being overshadowed by your dazzling appearance. Each of you looks positively flawless, especially you, Beth. Why, you look like you're ready for your first cotillion!"

Beth scrunched up her face and asked, "What's a cattle-on?"

Carl grinned as he replied, "It's a fancy dance back east where all of the ladies and gentlemen dress in finery and spend the evening dancing and talking a lot without saying anything."

Beth shrugged, then reached for his hand and said, "I'd rather go to the restaurant and have supper with you, Carl."

"And I'd much prefer spending the evening with you and your mother and Mrs. Wilson," answered Carl as he offered his left arm to Emily.

Barbara took Beth's other hand and the four stepped out onto the porch. They reached the boardwalk as quickly as they could, so the ladies could keep their dresses as pristine as possible.

It was a cool evening considering the time of year, and they arrived at the Pines Bluffs Hotel after the short walk, then crossed the lobby and entered the restaurant on the right. After passing through the wide, arched doorway, they were seated at a table near the kitchen door. There were already menus in place and many of the other tables were already occupied. After a few minutes, a pretty, smiling waitress arrived at their table.

"Hello, Mrs. Mathias," she said as she smiled at Barbara, "may I take your orders?"

"Hello, Nancy. It's good to see you again."

While Barbara was exchanging greetings with the waitress, Carl scanned the short menu. He had already made his choice and was waiting on the women. Not surprisingly, Beth, after consultation with her mother, announced her choice first, "Can I have turkey?"

Nancy smiled at her and said, "Of course. It comes with dressing, mashed potatoes, gravy, and cranberry sauce. Is that okay?"

"Are they good?"

"Yes. They are all very good."

"Okay."

Barbara ordered the prime rib, as did Emily. Carl was glad they had chosen the prime rib, as it was the most expensive item on the menu. He'd expected them to choose the cheapest item on the list. Carl also ordered the prime rib because he hadn't had any in quite a while and loved the cut of beef as long as it wasn't overcooked.

The waitress then asked, "Would you like some wine with your meal?"

Carl looked across the table and said, "Emily, I'm sure you have a more sophisticated palate than I do. Why don't you choose?"

Barbara looked at him with raised eyebrows and mouthed, "Palate?", as Emily asked for some California burgundy. Wine was not one of his areas of his expertise, right alongside embroidery.

Nancy took their menus before she left, leaving the diners to chat before their wine arrived.

"Ladies," said Carl, "if I digress from your local norms of proper dining etiquette, please do not hesitate to inform me of my error. A swift kick under the table should suffice."

Both women laughed and Beth just looked confused.

"You want them to kick you?" she asked.

"Preferably not. If they do, it's because I've made a mistake."

"My teacher doesn't kick me when I make a mistake, but she sure walloped Willy Jacobsen's behind when he pulled Sally Fremont's hair the other day."

"You know something, Beth. I'm glad you came along. I think you'll make tonight even more special."

Beth beamed at the praise as she looked at Carl and then her mother.

"Uh-oh," Barbara said in a hushed undertone.

"What's wrong?" asked Carl.

"There's a certain barber sitting at the bar. Just to your left and he's giving you the evil eye."

Carl didn't turn to look, and he knew who the man was and the reason behind his stare, but obviously Emily didn't.

Emily could see the barber and just the way he was looking at Barbara gave her the answer to any question she may have had.

Carl said, "Well, let him look. He's not going to ruin our dinner. Just act as if he isn't there and that'll probably irritate him even more."

Nancy brought the wine and three wine glasses, then popped the cork and offered the bottle to Carl. Carl simply nodded toward Emily, who sniffed the cork and nodded her approval. The waitress poured wine into the three glasses to the halfway point, then left the half-full bottle on the table before returning to the kitchen.

Emily and Barbara each tasted the wine with looks of satisfaction.

"Aren't you going to have some," Beth asked Carl.

"No, sweetie. I never developed a taste for alcohol. I tried it a couple of times, but I didn't like it. Did you want a sip to see what it tastes like?"

"Okay, just a little one."

"Is that okay, Barbara?" he asked.

"Sure. A little taste won't hurt."

Carl handed the glass to Beth who grasped it with both hands and slowly brought it to her lips.

As the wine hit her tongue, she spit it back into the glass and made a face, before exclaiming, "It tastes horrible! I thought it would taste like root beer!"

The three adults began laughing and even the couple at the next table joined them.

Carl moved the glass of unfinished wine to his side of the table and said, "That's why I don't drink it. I just never liked the taste. It's the same thing with smoking. I tried it once and darn near coughed my head off. I figured anything that caused that kind of a reaction wasn't worth trying again. What made it worse in both cases is that the cowboys I was with told me you have to develop a taste for it first. Why would I want to develop a taste for a habit I don't like to begin with?"

"Well," said Beth with a serious expression on her face, "I'm never gonna drink wine when I grow up and I'm never gonna smoke, either."

"Good for you. I'm sure it makes your mama very happy to hear it."

Barbara said, "Yes, it does. A little wine now and then is fine. You have to get used to the taste, and as long as you don't drink too much, it's okay."

As Barbara and Emily sipped their wine, Nancy arrived with their dinners.

Carl found the prime rib to be perfect with a side of juice that accentuated the rich flavor that didn't need to be an acquired taste.

Beth enjoyed her turkey, and Barbara was pleased to see that the portions for her daughter were smaller than for the adults. Beth was especially delighted with the cranberry sauce.

"Where does this come from," she asked Carl, whom she regarded as a much better teacher than Miss Garrison.

"Most of them come from the state of Massachusetts," Carl said, "from a place called Cape Cod. It's a long narrow piece of land that sticks way out into the ocean."

"That sounds exciting, Carl! Have you ever seen it?"

"Nope. I've just read about it in books, but I'd like to go see it sometime though. I've never seen an ocean either, but I think I'd really enjoy watching those waves crash onto the shore."

"Maybe you can take me and mama with you. I'd like to see that, too!"

"Of course, I will, Beth," Carl replied, smiling when he saw the excitement on the little girl's face and wondered if he just had unintentionally proposed.

Barbara hadn't missed his reply and had the same question. They'd been growing so close almost since the day they'd met in the store, but not a single word that had passed between them had contained the hint of affection. She already was certain how she felt about Carl but was desperate to know how he thought of her.

———

Thirty minutes later, as the waitress swept by to remove their plates, Carl asked, "Ladies, would you care for some coffee and dessert?"

Both women said yes to coffee but no to dessert.

He then turned to Beth and asked, "And what about you, Beth, would you like some more milk and dessert?"

"Do they have ice cream?"

"I'm sure that they do, but if I were you, I'd have some of that cherry strudel I saw on the menu. I haven't had any since I left home a long time ago. Would you like to try some? We'll share, okay?"

"That's a good idea because I don't have a lot of room in my tummy right now."

Carl ordered three coffees and an order of cherry strudel with a glass of milk for Beth.

After Nancy left, Barbara said under her breath, "He's still staring, and I think he may come over here and say something to you, Carl."

"Don't worry. I'll take care of it if he does."

Before Elrod Lydon could cause any trouble, the waitress arrived with the dessert, coffee and milk.

Carl cut into the strudel, then fed it to Beth as if she was a toddler again.

After a wide-eyed swallow, she smacked her lips and exclaimed, "Oh! That's way better than ice cream! Can I have some more?"

"Certainly, Beth. You eat as much as you like," Carl replied as he handed her the fork and slid the dessert plate before her.

She attacked the strudel with a vengeance while the two women watched with disbelieving eyes as Carl sipped his coffee and nursed a grin. It was an incredible sight to behold from a little girl who had just announced her tummy had reached its capacity.

Before long there was nothing left but crumbs and Beth took a sip of milk before she looked at Carl with a sudden look of guilt on her face.

"Oh, Carl. I'm sorry! I didn't share with you at all. Now you won't get to have any strudel like your mama used to make for you."

"That's perfectly okay," Carl said, "it was a lot more fun watching you munching down the strudel than it would have been eating it myself. Besides, it was my papa who made the strudel, not my mama."

"Really? Your papa cooked? I didn't know men cooked."

Beth was happy that she hadn't made Carl mad, but now she was worried about her tummy. It was protesting the added volume and she hoped it didn't send it all back.

"Yes, my papa cooked, and he was very good at it," said Carl, "Some of the greatest cooks in the world are men, you know."

"Really? Can you cook, too?"

"Not as well as your mama, but yes, I suppose I can cook a thing or two."

The waitress brought the bill and Carl slipped his wallet from his new jacket pocket and handed her a five-dollar bill for the $3.80 bill.

"Thank you, Nancy," he said. "I don't need any change."

Nancy gave him a broad smile as she accepted the banknote, then turned and left.

Carl was ready to stand and escort the ladies back to the boarding house when he sensed someone standing over him and didn't have to guess who he was. He could also tell from the alcoholic cloud that wafted over him that Elrod was drunk, which might complicate things as he'd be unpredictable.

Out of the corner of his right eye, Carl saw an index finger pointing in Beth's direction before he heard Elrod's slurred voice.

"You're makin' a big mistake, woman. He ain't nothin'. Nothin'! Next week I'm gonna be famous. Gonna be important. Then you'll wanna be with me, not with him!"

The finger whipped back to Carl and he could see that it was trembling.

"And you! Who the hell do you think you are? You ain't been here long and here you are sportin' a lady that don't know you for nothin'!"

Barbara prepared to say something, but Carl simply raised the palm of his hand, then turned to face Elrod Lydon.

"Now, Elrod, it seems to me that you've had a mite too much to drink tonight, and it appears that all that alcohol has removed your good sense. I invited all three of these ladies out to dinner because Mrs. Wilson's husband had been shot and I thought it would be polite to take her to dinner. Mrs. Mathias and her daughter came along because it would be improper for me to be seen alone with another man's wife. Surely you can see that this was the gentlemanly thing to do."

Elrod, well in the throes of a drunken stupor, grew even more confused after trying to follow Carl's logic.

"But that don't make it right. She's my girl first. I got claim!"

"Now, Elrod, nobody has claim over another human being, especially someone as intelligent and independent as Mrs. Mathias. I'm sure you didn't mean what you said just now, did you?"

"Well, maybe not. Not so's you put it. But...but..."

With the two buts, Elrod simply ran out of steam. He stared at Barbara one last time, opened his mouth to say something, then snapped it closed again and swaggered toward the door. By some small miracle, he was able to make it out of the restaurant without falling on his face.

"I think we should give Elrod a few minutes," Carl said, "either he'll make it home safely or go find a nice back alley and pass out there."

"That was the second time I've seen you do that, Carl," said Barbara, "I don't know how you do it."

"Call it a gift," he said, "let's finish our coffee and start digesting all that food."

They spent another five minutes finishing their coffee, and as the adults stood, Beth seemed to be a bit lethargic as she remained seated with a strained look on her face.

"Beth," Carl asked, "would you like a ride home?"

"Yes, please," she replied letting out a deep breath.

Carl took her hand to help her stand then swept her into his arms and let her rest her head on his shoulder as they left the restaurant. By the time that they reached the boardwalk, Beth was already asleep, which was the best remedy for her overstuffed tummy.

Carl walked as smoothly as he could as he carried his precious bundle down the street, listening to the soft sounds of her sleeping breathing.

Before they reached the boarding house, Emily said, "I'm going to go and check on Tom. I won't be long."

As Emily walked straight ahead, Carl and Barbara turned into the boarding house's walk.

After crossing the porch, Barbara opened the door and Carl carried Beth into the hallway as Barbara swept past him, then opened the door to her room which she quickly entered then turned back the covers on Beth's bed. Carl laid her gently down before Barbara removed her shoes and pulled the comforter over her daughter.

"I'll have to iron that dress before church tomorrow," she said, looking down at Beth's peaceful face.

"It's a small price to pay for having a daughter like Beth," said Carl as he gazed at her angelic visage before leaving the room.

Barbara followed him back out into the hallway where they stopped, then as they faced each other just inches apart, she said, "Thank you for dinner and for handling Elrod. I thought things were going to come to blows."

"You're entirely welcome for dinner, but Elrod wasn't about to start anything. Deep down he knew that he'd get hurt if he tried anything violent, so all I had to do was give him a reason to be able to back down without losing too much face. Of course, with that face, losing some of it might not be such a bad idea."

"That's true," she replied as she laughed.

Then she quickly grew serious and decided to ask the question that had been burning inside her since he'd answered Beth's question about the cranberry sauce. It would be awkward for her, but she had to know the answer.

She locked her blue eyes on his and said, "Carl, I know you were probably just telling Beth that you'd take us to the ocean because you didn't want to disappoint her, but it, well, your answer surprised me."

Carl had also realized that now was the time to make his own confession, and replied, "I never make a promise that I don't intend to keep, Barbara."

"Then you meant it when you said that you'd be taking us with you to see the ocean?" she asked softly.

Carl gazed into her eyes and answered just as quietly, "Every word, Barbara. The worst thing about seeing wondrous things is having no one to share them with. I rode down to Arizona some time ago and saw the sun setting over the Grand Canyon. It was one of the most beautiful things I had ever seen, but I had no one by my side to share the experience.

"But even then, it's only better if the someone you're sharing it with is the same person who you want to share your life, too. It's hard to explain. It's like having a really wonderful gift, but no one to give it to."

Barbara stepped closer to him, looked into his eyes and whispered, "I'd love to share those moments with you, Carl."

Carl put his arms around Barbara and said, "We've been dancing around the obvious for some time now. Emily noticed in her German comment days ago, and I don't want to keep hiding how I feel about you, Barbara."

He then leaned forward, their lips met as she wrapped her arms around him and kissed him deeply. After a few seconds, they separated and shared a few seconds just looking into each other's eyes.

Carl finally whispered, "It's only been a short while, Barbara, but I feel like I've known you my entire life. But do you know what makes it even better?"

She whispered in return, "I can think of so many things, but what do you believe makes it better?"

"It means that my mother was telling me the truth. For as long as I could recall, she told me that in this entire world, there is someone out there that is so perfect for you that you'll know it as soon as you see her. Now, my mind doesn't work like hers and I tend to be more pragmatic, so I downplayed the notion. She kept reminding me, but I never expected her to be right. Even after I started meeting girls and enjoyed being around them. Yet even as I did, her voice was never far away in my mind, and I never felt that instant recognition.

"I thought that I'd wind up a lifelong bachelor until I arrived in Pine Bluffs. Then, the moment that I saw you standing in the fabric aisle, I knew that she'd been right all along. I've never had any doubt about it, either, never a question. I just didn't want to offend you by telling you how I felt. Then, after you told me about how all those men chased after you, the last thing I wanted to do is make you believe that I was nothing but another one of them.

"It's dangerous to express such deep affection after such a short time and I was afraid that if I did tell you, I'd hurt you and then lose you forever because you thought I was just trying to talk you into my bed. I couldn't afford to take that chance, Barbara. I'd be willing to stay in your boarding house for another ten years just to be near you. I'd have done that rather than lose you. It sounds silly, doesn't it?"

"No, not at all and maybe I shouldn't have told you about those men. That first day, when I saw you with Beth acting like the father she never had before you even saw me, I knew that you weren't like the others. Since that very first day, I knew you were special. I'll confess that after I told you about them, I had already made up my mind that if it took going to your bed to keep you here, then I would have done it willingly and happily. Remember that time in the kitchen when you saw me shudder?"

"I remember it distinctly."

"When I saw you with Beth and you were both so happy, I closed my eyes and wondered how someone could come into our lives and so quickly become such a critical part of our lives. Then I wondered what would happen when you left and that's when I shuddered. The idea was so horrible that I couldn't face it."

"So, here we are, Barbara, you, me, and Beth. It's only been ten days since we met, but you already know that I love Beth as if she were my own daughter, and you probably know that I love you, too. When you think it's proper, I'd like to become Beth's father, and your husband."

Barbara's eyes welled up, and the tears rolled down her cheeks, but she wasn't about to wipe them away as she held onto Carl.

She smiled and stifled a laugh as she asked, "What's proper? Should we wait another few months or years to satisfy the expectations of others? We'd be wasting so much time, time that we could be spending together. Is that a good enough answer for you?"

"The best," he replied before kissing her again.

After their lips separated, he smiled at her joyful face and said, "I guess now it's safe to tell you what Emily said to her husband in German, the comment that turned me as red as a sunset over the Rockies."

Barbara smiled as she replied, "Okay. Let's have it. I think I might be able to guess, though."

Carl released Barbara, then as they walked toward the sitting room, repeated Emily's comment word for word, but in German.

They stopped at the end of the hallway where Barbara smacked him on the shoulder and started laughing.

"Try again, in English!" she snapped, amid her laughter.

With a grin, Carl said, "She thought you had your cap set for me and that I was thinking along similar lines."

"That's not as ribald as I had expected. When I watched you turning red, I had a much more, um, physical image in my mind. That's what made me blush, but I'll settle for what she said instead."

As much as he would have liked to expand on her interpretation of what Emily had said, Carl didn't go there because…well, just because.

Instead, he simply said, "When we see Emily, we should tell her that she has a very keen sense of observation."

"Observation about what?" Emily asked as she entered the foyer.

Carl and Barbara turned, saw her questioning look, and broke into laughter until, after almost a minute, Barbara confessed that Emily's German message had finally been translated.

Emily smiled broadly and said, "It's about time."

Then Barbara asked, "So, do you think you and Tom will be around for the wedding?"

"A wedding? Already? My! My! You two don't waste any time, do you? Of course, we will. Tom will be here tomorrow around noon. His head feels fine, and now he's just sore. Don't either of you spoil the surprise for him, either. I want the satisfaction of watching his face drop when I give him the news. Congratulations to you both!"

As Emily headed upstairs, Barbara stopped her and said, "I've got to finish moving your things to your new room. I moved most of them earlier, but I was in a hurry and left a few things in your old room. I think it's best if I do that. Why don't you talk to Carl for a few minutes while I take care of it, okay?"

Emily nodded as she had no great desire to return to the scene of the shooting, and she really wanted to talk to Carl about the startling revelation.

Barbara gave a quick kiss to Carl, then practically bounced up the stairs.

Emily and Carl walked to the sitting room where Emily took one of the easy chairs, and Carl parked himself on the couch.

Once they were both seated, Emily asked, "Now, Mister Ritter, how in the blazes did you and Barbara go from landlady and boarder to fiancé and fiancée so quickly? You both seemed to be attracted to each other, yet both of you seemed so determined to ignore it. I imagine that it had to do with your slip of the tongue at the dinner table."

Carl replied, "You are a wise woman, Emily. Yes, it was my answer about the source of cranberries that triggered the change, but we each had our reasons for holding back."

Emily glanced at the empty staircase, then asked, "What were yours?"

Carl began explaining his concerns about being lumped into the same group with the men who had been attempting to woo Barbara over the years for one reason or another.

He'd just about finished when they heard Barbara stepping down the stairs, so he stopped talking and then waited for her to enter the sitting room.

Barbara returned, said, "You're new room is all set, Emily."

Emily rose, replied, "Thank you, Barbara," then smiled at Carl before she quietly left the sitting room and climbed the stairs.

After Emily had gone, Barbara plopped herself down next to Carl, who immediately put his arm around her before she almost buried herself into to his chest and sighed.

"Do we want to set a date yet?" she asked.

"Well, there's a minister at the church tomorrow, right?"

She sat up straight and stared at him in mock outrage.

"Mister Ritter! Surely, you're teasing me! Why, so much has to be done! Plans needed to be made, and guests invited. I'm as anxious as you are, but fourteen hours seems a bit rushed!"

"I was just teasing you, ma'am. Besides, Tom wouldn't be able to attend. How does the end of September sound? The leaves will be turning, and the weather should still be nice."

"I was just teasing you as well and wouldn't mind if it was tomorrow, but the end of September sounds wonderful. I can start planning tomorrow after we talk to Beth."

"Speaking of Beth. Do I get to tell her? I'd really enjoy that."

"That would be perfect," she said as she smiled.

"One other question about Beth. Would it be okay if I legally adopted her? I don't know if you'd have a problem with her changing her name and all."

Barbara teared up again and said, "I wouldn't have it any other way. Thank you, Carl. You're making this wonderful day even better."

"Well, don't go selling yourself short. You're the reason this is a wonderful day for me. You are a wonderful woman, and I'd like to tell you again that I love you."

She smiled gently, and said, "I love you, too, Carl."

He leaned over and kissed her deeply, then she sat up and leaned onto his side as contentment reigned in the Mathias Boarding House parlor.

They sat unmoving for almost ten minutes, neither saying a word to disrupt the atmosphere as no words were necessary. Suddenly, Carl slid to his right and stood up.

"As much as I'd love to spend a few years sitting with you, I have a couple of things to do, and I think you should join Beth in getting some sleep. I know it's early, but tomorrow will be a busy day for both of us. A great day, too, I might add."

"It will be that, with many more to follow, I think," Barbara replied and smiled at him.

"Every single one, sweetheart," Carl said before leaning over, giving her a quick kiss, then leaving the parlor.

Carl left Barbara still smiling on the couch and headed upstairs to his room where he sat down on the bed completely astounded by what had just happened.

What a day! Now he'd have to make some serious decisions. He'd been putting them off until he had a good reason, and now he had one, and it was the very best of reasons. He undressed and laid down on the bed and didn't even go through his usual ritual of checking his weapons before he slid beneath the blankets.

At the moment, his guns were the last thing on his mind as it was chock full of images of Barbara and Beth. He felt he had no right to be this happy but was thankful for it, nonetheless. With those thoughts in his mind, he drifted off to sleep.

———

He snapped awake in the middle of the night, but stayed under the covers, his mind racing, and he found himself thinking of Elrod Lydon, of all people. *Why did he have that goofy barber on his mind?* As long as he was there, he began replaying the confrontation at the restaurant in his mind. *Why did Elrod think so highly of himself? Why had he told Carl that he was going to be famous and important?* He wasn't going to get there as a barber, so he had to have something momentous up his sleeve, but Carl couldn't connect him with the local plotline. But still, whatever Elrod was expecting to happen wouldn't happen by his own hand. Elrod hardly seemed the sort to do anything remarkable on his own. He wasn't his own man. He didn't have the sand to stand up to anyone or to take wild chances, so whatever it was that he thought would make him famous would need to involve someone else. Maybe it was that stranger on the Appaloosa. Carl recalled the stranger as he had come out of the barber shop with exactly as much hair as he'd had when he'd entered. This was getting interesting, but he still couldn't quite put his finger on it.

Carl spent another hour running different scenarios through his mind, and his best guess was that the plot had something to do with Jameson's assassination attempt. There had been three horses involved, so that meant three men. Now he had those three men, just nothing to tie them together, at least not yet. Carl's last thought before drifting back to sleep was to run his ideas by Tom, as soon as Tom was up and ready to talk.

CHAPTER 4

Carl had just awakened to feeble sunlight illuminating his room, stretched and slid out of bed, then threw on his jeans and headed for the wash room. After shaving and washing, he tiptoed back to his room and shut the door, took off his jeans, put on his slacks, and slipped on a new shirt. He hadn't been to church in months and found himself looking forward to it. He checked his watch, saw that it was 5:05 and thought Barbara might be awake preparing breakfast, so he left his room and headed down to the kitchen.

He found Barbara at the counter, making biscuits for breakfast. He knew no one else was awake, so he wrapped his arms around her as she turned and pulled her to him, kissing her as he did. After she pulled back, she laughed lightly as he noticed her flour-covered hands.

"Well, I can't recall a better way to start my day, Mister Ritter. Although you came very close to ruining your nice, clean shirt."

"I could live with such a consequence," he said, releasing her to return to the counter, "When do church services begin?"

"Eight o'clock. I'll have to go wake Beth shortly, as soon as I get these in the oven."

"I'll handle making the coffee. Anything else I can help you with?"

"Coffee's fine," she replied as she smiled, "are you going to continue to be this helpful after we're married? Or is this some elaborate ploy to maintain good standing with me?"

"I plan on doing anything I can to keep up that good standing for the rest of our lives," he said.

"That's the best answer I could hope for," she replied as she slid the biscuits into the oven and wiped her hands on her apron.

Carl turned to fill the coffeepot with water, and as he did, he felt her walk up behind him and wrap her arms around his waist. He turned, and she kissed him. It was a long kiss, and when they finally parted to take in some much-needed oxygen, she gave him a wide grin and said, "That's payback."

"If that's punishment, I'll make sure I commit a long list of indiscretions each and every day."

Barbara laughed softly then left the kitchen to wake Beth.

Carl filled the coffee pot and put it on the stove, took a small pan and filled it with water, then set it on the stove as well. While he was waiting for the water to heat up, he set out some plates, a bowl for Beth, and some cups and saucers on the table. There was no sense in using the dining room. The kitchen was nice and toasty, and he was sure Emily wouldn't mind the less formal atmosphere.

By the time the coffee was ready and the water for Beth's oatmeal was boiling, Barbara and Beth had entered the kitchen.

"Good morning, Beth. Are you ready for breakfast?" he asked.

Beth nodded and asked, "I think so. Are you cooking my oatmeal?"

"If you don't mind, and I'll make it the way I used to for myself, okay?"

"Okay," agreed Beth as she took a seat at the table and yawned.

"Is your tummy better now?" Carl asked as he made her breakfast.

"I thought I was going to pop last night, but it's okay now," she replied.

Carl smiled as he added the oatmeal to the water and began stirring. When it thickened, he added some honey and some cream and wished he had some raisins. They were always an unexpected treat for him when he was younger. He filled her bowl with oatmeal and put it on the table, then he cut a pat of butter and slipped it on top.

"Give it a minute to cool and then you can try it, okay?"

She smiled at him and nodded vigorously. Once he had moved away from the stove, Barbara took the lead and began frying some bacon, then took out the biscuits and slid them onto the counter, observing her daughter and future husband.

Carl sat down at the table next to Beth and glanced at Barb who nodded with an expectant smile.

"Beth, can I ask you a serious question?" Carl asked.

Beth tried out her best adult face and nodded.

"You know, Beth, I've only been here a short time, but I feel like I belong here. I love you very much, Beth. Did you know that?"

Beth forgot about being serious, smiled and answered, "You do?"

"Yes, very, very much. And I love your mama, too. Last night I asked her to marry me and she said yes. But before we do that, I want to know if it's okay for me to become your papa."

Beth's eyes grew wide as she quickly replied, "You're going to be my own papa? You're not going to leave? You're really going to take me and mama to see the ocean?"

Carl had to smile at the last question.

"Yes, to all three. I'd like to be your papa. I'm only going to leave if you and your mama come with me, and I will definitely take you and your mama to see the ocean."

Beth didn't know how to react. She turned to her mother, back to Carl, then back to her mother again in absolute, disbelieving joy.

She kept her eyes on her mother and finally shouted, "Mama! I'm going to have a papa!"

She dropped from her chair, the oatmeal forgotten, and ran over to her mother as she continued to shout, "I'm going to have a papa! I'm going to have a papa!" then flew into her mother's arms, half crying, half laughing.

Barbara matched her tear for tear and smile for smile as Carl watched without a word, accepting the joy for what it was and enormously pleased to be its cause.

After a minute or so, Beth squirmed out of her mother's grasp and ran back to Carl and jumped onto his lap, wrapping her thin arms about him in a surprisingly strong hug. Carl hugged her right back.

Beth whispered, "Now none of the other kids can make fun of me 'cause I don't have a papa. I'll have the best papa in the world."

"I have to be," Carl said softly, "because you're the best child any father could hope for. Now, I guess you'd better finish your oatmeal."

"Okay, Papa," Beth said, already completing the adoption before any paperwork was even started.

She smiled as she sat down in her chair and began to eat her father-prepared oatmeal.

Emily stepped into the kitchen and said, "It looks like I just missed another big event."

Carl commented, "You sure know how to time your entrances. You might even be clairvoyant."

Emily smiled as she took her seat at the table, saying, "Well, I'll let that be a mystery."

Beth turned with a mouthful of oatmeal and tried to exclaim, *"Cahl ith gone to be my papa!"*

She swallowed and repeated, "Carl is going to be my papa!"

"Well, aren't you the lucky girl, Beth. I'm very happy for you," Emily said with a big smile.

"Me, too," Beth said with a glimmer in her eyes.

As breakfast progressed, Carl reminded them of their planned target practice later in the day.

"We can do it right behind Barbara's house. There's a small hill without any other buildings around, so it's perfect for shooting. I only want you to take a few shots each, just to get used to cocking the hammer, aiming, and pulling the trigger. The whole training session should take less than an hour."

"After church, we can swing by and bring Tom back, too" said Emily, "he may want to watch."

"I need to talk to him for a while anyway, so after church, we'll all head over to the doc's and bring him home. If he feels up to it, he can join us in target practice."

"What do you need to talk to him about?" asked Emily, "You're not thinking of going to Rock Creek, are you?"

"No. Don't you worry on that front," said Carl, "strangely enough, it has to do with Elrod and his behavior last night. All drunkenness aside, it was what he said that got to me, especially the part about becoming famous. It even woke me in the middle of the night, as if my brain made the connection while I was asleep."

"I was wondering about that myself," said Barbara, "what could he possibly do to become famous? Invent a new hair style?"

"He's not much of a troublemaker on his own, and it was hard for me to develop a theory that fit. I have my guesses, but I'd want to run them past Tom. If he doesn't mind, I'd like both of you to be there when we discuss it. I'd rather that both of you learned of my suspicions, rather than keeping you in the dark. That's why I'd prefer you both to have some means of protection."

"I understand," said Barbara, "We'll try to be good students. Now, let's get ready for church."

An hour later, Carl, Beth, and the two ladies walked down to the end of the boardwalk, stepped off the boardwalk and took a short crossroad into the whitewashed church. The bell was clanging as they entered, and Carl was surprised at the size of the congregation as it was much larger than he expected. Pine Bluffs wasn't a big town, but it looked as though a third to a half of the entire population was present. He guessed it helped to have a monopoly on the local religion and estimated that only a few of the attendees were Presbyterian by birth or choice.

The service wasn't as long as some he'd attended in the past, and Barbara had been right in saying that the reverend wasn't a fire and brimstone kind of preacher. In fact, it was one of the more pleasant religious experiences Carl had ever had. He took note of some of the stares directed his way by some of his fellow worshipers as he stood or sat close to Barbara, almost giggling inside as he knew what none of them did.

After the last hymn was sung and blessings administered, Carl and the womenfolk exited the church and joined the congregation in shaking hands and exchanging pleasantries with the reverend.

"Let's go and see if Tom is ready. I think he'll probably drag us out of there," said Carl after thanking the preacher.

When they got to the doctor's house, Carl knocked on the door and Mrs. McNamara let them inside.

"Come to retrieve our wounded patient? He's a bit anxious to be free of us, I suspect," she said as they walked to his room.

"Tom is never one to stand still for very long," Emily responded, "he doesn't even sleep all night. It seems like he's always busy with something or other."

Mrs. McNamara opened the door to the third room on the left, then announced, "Mister Wilson, you have visitors."

Tom asked, "About time they got here. Can I have my shoes now?"

He had already dressed, but Mrs. McNamara had withheld his shoes until Emily's arrival to ensure he had an escort.

"I'll fetch your shoes provided you keep your voice down. Raise your voice and I may just shoot you again to teach you a lesson," said Mrs. McNamara.

The threat hit its mark as no further shouting was heard. Mrs. McNamara was a formidable force in her own home – and anywhere else, for that matter.

Carl watched as Tom put on his shoes and could tell by the man's grimaces that his side was causing him pain. Nevertheless, Tom persisted and rose to his feet.

"Mrs. McNamara," he said, "I'd like to thank both you and your husband for your care. I know I may not have been the most pleasant or accommodating patient, but that's just my demeanor. Both of you have been nothing but kind, and for that, I am eternally grateful."

With that, he took out a gold double eagle and handed it to her.

"Will this cover my bill?" he asked.

"Your bill is only half that," she said.

"Well, keep the rest for all the grief I caused you."

"You were perfectly fine," said Mrs. McNamara, "I just like joshing you because it keeps me going."

"Okay, folks," he said as he smiled at everyone, "let's get back to the boarding house."

After his pronouncement, Emily took his arm, then they all turned and left the doctor's house. Tom noticed that Carl held Beth's hand and had his arm locked around Barbara's arm as well. He cast a questioning glance at his wife, who smiled and whispered something in his ear.

"What? Already?" he exclaimed.

"I guess Emily told him our little secret," Carl whispered to Barbara as they strode a few feet in front of the Wilsons.

"It won't remain a secret very long," she replied with a smile.

As they entered the boarding house, Barbara noticed a yellow envelope tucked just inside the doorway, snatched it from the floor and read the name scribbled across the front.

After everyone had passed through the doorway, Barbara held out the message and said, "Tom, I believe this is for you. The writing is terrible, but you're the only one likely to receive a telegram."

She handed the telegram to Tom and he slipped it into his pocket as they adjourned to the sitting room.

Barbara said she'd go prepare lunch for everyone, but Carl said, "Can you put that off for a few minutes, Barbara? I'd like to share a few things with everyone."

The Wilsons aligned themselves on the couch, Barbara and Beth took the two chairs while Carl remained standing.

"First, I'd like to welcome Tom back to the clan. Life here is much more pleasant since the sudden departure of Mister Jameson, and Mister Jameson is precisely who I'd like to talk about. I'm not sure how current you are on the events that have transpired since his departure, Tom, but I can give you the short version."

"Emily has told me the basics," said Tom, "but I'd like to hear you fill in the gaps."

"That morning, the sheriff and I tracked Jameson away from the house, heading east. He'd been accompanied by two other men, and the two men had waited for him out behind the house in the alley while he did the job. After he jumped from the porch to join them, the three of them left in no particular hurry, which surprised me. They didn't fly off in a panic, they took the horses on a tranquil little trot away from the fresh crime scene."

"Any idea who the other two might be? asked Tom.

"I have my strong suspicions. One I believe is the rider of that Appaloosa. He and Jameson had similar suspicious mannerisms and I haven't seen the horse in question since the incident. The second man was about the same weight as the first because all the tracks were the same depth. I was in the dark for a time, but now I'm pretty certain that the third man was Elrod Lydon."

The group looked at him as though he had suddenly sprouted a pair of antlers.

It was Barbara who broke the silence.

"Carl, this isn't because he insulted me last night, is it?"

"What happened last night," asked Tom.

Carl replied, "While we were having a pleasant dinner at the restaurant, he showed up at the table and started spouting off. He was drunk, so I just talked him out of doing anything rash and he left."

"How bad was it," Tom asked Emily.

"I don't think it was as harmless as Carl said, but I don't believe we were in any danger."

Carl then said, "To answer your question, Barbara, my suspicions have nothing to do with his behavior. My suspicions have more to do with what he said."

"You mean his designs on becoming famous and important," she suggested.

"Yes," said Carl, "The first thing he ranted about was directed at Barbara. He was claiming that in the near future he'd be famous and important, which made no sense at all considering his line of work. But it did get me thinking. What could he be involved in that might bring him fame, or more correctly, notoriety, or infamy? The only thing I could think of is the unrest in Rock Creek. But that is a flimsy connection at best. What could he possibly do to make an impact there? But then I remembered that the first time I saw the man on the Appaloosa, he was coming out of the barber shop."

"I don't see your point," interjected Tom, "Lots of men when they first arrive off the trail go the barber to get cleaned up. You did yourself, if I rightly recall."

"I surely did," admitted Carl, "Barbara even noticed as much, but this guy didn't go in for a haircut. He came out of there just as hairy as he was when he went in. If he had business in the barber shop, it had nothing to do with getting himself quaffed."

"But Lydon's lived here for a long time," said Barbara, "Why would he get himself involved with two newcomers?"

"Maybe he knew the Appaloosa rider. In fact, I wouldn't be surprised if they were related."

"How did you make that connection?" asked Emily in astonishment.

"No one else here saw him," said Carl, "I had an up-close and personal view of the man. He was thin, but he had a very prominent nose. Remind you of anyone?"

A silence fell over the room as Carl continued.

"What if the man on the Appaloosa came to help Jameson and needed a local contact for supplies and information? If he had a relative in town, it would make the job much easier. That said, I still think they're all amateurs. Jameson made a poor choice of weapons to accomplish the job and didn't use enough powder for the load, and probably hadn't cleaned and oiled the pistol, or it wouldn't have jammed on him. He was planning on emptying the gun at you, Tom, which would have left him defenseless if someone pursued him after the attack, and then stealing a nag as a getaway horse. All of it was amateur hour stuff. Heck, I'm no gunman and I could have pulled it off cleaner than Jameson did."

"You may have something there," said Tom after a moment's reflection, "The Knights of Labor may be thugs, but they're also miners without any tactical skills."

"Sounding regimental there, Tom," Carl said with a grin.

"After high school I was in the army for a few years before going to college. Then I found a job with Union Pacific and I've been with them for ten years now."

"I trust that means you can handle a gun."

"Sure, I can. I don't own one, though. Lately, I've been thinking that I need to rectify that situation. I hear you bought two pistols for Emily and Barbara. I was a bit miffed with the idea at first, but after thinking about it for a while, it's probably a wise precaution. Emily said you'll be doing some target practice this afternoon. Mind if I join you? If you bring your Colt, I'd like to make sure my shooting skills haven't diminished over the years."

"Glad to have you along, Tom. That's about all I have right now. If I find anything else, I'll let you all know. It's better if we're all kept up to speed. I even want Beth to know, so we can keep her safe. Do you understand, Beth? There may be some bad men around, but I'll sit down with you and your mama tonight and we can go over some plans about what to do. Okay?"

Beth had her serious face on and nodded as she replied, "Okay, Papa."

Barbara smiled at Carl, stood up and went into the kitchen to make lunch as Beth trailed after her.

"So, Carl," said Tom, "I hear wedding bells are in your future."

"At the end of September," he answered with a grin, "We need to start making some arrangements."

"Congratulations. I'm happy for both of you, and if you don't mind, I'm going to take a minute to read this telegram."

With that, Tom pulled the telegram from his pocket and perused its contents. It must have been a long message because it took him almost thirty full seconds to finish.

He glanced up at Emily and then at Carl.

"The president of the railroad is upset. The attack on me and the growing tension in Rock Creek is forcing him to act, so sent a letter to the Territorial Governor, Francis E. Warren, in Cheyenne, threatened to notify the Federal government and was going to recommend sending in U.S. troops to pacify the situation."

"Did he give you any orders?" asked Emily.

"All he said to me was to get well and stay alert and I plan on following those orders."

After they had a quick lunch, Carl went to his room and put on his gun belt, checked his Colt, took the two loaded pocket pistols and a box of .44 cartridges for his pistol, then left his room and went downstairs again.

Once he reached the kitchen, he asked Barbara, "Do you have something we can use as targets? Old cans or something similar?"

She nodded and, after some rummaging around, filled a sack with about a dozen empty tins.

"What should we wear?" she asked.

"Both of you should be fine. This isn't going to be very messy and I'll handle most of the dirty chores."

"Can I come?" asked Beth.

"Okay," said Barbara, "but you have to stay behind everyone."

"Okay, Mama."

Carl took the bag of cans from Barbara and after finding the Wilsons, led the small crowd out the kitchen door to the open field beyond. A convenient oak tree stump stood about fifty feet in front of the hill and Carl put his Colt's ammunition on the stump and took ten steps toward the hill, looked around and found some loose branches then used them to erect a crude trestle using two thick branches and positioned another across some notches that he whittled using his pocket knife. The construction took him ten minutes, then he placed four cans on the top of the improvised support.

He returned to the stump and removed the two small pistols from the boxes.

"Ladies, these are .36 caliber Colt Navy Pocket revolvers. Each holds five rounds of ammunition. I've already loaded them, but I'm not going to train you to be marksmen. I just want you to be able to cock the weapon and pull the trigger."

Both women nodded.

Carl picked up one of the pistols and asked, "Who wants to go first?"

"I will," said Emily quickly.

Carl asked her to step toward him and handed her the gun.

"You may think it's heavy, but it's not too bad. In a dangerous situation, you won't even notice it at all. I want you to just point it at the cans, but don't put your finger on the trigger,"

She did as he directed. She held the pistol steadily, maintaining a level aim until Carl told her to lower the gun towards its target.

"Here's something I want you to understand very carefully. This is a single-action revolver. You can pull the trigger all day, but nothing will happen unless you cock the hammer first. Remember, it's a two-step process. Pull the hammer all the way back until it clicks, and then aim and pull the trigger."

"When it comes to aiming," he continued, "a lot of people try to sight the weapon like a rifle but that's a waste of your time. What you need to do is point it like you do your finger. Make believe the barrel is your index finger and you'll do fine. Are you ready, Emily?"

"I think so."

"Now I want you to raise the pistol. If you want to use your left hand to pull back the hammer, you can do that. Then point it at the first can on the right and slowly squeeze the trigger. You'll be surprised by the sound when it goes off, but also be ready for a kick. These guns don't have a big kick, but it'll be noticeable. Okay, go ahead and try it."

Emily brought the pistol level with both hands. She cocked the hammer with her left hand and squeezed the trigger. The pistol suddenly bucked in her hands as the pistol erupted with a report and a cloud of gunsmoke. She maintained control and asked where the shot went. Carl had been focused on her hands, so he turned to Tom and asked, "How far off, Tom?"

"Not bad. About a foot high and left, I think."

"Great job, Emily. For a first shot with short-barreled gun, you did really well. Did you want to try another?"

"Sure. It wasn't as bad as I thought it would be," she replied with a smile, secretly thrilled with her newfound ability.

Emily missed her second shot as well, but his time, Carl tracked the shot and noted that it had landed almost in the same place.

"That'll serve you well, Emily. Both shots were pretty close. If somebody were to get within twenty feet of you, you'd stop them cold. Barbara, are you ready?"

Barbara had been watching Emily and nodded, then stepped up to the stump and took her pistol. She mimicked Emily's two-handed approach, cocked the hammer then pulled the trigger. To everyone's surprise, the can flew off the stick.

"Barbara," cried Carl, "that's more impressive than you could imagine. You should be proud of yourself."

Behind them, they could hear Beth's enthusiastic applause at her mother's marksmanship.

"Good shooting, Mama!" she shouted.

"Okay, Barbara. Try another one. If you hit a second can, I'm going to give up shooting myself."

Barbara smiled at Carl and then turned toward the targets, and fired her second shot, only narrowly missing the can.

Emily and Barbara returned their pistols to the stump, both sporting wide grins.

"To be honest, I was a bit frightened about shooting a gun," said Emily, "I know how dangerous they are, but it didn't bother me at all! I'm actually proud of what I've accomplished today."

Barbara nodded in agreement as Carl said, "A gun is only a tool. How you use it makes it good or bad. Both of you will only be using these weapons to protect yourselves and your loved ones, and in that case, a gun is mighty good tool."

"So, are you going to shoot that big gun now," asked Barbara.

"I haven't practiced in a while, so I may be rusty."

"Are you making excuses, Mister Ritter?" Barbara asked with a mischievous smile.

"We'll see."

With that Carl walked up to the stump, quickly pulled out his Colt and fired three shots in rapid sequence, each bullet making a different can hop fifteen or twenty feet in the air, then quickly holstered his weapon. The whole exhibition lasted less than six seconds.

"Where did you learn to do that?" Emily asked in awe.

"I'm from Texas, remember. I've been shooting all sorts of guns since I was eight. Like anything else, it's a matter of practice. On the range while we were driving cattle, I'd practice most days. In fact, ammunition was my biggest living expense."

Carl walked back to the target, placed four more cans on the branch, and sauntered back.

"Want to try now, Tom?" he asked.

"I wish I had gone first, Carl. You're going to be a tough act to follow."

Carl filled the used chambers with fresh cartridges and handed the pistol to Tom.

Tom felt the balance of the gun and nodded, then drew it level and shot four times. He wasn't as fast as Carl but hit three of the four targets.

"This is a nice weapon, Carl," he said as he returned the Colt to Carl butt first.

Carl dropped it back into his holster and replied, "I've had it for three years. It's accurate and handles easily. So, do we call it a day, folks?"

They all agreed that it was time to return to the house, so Carl cleaned up the target area and then picked up the guns and ammunition from the stump. Then they all crossed the field to the house.

Once inside, Carl said he'd clean, then reload the pistols and give them back in a little while, then added, "What I'd recommend is that you each keep your weapon in a purse or something that is always nearby. It'll be right where you want it if you ever need it."

Both women nodded as they smiled at their newfound skill.

"I think I'll go to the gunsmith tomorrow to pick out a pistol," said Tom.

"That would be a good idea. You'd be at a severe disadvantage having an armed wife and no way to protect yourself from her," Carl said grinning at Emily.

Emily laughed and pointed a teasing finger at Tom, but at least didn't make a hand gun and pretend to fire.

After dinner, Carl stayed in the kitchen with Barbara, helped her with the dishes and pans, saying very little all the while.

When they'd finished cleaning up, he asked her to bring Beth to the sitting room.

Tom and Emily were waiting for them. as Carl sat down in a chair as Barbara walked in holding Beth's hand, then after Barbara sat down, Beth crawled into her lap.

"Now that we all know how to use pistols, we need to come up with a plan to provide safety for the ladies when us menfolk aren't here," said Carl.

"Here's what I've come up with. If either of you feel threatened while in the house, go to a place where there is no exit. A bedroom would be best. Sit on the floor with your back to the wall and keep your pistol nearby. If you're both together, that's better yet. We don't want Beth anywhere bullets may be flying around, so Beth, you have to pay close attention. If your mama tells you to run somewhere, you don't ask why, okay? You just go. Barbara, where's the safest place in the house for Beth?"

Without hesitation, she answered, "The cold room. It's dark and there's an empty barrel down there that she can climb into."

"Did you understand that, Beth?"

"Yes, Papa, I hide in the barrel sometimes when I'm pretending."

"Good girl. So, when your mama says to run, you just get yourself down into that barrel until one of us comes for you, okay?"

"Okay, Papa."

Hearing Beth calling him 'papa' made Carl feel warm inside and brought a smile to his face.

"Two more things. If there's a threat after sundown, darkness is your friend. You can hide in the dark better than anyone else can find you. They make noise by looking but you don't make any noise by hiding. Second, never believe a bad guy. I don't care what he promises, he's lying. He may tell you all he wants to do is talk, or that he'll leave after you give him some money or something, but don't believe a word of it. If you have a gun on him, hold it there. He'll be afraid and try to talk you into lowering the pistol, but don't give him any advantage. None of this should last long, but if something like this happens, Tom and I will be here before you know it, okay? We would never let anyone hurt you and I know that I'm being overly cautious, but I'd rather err on the side of caution than feel sorry later. Everyone understand the plan?"

Both women nodded somberly at the instructions.

"Tom, do you have anything to add?"

"No. I don't think there's anything else we can do."

"All right, then. Enough of this doom and gloom. Tomorrow is going to be a busy day. I have some things to attend to, so I'll be gone most of the day. Tom's going to buy himself a gun, so he'll be around if you need anything. Oh, and, Tom, now that I think about it, you may want to procure yourself a rifle as well. Probably a Winchester that uses the same cartridges as the pistol."

Tom nodded and added, "I'll probably pick up a whole rig while I'm at it."

"Good. If our martial conversation has run its course, let's get back to our normal Sunday way of life."

They were getting up to leave the sitting room when Beth spoke up.

"I didn't hear a marshal talking."

It took a few seconds for the adults to make the connection, but when they did, there was a rolling sequence of giggling. Beth had no idea what was so funny but seemed happy to cause those silly grownups to laugh.

Emily helped Barbara prepare dinner while the men waited in the sitting room discussing the advantages and disadvantages of a Smith & Wesson versus the Colt. After dinner, Carl took over assisting Barbara, and now that the tension of early romance was over, they were able to talk freely and simply enjoy each other's company.

At the end of the evening, Barbara tucked Beth into bed while Carl stood by and watched as Beth smiled up at him.

"Good night, Papa."

Carl smiled and replied, "Sweet dreams, darling."

Barbara blew out the lamp and walked with Carl into the hallway, shutting the door behind her.

"So, you'll be gone tomorrow?" she asked.

"Yes. It's nothing dangerous, I just need to tie up some loose ends, and no mysteries either, just regular stuff."

"Are you going to tell me what the regular stuff is or where I might expect you to be?"

"The details would bore you. I'll tell you when I'm finished. Tomorrow night, with any luck."

"What are you hiding from me, Carl?" Barbara asked suspiciously.

Carl extended his palms and replied, "Now, Barbara. Are you saying that you don't trust your future husband already?"

"Of course, I trust you. It's just that I don't want anything to happen to you."

"Let me put it this way. It has nothing to do with guns. I'll even leave mine up in the room. You have nothing to worry about."

"You're not getting yourself mixed up in that mining mess, are you?"

"Absolutely not. That's between the railroad and the government now. Not even Tom will go there."

"Well, all right then. Did you want to go and share the couch with me for a little while?"

An enticing smile crossed her lips as she had asked, so Carl brightened up at the suggestion, took Barbara's hand then they walked down the hallway together.

CHAPTER 5

After he'd finished his morning wash and shave, Carl headed downstairs. It was still early as the sun had just risen just a few minutes earlier, but Carl found Barbara sitting at the kitchen table with a coffee cup cradled in her hands. She looked up at Carl and smiled before he bent over and gave her a long kiss before standing up again.

"Good morning, ma'am. I have to admit I anticipate these mornings with more and more eagerness each day."

"Likewise, sir."

Carl poured himself a cup of coffee and sat down.

"Carl," began Barbara, "what are we going to do after we're married?"

"Well, I'd like to know something first. How attached are you to Pine Bluffs?"

"I was never keen on the idea of staying here in the first place. That was John's decision. He didn't want to live in a big city because he felt there was too much competition. As for the house, its only pull on me is that it was here I raised Beth and it's all she knows."

"Do you think we ought to talk to Beth about this? Because I've thought this through and I'm thinking of taking Tom up on his offer. It would mean a move to Omaha, but it would be a good-paying job and I'd be better able to provide for you and Beth and that's important to me."

213

"Carl, I don't think Beth would mind the move at all," said Barbara, "She could be with her papa and mama and find a lot more to experience. Are you sure it's what you want?"

"I'm absolutely positive. Of course, I'd have to break it to Beth that there's no ocean in Omaha, but there is a really large river by way of compensation."

Barbara stood, then leaned over and put her arms around Carl's shoulders and whispered, "Thank you for everything you've given to Beth and me. You've given us both a life we could never have hoped for."

Carl looked into those same bright blue eyes that had mesmerized him at first sight.

"You've done the same for me," he said, "I could never imagine a life without you and Beth in it."

They shared a long kiss before Barbara wiped her eyes with the back of her hand and said, "Well, I'd better start making breakfast."

Carl turned, just in time to collide with Beth.

"Good morning, Papa!" she exclaimed.

She reached out for a hug and Carl picked her up. When he held her at eye level, he asked quietly, "Bethany, I was talking to your mama this morning, and after we get married, we'll be leaving here and moving to Omaha. Is that okay?"

"Really? Do they have an ocean there?"

"No. Just a great big river. We'll get a house near the river, but we'll still have to go to the ocean for a visit. I just wanted to be sure you'd be okay leaving all your friends."

"That's okay. I haven't been in school very long anyway. And besides, you are my best friend."

With that pronouncement, Beth hugged him even tighter.

He put her down and she trotted over to her mother and began chatting about Omaha, rivers and Carl. Carl figured it was time to get ready for the day, so he returned to his room and picked out some items he thought might be necessary for the day's journey as well as a letter to his parents, letting them know of his pending nuptials, along with a lengthy description of Barbara and Beth.

He returned downstairs with his saddlebags slung over his shoulder and entered the dining room. A seated Tom acknowledged Carl's arrival with a wave of his hand.

"I'm heading over to the gunsmith's in a bit. Any last-minute suggestions?"

"Just one. Tell him you want to go out back and fire a few test rounds before you buy anything. Some guns feel right but pull to one direction or the other."

Emily and Barbara entered with breakfast and Beth followed behind carrying a basket of biscuits. They all sat down and had a cordial breakfast with enough joshing to bring out mild embarrassment and feigned indignancy by the recently betrothed couple. The friendly teasing reminded Carl of mealtimes with his family back in Texas. He missed those days and was overjoyed to experience them once again.

Barbara got Beth ready for school while Carl checked his watch. It was 7:35, and he had to get moving, but waited for ten minutes to finish his coffee and make small talk with Tom and Emily. Finally, he rose, bid farewell to the Wilsons and headed down the hallway. The door to Barbara's room was open and

Beth was all dressed up for school, so he rapped on the doorjamb and asked, "May I enter, ladies?"

"Well, seeing how you asked so politely," said Barbara, "I suppose that you may."

Carl picked Beth up in his arms, gave her a light kiss on the forehead and said, "I won't be here when you get home, but I'll be back later, okay? I'm just letting you know in advance, so you don't get worried."

"Okay," she nodded.

Carl settled her back down and turned to Barbara, extended his arms, wrapped her in a tight hug, and gave her a quick kiss.

"I'll be back late. I'll explain everything when I get back. I promise."

"I'll hold you to that," she said with a smile.

Carl smiled back at her and walked out to the hallway where he left his saddlebags, picked them up and tossed them casually over his shoulder.

"Goodbye, ladies. I'll see you later this evening," he said, then waved on his way out the door.

Carl then entered the livery and spent some time chatting with Ethan, gave Jules his treat and a second cube of sugar because he felt like he'd been neglecting his friend.

He left the livery stable and walked to the train depot to wait for the morning train heading west, which left at 8:15. The eastbound train arrived at 8:30 at night and he planned on being on that train as well, as he sauntered up to the ticket window and bought a round trip ticket to Cheyenne, then he took a seat on one of the platform benches and waited.

A short time later he heard the whistle of the incoming train and could see the tall stack of the locomotive belching clouds of smoke as it approached. Carl knew by its shape that it was a coal burner. The days of the fat-stacked wood burners was coming to an end as progress was coming rapidly towards the close of the century, and it was a be a fine time to be an engineer. There were lots of things that needed building.

The train huffed to a halt and the few passengers that were exiting at Pine Bluffs dismounted the passenger cars. Carl boarded the train and found a seat by the window as the train took on water. Most of the people on the train were headed to either Cheyenne or Laramie, but perhaps a few were headed further west to San Francisco. But his was a short trip for him and he'd only be on the train for about an hour before it reached Cheyenne.

Carl almost fell asleep against the window pane because there wasn't much to see. The land was level and, except for a few cattle scattered here and there, not terrifically lively. He imagined it was a lot like being on an ocean, at least a calm ocean.

He arrived in Cheyenne at the scheduled time and was surprised to see how built-up it was. This was the largest city he had visited since Kansas City. There were cobblestone-paved roads and gas lights along broad boardwalks. Most of the buildings near the depot were three or four stories and were made of brick. The streets were lined with stores and eating establishments and there was even a theater and opera house. He wondered how Omaha would compare and imagined it was a step up.

His first stop was the Western Union office. He wired his bank in Kansas City for three hundred dollars, then he sent a telegram to New Braunfels:

GUS AND BERNADETTE RITTER NEW BRAUNFELS TEXAS

GETTING MARRIED SEPTEMBER 30 IN PINE BLUFFS WYOMING
HOPE YOU CAN MAKE IT
LETTER COMING WITH DETAILS
MAMA WAS RIGHT
LOVE

CARL RITTER MATHIAS BOARDING HOUSE PINE BLUFFS WYOMING

He told the telegrapher he'd be back in an hour to receive any replies, then walked down the nearest boardwalk and began exploring the stores and shops. He found a newsstand and bought the latest edition of the *Cheyenne Daily Sun*, then walked to a nearby restaurant and ordered a cup of coffee as he read the paper. Again, the local news was filled with talk about the unrest in the mines and how it was spilling over into Laramie and Cheyenne. The editor had written a piece on the violence and suggested it was time for the governor to step in and have Federal troops called in to quiet the situation. Carl wondered how bad it was going to get and what part Jameson and his two partners had in the whole thing. By the time he had finished reading and drinking his second cup of coffee, he realized that it was already ten o'clock, so he tossed a quarter onto the table and returned to the telegrapher's office in case the bank was faster than he expected.

As it turned out, they were even faster as the wire had been received twenty minutes earlier. He knew any reply from his parents would go to Pine Bluffs, so he accepted the voucher, then had to stop at the First National Bank and cash it before he started his shopping.

With the cash in his pocket, the first place he needed to find was a large clothing store and was surprised to see a store of this size so clearly specialized in just clothing in Cheyenne but appreciated the wide selection when he entered. He wandered the store until he found a young woman clerk who would know more about what he needed than a man.

"Excuse me, ma'am. I have no idea what I'm doing, so could you help me?"

"How can I help you, sir?" she asked as she smiled.

"Well, I need to buy some silk fabric for my fiancée. I have no idea how much she'll need to make a dress or what sort of material would be best."

"Well, you could buy her some silk, or if you'd prefer, I'd recommend buying her a readymade dress. It would save her a lot of time and she'd really like it better, I'm sure."

Carl was really lost now. *A dress? What did he know about dresses?*

"That would be nice, I think. But I have no idea what she would prefer."

The clerk smiled at him and said, "Follow me."

She escorted him to the ladies' clothing department and Carl was feeling more lost by the moment. Here he was standing there in his jeans with a Stetson on his head in a jungle of dresses and many of the lady shoppers glanced his way.

"Do you see anything you like?" she asked.

Carl looked around at the mannequins sporting various attires and was about to give up when he noticed a silk dress that was sky blue like Barbara's eyes with cream-colored panels.

"That one looks nice," he said.

"Very good choice, sir. Can you tell me what size you'll need?"

Just when Carl thought he was out of the woods, too.

"I'm not quite sure on that. She's about two inches taller than you are and I think she probably weighs around a hundred and twenty pounds or so. I haven't picked her up or anything, but that'd be my best guess."

"Well, I think I can get a close fit. She'll be able to make any alterations she may need. Did you want anything else to go with it?"

"Well, she's going to need all of those frilly things that women wear with nice dresses."

"Of course. I'll pick out everything she needs. Don't you worry about a thing. Anything else?"

"Well, I'd like to get another nice dress for her daughter. She has a wonderful little girl about this high," he said, holding his hand just above his waist, "I'd like to get a nice dress for her, too, and include all of those same frilly things she'd need."

The clerk walked down an aisle to the girl's section and showed Carl the assortment of children's wear. Carl spied a cute emerald green silk dress with lighter green accents.

"How about that one," he asked.

"Of course," she said as she jotted something down in a notepad, "Will there be anything else?"

"Do you have jewelry here, or do I have to go to a different store for that?"

"I'd recommend you try Zenner, Jackson, and Buechner. They're just next door and they make their own jewelry."

"Thank you. I'll go there next."

"It'll take me about thirty minutes to get your order together. Why don't you fetch your jewelry and I'll have everything ready by the time you return?"

"Thank you, ma'am. I'll do that," he replied as he tipped his hat, and quickly left the clothing store to head for the jewelers, which shouldn't be too bad.

It was easy to find the jewelry store as they had a large sign hanging over the boardwalk.

As he entered, he was struck by the rows and rows of display cases filled with all manners of rings, brooches, necklaces, and other glittering merchandise.

"Can I help you, sir?" asked a voice to his right.

He saw a middle-aged man sporting a fine, gray suit with large mutton-chop whiskers bordering his oval face.

"Yes, I would like to see some engagement rings and wedding band sets."

"Of course, sir. My name is Hiram Jackson and I'll be more than glad to help you."

Mister Jackson showed him a case filled with rings. Most had diamonds, some had other stones of different colors while others featured combinations of both.

"So, does anything catch your fancy?"

Carl scanned the display, unsure of what he was looking for. He was just about to give up on the first tray when he saw a diamond ring with a sapphire on each side. It wasn't the biggest set in the box, but he thought it was the most elegant, just like Barbara.

"That one," he pointed, "The one with the sapphires."

Mister Jackson took out the ring and examined it.

"Very good taste, sir. It's a very well-cut stone. It's a bit pricy, though, at one hundred and ten dollars. Is that okay?"

Carl imagined that Mister Jackson had taken one look at his jeans and Stetson hat and thought his customer was in over his head.

"That's fine. Now the wedding set. That should be simple. I just need two gold bands to match the band on the engagement ring."

Mister Jackson showed him a matching set, then had Carl try on the man's ring to make sure it fit. He advised Carl to try the engagement ring and Barbara's wedding band on his pinky finger to see whether they fit. Both rings slid easily on his finger, if a bit loosely. Jackson assured him that larger rings are easier to work with if they needed resizing later.

As Carl was getting ready to pay for his order, he glanced down at the display to his left and noticed a beautiful turquoise necklace. It was simple, but elegant, and told the cashier to add it to his order. He also selected a second, smaller turquoise necklace for Beth. His total bill was just under one hundred and seventy dollars, putting a serious dent in his wallet, but he hadn't expected to return with a lot of cash and he'd already had over two hundred dollars before he left for Cheyenne.

He thanked Mister Jackson and took his packages with him as he crossed the street, reentered Smith and Harrington's department store and went directly to the women's department and found the same young woman clerk near the counter. She smiled and led him to a larger counter in the back of the store where he was confronted with a towering stack of boxes. He hadn't expected such a massive quantity of female attire.

"How am I going to get all of that back to Pine Bluffs?" he asked in astonishment.

"It's not a problem," she said, "We can crate them up and have them taken to the depot for you. Would that work?"

"That would be fine. When you do, can you have the two dresses put on top?"

"Of course, sir. It won't be a problem at all."

He paid his bill and it wasn't as expensive as he thought. After paying for everything, he still had over two hundred and fifty dollars left. He thanked the clerk for her help, shook her hand, and slipped her a five-dollar gold piece. She told him it wasn't necessary, but he assured her that she had saved him from embarrassment and that alone was worth every penny. She laughed and thanked him for the tip.

Carl stepped out into the blinding noontime sunshine then left the store and walked to S.S. Ramsey Restaurant, had lunch and spent the rest of the afternoon taking in the sights.

After a big dinner at the same establishment, Carl walked down to the depot, and was gratified to see a large crate sitting on the loading dock marked Carl Ritter, Pine Bluffs, Wyoming. He went into the office, paid for the shipment, then sat on the platform waiting for the train, which arrived just twenty minutes later.

By the time he stepped onto the platform at Pine Bluffs, the sun was down, but the sky was still light. He had to wait while they unloaded his crate, then asked if someone could take it to Mrs. Mathias' boarding house. He was assured that it would be taken care of and he headed in that direction, his exhaustion bolstered by his excitement. He was hoping he had made the right choice in dresses. *What if they didn't like them?* Women were more particular about such things. Men would wear damned near anything short of dresses, if one disregarded kilts and probably togas.

As he opened the door, Beth welcomed him with a shout from her room.

"Mama, papa's home!"

Then he heard the scuffling of small shoes as Beth rounded the corner of Barbara's room and threw herself into his arms.

"Glad to see you too, Beth," he said as he hugged her.

Barbara came around the corner from the kitchen and smiled.

224

"Glad to see you all in one piece."

Before he could answer, there was a loud thump on the front porch and Carl set Beth down.

"Just a second," he said, "I've got to take care of something."

Amid curious glances from both mother and daughter, Carl turned, then opened the door and reached into his pocket, handed a coin to a porter and then closed the door again.

"What's that?" asked Beth.

"I had to go and pick up an old saddle of mine and it's sitting in a crate out front. Want to see it?"

"A saddle? You took all day to get a saddle?" Barbara asked suspiciously.

Carl began to suspect that the ruse wouldn't last long.

"I'll need a screwdriver. Barbara, can you find one for me, please? I'll go get the crate."

She went back to the kitchen to get the tool while Beth stood watching as Carl lifted the crate, then struggled to guide the awkward crate to the sitting room, but once there, he carefully lowered it to the floor. Barbara walked in, screwdriver in hand, and handed it to Carl who had taken a seat on the couch behind the crate.

"Okay, ladies. I'll need you to sit on the down while I get this thing opened."

Both were intrigued. Beth was because she wanted to see what the saddle looked like and Barbara was curious to see what Carl really had hidden in the mystery box, not thinking for a moment that there was some ancient piece of leather.

The top of the crate creaked as its nails worked their way free, then Carl pulled the lid back and looked inside.

He feigned surprise and exclaimed, "Why this isn't my saddle at all! The railroad must have mixed up my crate with another one completely!"

Beth looked disappointed, and Barbara felt vindicated, but still curious.

He reached inside and pulled out a box with Smith and Harrington printed in large letters along its side.

"What's this?", he asked, holding the box in his hands, examining it closely.

Barbara took one look at the box and knew that there had been no mistake. She recognized the name of the largest clothing store in Cheyenne and felt her heart pick up its pace.

"Carl, what have you *really* been up to?" she asked.

"Obviously," he said, "I'll have to go back and find my saddle. Maybe you should open these and tell me what they are, so I can describe them to the railroad clerk."

Barbara reached for the first box and slowly opened it as Carl caught his breath, knowing this could end in utter disaster.

Barbara gasped as the blue and cream silk dress was revealed and she slowly lifted it from the box and held it out before her disbelieving eyes.

"Carl," she said breathlessly, "this is exquisite. Why? How?"

"It's for you. It had to be, Barbara," he replied quietly.

She lowered the dress into the box, then set it on the floor, stood, took a short few steps, sat next to him on the couch, wrapped her arms around him, and started crying. Carl leaned his face on the top of her sobbing head. He guessed that he'd done okay as Beth watched them both, mystified.

Barbara finally pulled back and wiped off her wet face.

"What's in the other boxes?" she asked, her voice still trembling.

"Only one way to find out."

Carl reached in and produced a smaller box, and Barbara watched as he handed the box to Beth.

"Now we couldn't have mama all dressed up without our beautiful daughter wearing something to match, could we?"

"This is for me?" Beth asked, her eyes wide.

Beth whipped the top box cover off, then pulled out the green silk dress and held it in front of her.

"Mama, isn't this beautiful? It makes me feel like a princess!"

"You *are* our princess, Beth," Carl said.

She ran up to Carl and hugged him.

With that, Barbara pulled out another large box and opened it.

"How did you ever know how to buy all these things?" she asked between tears as she began to see the fine undergarments.

"I just told the sales lady to add all of those frilly things that females needed, and she took care of the rest while I ran away. I gave her a nice tip, too, because she saved me from being permanently red-faced."

Both ladies, young and old alike, let out a giggle at his admission.

"Well, ladies, I'm not guessing what else is in the remaining boxes, and to be honest, I don't have a clue, and I'd like to leave it that way. But I think that having nice dresses is only the cake. You still need some dressing."

With that, Carl reached into his saddlebag and pulled out the two boxes with the turquoise necklaces. He handed one to Barbara and the other to Beth. He had marked them with a pencil, so he knew which necklace was inside. Beth opened hers first and squealed as Barbara opened her box, saw the necklace, and closed the box as she shut her eyes and tears began to stream down her cheeks again.

Beth looked at Barbara and said, "Mama, why are you crying? Don't you like yours? I like mine a lot. It's so pretty!"

"Yes, sweetie," she said her voice choked with emotion, "I like mine, too, but I'm crying because I'm so happy. No one has ever given me jewelry before. I think it's just so beautiful."

She looked up at Carl through misty eyes.

"Thank you," she said, "Thank you from the bottom of my heart."

Carl was too close to tears himself to do anything but nod in return.

Tom and Emily walked into the room, evidently overhearing the ruckus downstairs, noticed the crate and open boxes around the room, and Barbara's red, teary eyes.

"Carl, what have you done to these poor ladies?" Tom asked as he grinned.

"Beats me. I thought I was opening a crate with my old saddle in it, but all this other stuff was in there instead. It turns out it's all a bunch of women's clothing, and I figure it can be put to better use here, so I'll let some other fella explain to his womenfolk why they were expecting dresses and got an old saddle instead."

Emily walked over to Barbara who was showing her the blue and cream silk dress.

"Oh, Barbara. This is extraordinary! Did you pick it out?" she asked in amazement.

Barbara shook her head and nodded toward Carl.

"You're kidding. That galoot actually chose all of this? What is happening in this world? He's got the womenfolk shooting guns while he's out traipsing around buying women's dresses!"

The women broke out in laughter as Carl held up a pair of denying hands.

Emily smiled at Carl and said, "You did all right, cowboy."

"Thank you, ma'am," he said, bowing at the waist.

Barbara showed Emily the necklace, eliciting more praise for Carl.

"Thanks, Carl," said Tom, "Now I've got to live up to this, you know. You are making my life more difficult than it needs to be."

"Maybe I'll continue the tradition in Omaha, if you'll let me."

That caught Emily by surprise, and she wheeled around to face Carl.

"So, you've decided to accept my offer?" asked Tom.

"I believe so. I'll have a wife and daughter to support and I think they'll both be delighted to have you as neighbors."

Emily beamed as Carl and Tom shook hands.

"We'll finalize all of the details later, Carl. I'm just glad you've decided to join us. You'll never regret it."

"I know I won't. For more reasons than one."

Then Carl said, "Before we do anything else, I need to get something from the kitchen. Beth, can you stay here with Uncle Tom and Aunt Emily for a few minutes?"

Tom and Emily smiled at their newfound titles as they looked at Beth.

"Okay," replied Beth, "I want to look at my dress longer anyway."

Carl gestured at Barbara to join him in the kitchen. Once there, he picked up the still-hot coffee pot and set two cups on the table, filled the cups and sat down across the table from Barbara.

Carl reached in his saddlebag and pulled out the smallest box of all as she stared down at the coffee thinking of what she could say.

"Now, Barbara. I seem to be spending way too much time making you cry, and I don't want to subject you to it anymore."

"Carl, that's silly. There are bad reasons to cry, and there are good reasons. Tonight, was full of nothing but the best reasons of all. It wasn't the dress or the necklace, it was knowing that they came from a man who loves me and is willing to show that love to me and the rest of the world. So, if I was crying, it was because my heart was full."

"Well," he said quietly, opening the box in front of her, "then I guess I'm about to cause you more tears."

Barbara stared at the exposed diamond and the sapphire ring nestled in the small blue box and couldn't find her speech as her eyes focused on the precious stones for almost a minute before she finally looked at Carl.

She breathlessly said, "I don't know what to say. This is totally unexpected."

Carl removed the ring from the box and took her left hand, slid the ring onto her finger noticing that it wouldn't need resizing as it fit perfectly. Barbara slowly lifted her hand and just stared at the ring.

"I thought we were just going to get married and have rings at the wedding," she whispered.

"I couldn't risk that. This way every man who sees you will know that you're spoken for. I won't have to worry about you suddenly having a change of heart and throwing me over for Elrod."

After a short, subdued burst of laughter, Barbara began to cry again, so Carl stood, walked to her side of the table, took her hands and after she rose, enveloped her in his arms let her continue to weep between kisses.

Back in the sitting room, Beth looked up at Emily and asked, "What are mama and papa doing, Aunt Emily? They've been in there for a long time."

Emily smiled at Beth and said, "Unless I'm mistaken, your papa is giving your mama a ring."

"How do you know that?" asked Tom incredulously.

"It's the only reason I can imagine that Carl would need to see her privately. Well, at least it's the only something that can be done in the kitchen when other people are around."

"Woman, you have no shame," said Tom with a chuckle.

A moment later, when Barbara and Carl entered the sitting room, Tom noticed the engagement ring on her finger and rolled his eyes at his wife.

"Barbara, that is a beautiful ring," exclaimed Emily.

Barbara, absolutely effervescent, proudly displayed the ring to Emily.

"I'm going to need you to teach my husband a few new tricks," Emily said to Carl.

Carl looked over at Tom and mouthed, "I'm sorry," knowing Tom was in a bind now, for sure.

As it turns out, he wasn't. Right after Emily closely examined the ring, she turned to Tom and said, "With all of the joy in the room, I suppose it would be okay to tell them?"

Tom nodded, a broad smile on his face.

"We are going to have a baby," announced Emily barely able to restrain the obvious joy in her voice.

There were high-pitched squeals and smiles all around, but Carl and Tom just grinned in an accepted manly reaction.

"We'd been trying for years," said Emily, "but now that we've finally been blessed, we couldn't be happier."

Carl shook Tom's hand and then hugged Emily.

"Congratulations to you both," he said.

Even Beth knew what was going on this time and felt proud of herself for growing up.

"It's been an exciting night," Carl said, "but it's getting late and someone named Beth has to go to school tomorrow."

Beth insisted that she had the stamina to stay up with the adults, but Barbara wasn't about to let her have her wish, as she took Beth's hand and led her to their room.

"Well, folks," said Carl, "I'm heading off to bed. It's been a long day."

"Maybe," agreed Tom, "but you may never have a better one."

With a smile, Carl left the sitting room and headed down the hallway. He arrived just as Barbara was explaining to Beth that she couldn't sleep with her necklace on, and as mothers always do, Barbara prevailed and placed the necklace in a special drawer.

Carl stood with the corners of his mouth turned up as Barbara turned to him, then stood, embraced him, gave him a long kiss, and said, "Good night, Carl. I can't thank you enough for all you've done for Beth and me."

"You know we'll all have to take a trip to Cheyenne to pick up all of the other things you'll need, like shoes, a coat, and other things. I think Beth would really enjoy the trip."

"I will, too," she said, "Goodnight, Carl."

She gave him one last kiss before he turned, left the hall, climbed the stairs and entered his room.

He had begun the day with so much uncertainty, and that uncertainty had persisted throughout the day. As it turned out, everything went even better than be could have possibly expected.

He walked down to the wash room and cleaned up before sleep, returned to his room, switched off the lamp on the dresser, undressed, and laid down on the bed. It was unseasonably warm for the last day of August, so he slept on top of the blankets. He drifted off to thoughts of Barbara running through his head, the best possible way for him to slip off to sleep.

It seemed like he had just fallen asleep when both of his eyes snapped open. *What woke him this time?* He didn't hear any footfalls in the hallway but sat bolt upright and looked around the moonlit room. Nothing seemed out of place until he heard a very light tapping at his door. He stood, opened it a crack and peered out into the dark hallway. Without making out a thing, he detected that light lilac scent that he always smelled when he had his face close to Barbara's hair.

"Barbara?" he whispered, "Is that you?"

ROCK CREEK

He saw her hand on the door and he opened it wide enough for her to enter, then she slid inside and closed it again. She was wearing her night dress but no shoes.

"Is everything okay?" he asked.

She took a step forward until she pressed up against him and put her arms around him.

She whispered to him, "Everything is wonderful," then asked, "Carl, make me your wife tonight? I can't wait any longer."

Carl felt her breasts against his chest and knew that he wanted this woman more than he had wanted anything in his life. He'd been denying that part of his deep appreciation for Barbara because he knew that he wanted it so badly. Now, he understood that she felt the same way.

He whispered back, "Barbara, I've wanted you so badly that I thought I'd lose my mind."

"Then don't," she whispered in return and kissed him passionately.

He slid his hands across her, feeling her perfection as he began to kiss her on her slender neck.

Barbara was no bashful, inexperienced young girl, but a hungry, sensual woman who was offering herself to the strong, masculine man that she loved and who loved her. It had been more than seven long years since she had been with a man, and now, she was able to release all the frustration that had been building each month and found herself at last feeling someone as passionate about her as she was of him. It was a thrilling and liberating sensation.

Carl found himself initially overwhelmed by Barbara's level of desire, but soon let himself get totally immersed in Barbara to her incredible pleasure.

When he did, Barbara let herself go and Carl let her know without another word, just how much he loved her and desired her.

When they finally reached that ultimate level of pleasure, Barbara found her toes curling and her eyelids fluttering as she held Carl tightly.

Carl thought he might pass out he was so lost in Barbara's passion.

When they finally lay intertwined in each other's arms, bathed in sweat, Carl whispered to Barbara, "I love you, Barbara. I can never fully express just how much I wanted you."

Barbara kissed his chest softly and replied quietly, "Oh, I think you have, my husband. I've never experienced anything like that before and I thought I'd lose my mind."

Carl stroked her skin with the backs of his fingernails as he asked quietly, "Then you wouldn't mind if we did it again?"

Barbara looked up at his face in the moonlight and whispered, "Oh, please tell me that you aren't joking. Please?"

Carl leaned down kissed her and took her hand in his and showed her that he wasn't close to kidding.

After expressing her gratitude to the deity for this man beside her, Barbara slid onto Carl and began kissing him with increased fervor and let him know without question that she was as ready as he was.

Neither got much sleep that night and when the first tendrils of sunlight began showing in the eastern sky, they made love once more before Barbara reluctantly had to slip back into her nightdress and sneak out of his room, wagging her fingers as she smiled, closing the door behind her, leaving an exhausted and very happy Carl smiling back at his wife in all but name.

––––––

Five miles northwest of Pine Bluffs, Jameson and Emerson Lydon sat in the miner's shack that Emerson had found for them in his scouting mission. They had a small fire going on the dirt floor because the nights were still chilly at this altitude, and neither of the two was very happy about their current circumstances.

"We need to head for Cheyenne," Emerson said, "and before we go, we need to take the back way into Pine Bluffs, go see my brother, and press him for information. It'll take us a day to get to Cheyenne and from there we can find the best place to set up the dynamite."

"Let's go, then," said Jameson as he threw off one of the almost useless blankets.

CHAPTER 6

An hour after sunrise, Barbara was downstairs in the kitchen making breakfast as Carl came downstairs, acting casually, though both knew that things had changed rather dramatically overnight.

Carl snuck up behind Barbara and planted a kiss on the back of her neck. She just arced her neck to the side to let him know that she approved, and even encouraged him to touch her as she said without turning, "Good morning, my husband."

He whispered into her ear, "Good morning, good wife."

He gave her another quick kiss, and exhaled before he went to the stove, picked up the coffee pot, poured himself a cup then set a second cup on the table, filling it with coffee and adding a teaspoon of sugar before Barbara smiled and took the coffee.

Barbara said, "I see that I already have you domesticated."

"Just trying to stay on your good side, ma'am."

"I don't think you'll have to worry about that for quite some time. Carl, you'll never really know how special you made me feel since the moment you returned until I left your room. I've never felt more like a woman than how you made me feel. Even thinking about it gave me goosebumps this morning."

"Trust me, Barbara. I know the feeling, and I've never felt anything like it before and can't wait until we try it again."

Barbara was smiling and about to make another suggestive comment, but before she could respond, Beth shuffled sleepily into the room.

"Mama, where did you go last night? I thought I saw you going somewhere when it was dark."

Before Barbara could reply, Carl answered the dangerous question.

"That was my fault, Beth," said Carl, "I hadn't had any supper, so your mama wanted to take care of me."

"Oh, that's good," said Beth, "I don't want my papa to be hungry."

"I knew you'd understand, Beth. You're a smart girl. I was very hungry, and your mama gave me everything I needed."

Barbara stifled a laugh as she turned her back to Beth and Carl.

Beth smiled at him and plopped herself down at the table. Barbara had regained her control and set a bowl of oatmeal in front of her daughter, along with a glass of milk, then glanced at Carl and shook her head with a smile, before she returned to her cooking.

Carl turned to see Tom and Emily approaching from the hallway.

"Morning, folks!" he called.

"Good morning, Carl," said Emily with one of her knowing looks, "Sleep well?"

Carl sensed mischief behind her question and knew that he couldn't slip anything past her, especially with the amount of noise that he and Barbara had made.

"As well as could have been expected."

"I imagine that's so," replied Emily, "it was very noisy last night, it must have been owls or something."

Carl held back his smirk and just replied, "I guess so. It is their mating season, after all and they can be quite noisy at times."

Barbara squelched a laugh from the near the cookstove, but Emily didn't bother squelching hers.

Tom seemed to miss the undertone of the conversation, and it was just as well.

"So, Tom, what are your plans for the day?" Carl asked.

"I was thinking of getting in some more target practice with my new guns."

"That sounds like a good idea. Maybe I'll join you."

After Beth had gone to school, Carl and Tom stepped out back. Carl took along the empty crate from Cheyenne and for almost an hour they practiced firing at the crate, then they went inside to clean and oil their weapons.

While they were busy shooting their guns, Barbara and Emily shared information, and even though she had heard the noises, Emily was stunned when Barbara had commented on the frequency of their lovemaking. As their men returned from shooting, both women just smiled as they passed, then quickly resumed their quiet discussion.

After they had their guns cleaned, Carl headed down to the mercantile and Tom went to find Emily.

Carl bought some screws, a handful of tools, and returned to the house. Once he was upstairs, he removed some loose wood fragments from the burst-in door jamb and then lifted the door to align the hinges and fitted the longer screws in place and tightened them down. He tested the door's alignment, found it fit well, then opened and closed the door a few times, and once he was satisfied with his repair, went back downstairs.

He found Barbara in her room trying on her new dress and stood there admiring the view for a few seconds before she turned and laughed.

"You're beyond beautiful," he finally said, "you are stunning, Barbara."

She beamed at him and replied, "Well, it's a gorgeous dress. You do know it's silk, don't you?"

"That's what the lady said, but trust me, it's not the dress. It's you."

"You sure know how to make a lady happy, don't you?" she asked.

"I never say anything I don't mean. Barbara, you are simply the most marvelous woman I've ever known, not to mention the most beautiful."

"Well, thank you, sir. I love the dress, but I love you much more."

"You know that I love you, too. When I wandered into that store, I wasn't sure what to do until I saw that blue silk dress. It mirrored the blue in your eyes, so I knew it was the one for you.

When we go to Cheyenne, you'll have to go spend some time in that store, look around and find a little something for yourself."

"I intend to, but I doubt if I could run into anything that I'd like more than this one."

"In the meantime, I just repaired the Wilsons' old door, and you won't even be able to see where it was damaged. All it took was some longer screws."

"Is there no end to what you can do to make me happy, Mister Ritter?"

"Hopefully there will never be an end, soon-to-be Mrs. Ritter."

Just then, the front door swung open and Tom entered with a concerned look on his face.

"New telegram from the main office, and it's serious. The Knights of Labor have upped the ante. They've killed one Chinese miner and injured another. It's only going to get worse. Oh, and there was a wire for you."

Tom handed a folded yellow sheet to Carl.

Carl opened the wire and read:

CARL RITTER BOARDING HOUSE PINE BLUFFS WYOMING

HAPPY FOR YOU
MAMA AND I WILL BE ARRIVING BY TRAIN SEP 21
MAMA SAYS SHE KNEW YOU'D LISTEN
CAN'T WAIT TO MEET YOUR BRIDE
LOVE

GUS RITTER NEW BRAUNFELS TEXAS

"My news is a little better than yours," Carl admitted, handing the telegram to Tom.

After he read the wire, he said, "That's great news, Carl. Planning a big wedding, then?"

"No. It'll be a small affair. My parents will be here, and I'll ask Barbara if she wants her parents to come. Other than that, you and Emily will be our only guests, and I'd be honored if you'd be my best man."

"I'd be the one honored, Carl," said Tom, "I even have a suit packed away somewhere upstairs."

"I've got to take care of that myself," said Carl, "I think I can do it when I take Barbara and Beth shopping in Cheyenne."

"If you're going to do that, I'd be crazy not to take Emily along shopping," said Tom, "Take the word of an old married man and let the ladies go off on their own. Too much exposure to shopping would only drive you crazy."

"I know what you mean," laughed Carl, "I was really out of my element in that store."

Carl told Tom that he was going across to the livery to check on Jules and invited him to come along. Tom nodded and followed Carl out the front door.

As they started down the walkway, Carl spotted Fred Jenkins headed their way. The man was almost unrecognizable as he he had cleaned up well.

"Fred, you look great," said Carl as he approached.

Fred wore a peculiar half-smile, half-grimace.

"Well," he said, "folks sure are treating me nice now, but I still don't feel quite right yet, bein' all clean and everything."

"You'll get used to it, Fred. Trust me."

"Maybe. But no matter. Say, I heard sumpin' that I figgered you might want to know."

"What's that?" Carl asked.

He leveled a finger at Tom and said, "I know him. He works for the railroad. And when I was sittin' in the bath in the back of the barber shop, I heard a ruckus goin' on inside the shop. I seen two skunky-lookin' fellers go in there just before the shoutin' started and ol' Elrod wasn't happy with 'em, I don't think. He wanted to go with 'em, but they was mad at him for bein' a drunk and loudmouth and not keepin' his mouth shut. They said they was gonna handle the job by themselves and told him to stay put. Then they said he didn't know nothin' about dynamite no how."

"*Dynamite*?" asked Tom with wide eyes.

"That's what one of 'em said. Then he said just give him the supplies and get back to cuttin' hair. Then them two came out, stared really hard at me for a second and then walked out the back door leavin' it open, hung this food bag on the saddle and rode out together."

"Fred, did one of them ride an Appaloosa? You know what they look like, right?" Carl asked.

"'Course I do. One was an Appaloosa, the other was a roan mare. One feller I didn't know and the other one was that man that stayed in the boarding house with you all."

Carl and Tom exchanged glances.

"Thanks, Fred. You did right by letting us know. I think they're up to something."

"Are they gonna rob a bank?"

"No, I suspect it has something to do with the railroad."

"Well, if there's anyone who can stop 'em, it's you, Carl. You're a good man."

"Thanks, Fred."

Carl reached into his pocket, pulled out a coin and handed him the five-dollar gold piece.

"That's for doing the right thing. Doing right always deserves a reward."

"Thanks kindly, Carl."

Fred turned and headed down the road holding the coin in front of his face as he walked.

"Let's go inside and figure out what they're planning," Carl said to Tom, "and how we can stop them."

Tom nodded before they returned to the house and found Emily and Barbara still chatting in the sitting room.

"Ladies," said Tom, "we've encountered some disquieting news that will require us to act. I'll fill you in and you can join the discussion about the planning we'll need to do."

"Go ahead," said Barbara.

Tom told them of the telegram and the ensuing discussion with Fred Jenkins.

"Are you sure Fred's right," asked Barbara, "He may not be the most trustworthy source of information."

"If you had seen him, Barbara, you'd have been shocked," said Carl, "He's all cleaned up and his behavior is that of a different man completely. He's trying to prove to everyone that he belongs here and I'm sure that his information is accurate. He has no reason to lie."

"What happened to him?" asked Barbara.

"Carl happened," Tom said with a laugh.

Barbara understood immediately, and Emily remembered the Elrod incident and figured it out herself.

"We have two guys with dynamite in their possession that are going to try to cause harm to the railroad," said Carl, "Any ideas, Tom?"

"That's what has me stymied. If they have the dynamite and want to hurt Union Pacific, why haven't they done anything yet? They've had plenty of opportunities."

"Think about it, Tom. It isn't the railroad itself they're after. In fact, the railroad is their life's blood. No railroad, no jobs," said Carl, "No, they want to intimidate the railroad into doing what they want. Judging by what I read, they want the Chinese out and their wages put back to what they were before the Chinese arrived. The real question is, what's the best way to intimidate the railroad into meeting their demands? They tried to kill you but failed. They wanted you dead because you are a railroad executive and make decisions about what the railroad does, but even then, they waited."

"I make those decisions to a degree, but all I can really do is make suggestions. The president makes all the real decisions. If it was up to me, I'd separate the Chinese and white miners. Let them run their own camps, get rid of the company stores and let someone go in there and set up a store with honest prices. But they wouldn't listen to me anyway because it means more profit heading their way. At least in the short term."

"Can you just send a telegram to headquarters advising them of the threat and let them take care of it?" asked Emily.

Tom shook his head and replied, "Not enough information. At most, they'd probably send a railroad agent or two to investigate, but by then, it'd be too late. Besides, they might think I'd lost my marbles and fire me."

Carl said, "The other problem is that they have a full day's head start in whatever they're planning to do. My guess is that they're still waiting for some trigger event to set their plan in motion. I don't know what it is, but my gut tells me it's something to do with Rock Creek."

"That sounds logical enough," said Tom, "but the train for Cheyenne has already gone. If we need to go anywhere, it'll be by horseback, and I don't have a horse."

"We can rent you one. I know Ethan has at least three that he keeps for rentals and at least one of them looks pretty sturdy, too."

"Let's see what happens and be prepared to move if we have to."

"What can we do to help?" asked Emily.

"Cheyenne is only forty miles away. If we ride quickly, we can make it there in four or five hours. Of course, we wouldn't be able to ride back tonight, so you probably won't see us until tomorrow. With the two bad guys out of the picture for the moment, you all should be safe, but be careful anyway."

The women nodded, but still looked at each other with concern.

"I'm going over to Hank's to pick up some supplies," said Carl, "I'll be back in a few minutes."

Tom joined him as they left the house.

"What a difference a day makes," remarked Barbara as the two men made their way out the door.

———

Tom and Carl stepped into the general store. They were stocked up on ammunition but bought another box of .44s just to be on the safe side.

Carl asked Hank if he had any field glasses.

"Yup, got a used pair that some feller traded me for a box of tobacco. Been here for a while, though, so I don't know how much use they are."

Carl examined the field glasses. The exterior was rough and battered, but the optics were outstanding.

"These will be fine. How much?"

"Three dollars. That's more than that danged box of tobacco was worth."

ROCK CREEK

They each bought a wool jacket, because they knew it would get chilly on the trail at night, then Carl paid for the order before they returned to the boarding house at noon, had lunch and the men decided to head over to the livery to see about the horse rental.

Ethan showed them the three horses. Two looked exhausted, suitable only for local trotting, but the third was the tall buckskin, five or six years old, that Ethan was proud to show them.

"Ethan," said Carl, "we'll be needing the buckskin for at least a day, along with a blanket, saddle, and bridle. We'll need a scabbard as well."

"No problem," said Ethan, "It'll run you three dollars a day. That's my best horse. I'd let you have one of the others for half that."

While the men considered these terms, Ethan pointed out the worn-out bay on the right and said, as if by an afterthought, "by the way that's the horse that was stolen. He wandered back here this mornin'."

"Glad you got him back. But you can keep him," said Carl, "We'll need the buckskin. We have to be sure that we get where we're going."

"I figured as much," chuckled Ethan.

Tom handed Ethan three dollars and told him he'd get the horse back tomorrow.

As they walked back to the house, Carl said, "You know, we may not even need to go anywhere, but the odds are that we will."

They took their purchases back to the house, returned to the kitchen and found the women having coffee at the table.

Tom told Emily there was something he needed to talk to her about and escorted her up to their room.

Carl took her seat and looked at Barbara while she smiled back at him.

"Well, I thought I'd like to add to your good mood," he said as he pulled out the telegram and handed it to her.

After reading it, the smile faded from her face.

"Carl I'm worried," she said, "I mean, I am a widow and I have a child. Won't your parents be embarrassed in your choice for a wife?"

"Now that's just about the silliest thing I've ever heard come out of your beautiful mouth," said Carl, "Let me explain something. My parents are not judgmental. In fact, they despise those that are. What they do understand is the value of love. Reread the telegram and notice two things. It says that my mother knew I'd listen to her, just like I told you, because she knew the standard that she had set for me and knew I'd never settle for less. And notice how the telegram ends. Love. That's what's important to my family, and I am here to tell you, however worried you may be, that they will love you as much as they love me and my brother and sister. You will be welcomed with open arms. Now do you understand, soon-to-be Mrs. Ritter?"

Despite her look of uncertainty, Barbara nodded and smiled at him.

"Now that you understand how much you will be loved, I need to ask you about your family. Did you want any of them to come to our wedding?"

Barbara shook her head.

"No," she said, "They are pleased that I'm in Wyoming and not in Texas. They didn't approve of my first marriage, and I'm sure that they wouldn't approve of this one. I think they wanted me to be an old maid schoolmarm."

"Well, I, for one, am very glad they didn't get their wish."

He stood up, walked over to her, and gave her a quick kiss on the forehead.

———

Krueger knew that this was the day. He had directed some miners to step up their attacks on the Chinese and knew that Jameson and Lydon were in place to intercept any attempt by the railroad to interfere, and he needed to provide that impetus.

He called in his closest union confidants. These were the men who would do anything he asked, any time he asked, and the anytime was now and he was about to ask for everything.

As the men filed into the union hall, Krueger greeted each of the men in turn. Then he outlined his plan. He wanted them to form two groups. He would lead one group, and his most trusted lieutenant – a true thug with the very Irish name of Patrick McCarthy – would lead the second. The first group would move into Chinatown killing any Chinks that got in their way. The second group would block the bridges out of Chinatown so that no others could escape. Krueger told them he would set everything in motion and for his men to wait for his order. They all murmured agreement and filed out.

As Krueger stood up, a member of his inner circle came barging in the door with a hand clenched in the hair of a Chinese miner.

"Krueger, I found this Chink snooping around out back, and I think he understands American, too."

Krueger eyed the Chinaman and was surprised that the captive didn't seem as terrified as ought to have been. Either this man was heroically brave or just plain stupid.

"That so, you slanty-eyed bastard? You been spyin' on us, have you?" he shouted.

Dak Lee pretended he didn't understand a word, but he knew that it wouldn't matter if he did or did not. Either way, he didn't think he'd live long enough to see the moon rise again.

Krueger didn't expect an answer. So, Krueger walked to the door and ordered his minion to bring the man along. They dragged Dak Lee out the door into the dirt yard and threw him to the ground. Once on the ground Krueger began kicking him about the midsection and Dak Lee curled up into a ball, knowing that resistance was useless as he endured one vicious kick after another. Some of the other miners had seen Krueger pummeling the prostrate miner and came to join in the fun. Soon Dak Lee felt himself being kicked by heavy boots and struck with thick staffs that some of the miners carried for balance. He lost consciousness after three minutes of abuse, and after two more minutes of beatings, he died.

A lone Chinese miner ran to Dak Lee's defense and was rewarded with a series of cracks from white miners' staffs. He too hit the ground and probably would have suffered the same fate if a white foreman hadn't intervened.

ROCK CREEK

The miners were all told to get back to work by the foreman, but they ignored him. Their blood was up. The foreman took no chances, as he guided the bloody Chinese miner back to where a group of his fellow Oriental miners had assembled and together, they returned him to his house.

Krueger told all his men to go home and grab anything that could be used as a weapon and said to meet him at this very spot at one o'clock sharp. A festive atmosphere broke out as the white miners returned to their homes to arm themselves.

An hour later, they reassembled and marched toward Chinatown. The Rock Creek Massacre was less than two hours away.

CHAPTER 7

Carl awakened just before dawn. That damned internal clock of his never seemed to transition off cowboy time. He washed and shaved then returned to his room, got dressed and went down to the kitchen. Barbara wasn't there yet, so he put some wood in the stove and filled the coffee pot with water, then then filled a pan with water and set it next to the coffee pot for Beth's oatmeal. Just as the coffee pot was ready to boil, Barbara entered the kitchen, and Carl turned, greeted her with a quick kiss and asked if she'd like some coffee before preparing breakfast.

"Well," she said, "as you've already made the coffee, I suppose I can spare a couple of minutes."

Carl took her at her word and filled her cup with coffee and then his. After replacing the coffee pot, he sat down and smiled at her.

"Carl, I'm sorry for worrying so much about your parents. I should have known better. I know you so well and no one as wonderful as you could have been brought up by parents any less caring than yours."

Carl replied, "That's not always true, you know. I've known some real stinkers that grew up in great families. I've also known exceptional people raised by tyrants. Look at you. It sounds like your parents never appreciated how intelligent or how special you are. Yet you spent almost seven years alone, raising an incredible little girl by yourself. How can anyone so perfect as you come from parents who don't recognize it? I was very fortunate to be able to appreciate my mother and father, and to learn from what they told me and how they lived their lives. Wait until you meet them. My father is just what you'd expect for a blacksmith. He's not tall, but he's as strong as a bull and if you didn't know him better, you'd think he's as fierce as one, too. My mother is the complete opposite. She's tiny, just a bit over five feet tall and weighs less than a hundred pounds. I could pick her up when I was eight. She laughs a lot and has a great singing voice, yet she controls her bull of a husband like a matador. He doesn't know it, either. And there was always humor in our family. Not the mean-spirited kind of humor. Just the gentle ribbing that comes from people that know you love them and are just having a little fun."

"It sounds like you had a wonderful childhood."

"I did, and I know it. I even knew it when I was a boy. I worked in my father's smithy and helped my mother with the chores. School was fun because my parents made it fun. After high school, they insisted I go to college. Engineering was my choice, not theirs. I've always built things, either in the smithy, in the wood shop, or in my mind. Now, with the Union Pacific, I'll get back into doing just that, and I owe all of that to you. If I hadn't met you, I'd still be searching for what to do with my life. Now I know, and I know who I'll spend the rest of my life with. And for that, I thank you, Barbara."

"You're welcome. It was the least I could do."

She put her hand on his as Beth came in to have her oatmeal. Carl told her that he'd add a secret ingredient one day that she would really like.

"Promise?" she asked.

"Of course. Maybe I'll buy some in Cheyenne when we go up there to do our shopping. They don't sell it here."

"What is it?"

"I can't tell you or it'll ruin the secret," he answered with a grin.

After they'd seen Beth off to school, Tom went to the telegraphers to see if there were any messages and returned with the expected yellow sheet ten minutes later and handed it to Carl without a word.

ROCK CREEK

T WILSON MATHIAS BOARDING HOUSE PINE BLUFFS WYOMING

MINERS NOT WORKING AT ROCK CREEK
WHITE MINERS AT ROCK CREEK BLOCKING BRIDGES
EXPECT TROUBLE SOON
BE READY TO GO TO ROCK CREEK

OFFICE OF THE PRESIDENT UNION PACIFIC RR OMAHA NEBRASKA

"This doesn't look good," said Carl, "This sounds like a planned event, not a spontaneous uprising. I think we'd better get ready to move on this. Do you think they'll send you in or not?"

"I don't know. I'm not even sure they know what's going to happen. They've stayed out of the situation for so long, it's like they're reading about it in a novel."

They both knew that once the killing started, it would set off a chain of events that would take a long time to bring to a halt.

The news didn't take long in coming. Ninety minutes later, there was knock at the door and when Tom opened it, he found the same pimply-faced teenaged boy standing at the door with a telegram for Mister Wilson.

Carl knew it must be urgent for them to send it so quickly.

Tom tipped the boy and rushed the telegram into the sitting room.

He opened it and read:

T WILSON MATHIAS BOARDING HOUSE PINE BLUFFS
WYOMING

WHITE MINERS AT ROCK CREEK RIOTING KILLING AND
BURNING
PREPARING SPECIAL TRAIN WITH EXECUTIVES OF
UNION PACIFIC
WILL PICK UP GOVERNOR AND CONTINUE TO ROCK
CREEK
TRAIN WILL NOT STOP AT PINE BLUFFS
MAY SEND FOR YOU LATER

OFFICE OF THE PRESIDENT UNION PACIFIC RR OMAHA
NEBRASKA

"Here's the event they must have been waiting for," said Tom.

Carl read the telegram and handed it to Emily who read it and
then gave it to Barbara.

"I'll send a reply to headquarters and warn them about the
threat. Then we have to get moving. That train will take about
nine hours at speed to get to Cheyenne. We may be able to find
out where they're planning on planting the dynamite and foil
their plans before they can light the fuse."

Carl went to his room, grabbed his Winchester, his
saddlebags, and strapped on his Colt. He made sure the newly
purchased field glasses were in the saddlebags along with his
spare ammunition. Food didn't concern him, but he grabbed his
canteen and put on his new wool jacket, too. It may be warm
now, but he wouldn't count on it after the sun went down.

By the time he got downstairs, Tom had already packed his
things, and both went into the kitchen to fill their canteens.

Barbara had two sandwiches for each of them wrapped and handed them to Carl before she gave him a quick kiss.

"Come back to me," she whispered.

"Always," he replied.

Tom stepped into the sitting room and kissed Emily goodbye and reminded her to take good care of his son while she reminded him to return to their daughter. He smiled and joined Carl as they walked out to the road.

———

In Cheyenne, Lydon and Jameson were sitting in Strom's Saloon when they heard excited talk among some of the patrons. Jameson caught the words 'Rock Creek' and his ears perked up, rose to his feet and joined the agitated crowd.

"What you fellas sayin' 'bout Rock Creek," he asked, "I know some folks out there."

The most vocal man in the crowd, a thin man with the appearance of a stork, replied, "Sure 'nuff, mister. Bad things happenin' there. Miners are riotin' and killin' Chinese all over the place. Governor Warren asked President Cleveland for Federal troops and the U.P. is sending a special train tonight with some high-ups to get the mess settled. The governor is going to get on the train when it shows up and they'll be heading out thataway together."

"Sounds bad," said Jameson, tucking his delight firmly away. Glad to see that Krueger finally got off his ass and did something that should have been done a long time ago.

He returned to his own table and filled Lydon in what he had learned.

Lydon shot him a grim look and said, "Time is wastin'. This is the time we make things right."

Then he stood and motioned for Jameson to follow. Jameson rose from the table and they walked out to their horses. They already had some food and water packed, and Lydon threw the saddlebags containing the dynamite over his Appaloosa before they mounted and rode west.

————

Back in Pine Bluffs, Carl and Tom stepped across the road to the livery stable, Ethan saddled the buckskin and Carl did the same to Jules. Jules seemed to sense the urgency and was anxious to get under way.

Tom stopped to send a telegram notifying the home office of the threat but knew that the train had already departed and wouldn't slow down except for watering and more coal. He wasn't sure that they would let speculation about a perceived threat stop them either. Threats these days were a dime a dozen.

The two men headed west on their horses along the roadway that paralleled the rails. They made good time because the road was well-maintained, and the weather was in their favor. They kept the horses at a medium trot, to keep from tiring them excessively, yet as they were riding, they kept an eye on the condition of the rails, the ties, and the railway bed. It took them a little longer when they came to a trestle crossing a gully and had to make sure it hadn't been tampered with, but a quick inspection failed to indicate any problems. Tom was grateful for having an engineer with him to verify the safety of the rails.

After twenty or so miles, they dismounted and let their horses rest, then fifteen minutes later, remounted and continued their ride. They didn't talk much as little that needed to be said and their concentration was on the rails.

The shadows lengthened as they arrived outside of Cheyenne.

"Do we go and notify the governor's office or press on?" Carl asked.

"Let's keep going. Either the railroad will let them know, or they won't. It won't make any difference anyway."

It was nearly dusk, and they were about three miles past Cheyenne and coming up on a large trestle. Carl noticed a light to the right of the tracks about a half mile ahead and signaled for Tom to hold up. Carl dismounted, and Tom followed suit.

"Looks like a campsite, don't you think?" Carl asked.

Tom replied, "That'd be my guess."

Carl pulled the field glasses out of the saddlebag and scanned the area. When the light popped into view, he spotted two men crouched beside a fire and handed the glasses to Tom.

"Looks like we found our guys," said Carl.

"I believe you're right," said Tom, lowering the glasses, "So, what's the plan?"

"My guess is that they know about the train and probably expected the railroad's reaction to their riot. Having the governor thrown into the mix makes it even better for them. Think about it. Railroad execs and governor killed when one of their own trestles fails. It'd put Union Pacific in a bad spot."

"It also means that they won't blow up the trestle until after the eastbound train comes through in a couple of hours or so."

"I think our best bet is to leave the horses about a quarter mile from their campsite and walk in on them. I don't want to spook their horses and let them know we're close."

"Let's go," said Tom.

They led their horses to a small copse of trees on the north side of the tracks and looped the horses' reins around a low-hanging branch. Rifles in hand, they crept toward the fire. About fifty yards away they could hear conversation, but it was too low to be understood.

Carl motioned to Tom to move off to his left, closer to the tracks. They were about twenty yards apart as they approached the fire. Carl cocked his Winchester and could hear the sound of Tom's Winchester's hammer being locked into position. Both men sitting in front of the fire froze and turned with the sound.

"Evening, boys!" Carl shouted as he stepped near the fire, his carbine's muzzle pointed in their direction.

The Appaloosa rider spoke first, saying, "What the hell do you want and why are you pointing that cannon our way. We ain't done nothin'."

"Well, that must be my mistake. It seems we may have mistaken a couple of innocent campers for the idiots planning on blowing up this trestle before a special train arrives."

Lydon shouted, "What the hell are you talkin' about? We're just mindin' our own business and you come into our camp threatenin' us. We should call the law down on you for that!"

"See how that works out for you. Your sidekick over there tried to kill a man in Pine Bluffs. Isn't that right, Mister Jameson?"

"Ritter, ain't it? I didn't shoot nobody, and you know it. You're just loco," Jameson replied with sneer.

"I could be wrong. But we could just ask the man you tried to assassinate," said Carl, "Tom, does this look like the wayward gentleman who tried to fill your hide with lead but had his gun jam after two piddling missed shots?"

The Appaloosa man jerked his head at Jameson, and shouted, "You said he was dead!"

"I put two rounds into him," bellowed Jameson, "That's more than enough!"

"You used a .32 caliber pistol," said Tom as he walked steadily toward the camp, "It didn't do much damage at all beyond giving me a headache something fierce and a sore rib or two, but you'll hang just the same."

Lydon was desperate and decided to turn on his partner.

"If he's what you come for, take him. It don't bother me none. I don't cotton to assassins."

Jameson exploded, yelling, "You back-dealing bastard!"

He pounced upon his ex-partner before Carl fired a round into the air and quickly levered a new cartridge into his Winchester. In the stillness left in the wake of the loud report, the two men ceased their fracas near the fire and looked up at Carl as the expended brass dinged when it bounced off the rail.

"Keep them covered, Tom. Gentlemen, do either of you possess any weapons?"

Both shook their heads.

"Tsk! Tsk! Boys, you shouldn't be telling any lies to me now," said Carl, "I know Jameson probably has that worthless .32 stashed in his belt somewhere, and if I were a betting man, I'd wager that you have one as well, although I'd hope that you had something a mite more impressive."

Carl had them both stand and pull up their jackets. Each had a pistol tucked into the belt behind his back, so he told them to reach with their fingers only and slowly drop their guns to the ground. Jameson complied, but Lydon grabbed the grip of his pistol, and his jacket flew loose as he tried to bring it to bear, but Tom's Winchester roared and Lydon felt the bullet snatch his loose jacket, punching a clean hole through the back, and he suddenly had a change of heart and dropped the pistol to the ground. Carl snatched the two revolvers where they had fallen and hurled them both down into the gully.

Carl had Jameson turn around, reached into his saddlebags and pulled out some pigging strings that all cow hands kept handy. He tied Jameson's hands behind his back and, once the man was fully secured, did the same to the Lydon.

"Tom get these morons onto their horses. I'm going to check and see if I can get that dynamite away from the trestle."

Tom nodded and had the two men shuffle toward their horses.

Carl stepped down toward the gully from the campsite, figuring the fuse had to be close at hand. They must have been keeping the fire going to provide them with a source to light it, and as he suspected, about twenty feet from the fire, he spied the fuse. It was being held in place by two heavy rocks, which Carl kicked over, then lifted the end and traced the fuse toward the trestle. Even in the waning light, it was easy to spot the four sticks of dynamite. They were placed on a close cross member. It was a perfect location as the charge would have brought down the entire front section of the trestle, which would have created a total disaster. Carl took out his pocket knife and cut the heavy twine that the men had used to bind the dynamite to the support, pulled the dynamite away, removed the blasting cap and wrapped it in the fuse.

He hefted the four sticks of dynamite in his left hand as he returned to where Tom was keeping an eye on the prisoners.

Carl came up behind him and said, "Found the dynamite. We'll need it for evidence."

Tom nodded, then they walked the men to their horses, and had to assist the two bound men into their saddles. Lydon was ejecting a steady stream of curses, threats, and insults directed at Carl, Tom, and their families while Jameson just scowled at them both. After listening to Lydon's ranting for about three minutes, Carl dropped back, pulled his Colt and cracked him in the head with the barrel. It didn't knock him unconscious, but it did shut him up.

"What did you guys think you were going to get out of this, anyway?" Carl asked Jameson.

Jameson wasn't about to say anything incriminating, but that didn't mean he'd be quiet either as he replied, "That's for you to figure out. But the joke's on you, too."

"What joke? We stopped your plot and you're both headed to jail," Carl said.

"Maybe. Maybe not. You don't have anything on us. Besides, Emerson's brother may get even with you anyway."

"His brother? And who is Emerson?" Carl asked.

Jameson nodded toward the other man.

"That there's Emerson. Emerson Lydon."

"Elrod's brother. I would have guessed they were cousins."

"He's his younger brother, but all he did was provide us with food and supplies. He's a perfectly worthless bastard, but he sure does hate your guts. After we left, he said he was going to go and drygulch your sorry carcass and take your girl away."

Jameson started laughing and added, "And here you are out here tryin' to be the hero. You'd better let us go. You got the dynamite, so we can't do nothin'. You gotta go and stop that freak brother of his from doin' what he wants to do."

Carl thought he might be bluffing but couldn't take the risk.

"We need to pick up the pace," Carl said to Tom, "We need to get to Cheyenne before the eastbound train leaves."

Tom had overheard the boasts from Jameson and knew the uncertainty it posed.

"Right. Let's go. It only has to take on water in Cheyenne, so it'll only be in the station for fifteen minutes or so."

They put both horses into a trot and were just arriving at the depot when they heard the whistle of the eastbound train behind them.

"I'll get these guys down to the sheriff's office," Carl shouted, "You need to hold up that train!"

"I can do that!", Tom shouted back and turned the buckskin toward the depot's office.

Carl took the lead of the two horses, picked up the pace and pulled up to the sheriff's office near the courthouse. He called out to a passing pedestrian and asked him to bring out the sheriff. At first, the stranger took Carl for a crazy man, then he reasoned that even if the man was crazy, he was a crazy man who was armed to the teeth and did as he was asked.

The sheriff emerged a few seconds later and asked, "What do you need?"

Carl related the tale and showed the sheriff the dynamite, what the two men were planning, and added an abridged story of the attempted murder. He told the sheriff that he had to get back to Pine Bluffs as soon as possible.

The sheriff advised him that he needed to stay in Cheyenne to sign the complaint, and Carl suggested that he simply put the men in jail for the time being, and he would return tomorrow to sign the complaint along with Tom Wilson of Union Pacific. When the sheriff asked where Mister Wilson was, Carl told the lawman that he was holding the train for him.

The sheriff weighed his options for a moment, then caved to Carl's request. With a doff of his Stetson, Carl jumped back in the saddle and raced to the depot.

The sun had vanished, but Tom had done his job, and Carl could see the locomotive still sitting at the depot hissing steam in large clouds as he raced to the depot, hauling Jules to a stop just before they reached the tracks.

Tom spotted him as he hung from the open door of a stock car and yelled, "Bring your horse over to the stock car! We're riding in here."

Carl didn't question their accommodations, but dismounted and led Jules to the stock car, walking him up the ramp as the whistle sounded and could see Tom waiting with the buckskin inside the car.

As the train picked up speed, Tom asked, "How'd it go with the sheriff?"

"It could have been speedier. I thought he was going to keep me there to sign a complaint, but I promised him I'd be back tomorrow. When he heard you were holding the train for me, he let me go. By the way, we don't have tickets."

"Tickets? You have to be joking. This is my railroad. I may not own it, but I'm high enough that I never have to pay fares."

"Handy enough on this occasion. What's the plan when we get to Pine Bluffs?"

Carl replied, "When we arrive, we'll take the horses and leave them outside the livery stable. Leave your rifle in its scabbard. You go in the front and I'll go around the back. Have your pistol drawn. If he's not there, then we don't have a problem. If he is, then we'll deal with the issue as we come to it. One other thing. When you get there, kick off your boots. I'll do the same. We'll both need to be quiet."

Back in Pine Bluffs, Emily was in her room reading while Barbara was downstairs in her room with Beth, both of them admiring their new dresses. Everything was peaceful and quiet when she overheard boots on the front porch, and she cast an eager smile at Beth.

"Sounds like your papa's home," she said.

She got up to welcome her man, but as she turned into the hallway, she was stunned to see Elrod Lydon's hideous nose peeking in through the door. She screamed, and raced to the front of the house, rammed her back against the door, slamming it closed and slid the locking bolt home, then ran back to her room, turning out every light on the floor as she did, the incessant pounding at the front door echoing in her wake.

She locked eyes with Beth and said, "Remember what your papa told you to do?"

"Yes, Mama. I have to go to my barrel."

"Go now. Run to your hiding place and stay quiet."

Beth needed no further orders. She scampered into the darkened kitchen, flew down into the cold room, and climbed into the barrel.

Barbara quickly returned to her room and did as Carl had instructed, took her purse containing the pistol, and sat down in the corner facing the door, pulled out the pistol and held it in her trembling hands. The only light left in the house came from upstairs and could hear Lydon smashing at the door and knew the door wouldn't hold much longer.

The upstairs light went out as Emily turned out the last upstairs lamp putting the entire house in pitch blackness. With a blast, the front door's latch gave way, and Barbara knew Lydon was in the house. She waited, taking deep breaths, trying to keep calm, but no matter how hard she tried, she couldn't keep from shaking.

She heard boots thumping across the floor and could tell Lydon was feeling his way around the house. He would know the basic layout but wouldn't know which room was hers. She heard his steps as he headed unevenly up the darkened stairs and reached the upstairs corridor. He must not know about the downstairs bedroom.

She could hear him open one door then shut it again, walk slowly down the hallway, with no apparent attempt to be quiet as he searched each of the bedrooms.

When he opened the next door that Carl used, he cursed, but lingered there. Barbara had heard his cursing and wondered why he seemed so angry. *Was he looking for Carl?* He surely sounded disappointed in not finding him in his room, but after another minute or so, Lydon continued his search.

Emily heard the same searching sounds that Barbara heard and, like Barbara, was sitting with her back against the wall with her revolver. When Elrod's search reached the adjoining room, Emily knew she was next, then cocked her pistol and waited. Her hands were shaking as well, but not as badly as Barbara's.

Barbara heard him open the third door – Emily's room – and a shot rang out. She hoped that Emily had hit him, but then heard footsteps racing down the stairs in terror, accompanied by a string of profanities, then as it reached the next to the last step, Elrod stumbled, and sprawled in a heap in the hallway. She heard him groan and could hear him crawling his way down the hall. Then all sounds ceased, and Barbara began to hope that Elrod was dead but kept her hands on the pistol. She just wasn't sure. But her shaking had subsided after the initial shock of the intrusion. Now, she just waited in the dark, her back against the wall.

Carl and Tom had just tied their horses to the rail when they heard Emily's shot echo from the darkened house, and both took off at a dead run and quickly passed through the open front gate. Carl raced to the back of the house while Tom headed for the front. Each of them took a few seconds to remove their boots before entering the house.

Carl entered the kitchen, and even in the darkness, he knew where he had to go first. He stepped quietly across the floor and down into the cold room, then after reaching the bottom step, he whispered, "Bethany?" A second later, he heard her relieved response when she whispered back, "Hans."

Carl crouched next to the barrel and leaned over the open top.

"Bethany, where is your mama?" he whispered.

"She's in her room. That ugly man broke in. I think he's trying to hurt mama."

"He won't. You stay here. I'll be right back."

Tom had seen the splintered doorjamb at the front door and stepped across the threshold, unable to see anything in the darkness, but he knew his way upstairs. He had to make sure Emily was safe while Carl would take care of first floor. He tiptoed up the stairs in stockinged feet. When he reached the top of the stairs, it occurred to him that Emily might be sitting in her room, armed with her pistol. He had to be careful. This could result in a sudden and violent end to their marriage.

Meanwhile, Carl had stepped back into the kitchen and stepped silently across the room.

Elrod had been stunned by the sudden trip and fall and, despite his bruises, managed to stand and decided to try the downstairs rooms, which was an almost insane thing to do after having just avoided a gunshot, but he was obsessed with killing Carl and he had to be in one of the downstairs bedrooms, probably already sleeping with Barbara and it overwhelmed any rational thoughts.

Elrod had seen Tom's shadow going up the stairs and momentarily thought about shooting him, but he was too short to be that damned Ritter. He only had four rooms to check on this floor and knew he had to be here.

Barbara's nerves had just returned to just excited when she heard the approaching footsteps. She could hear muffled yet obvious movement outside her door and began to panic. *Was it him?* She raised her pistol. *What could she do? What if it wasn't him? What if it was Carl or Tom or Emily?*

A shadow even darker than the darkness of the hallway entered the room and she didn't know whose shadow it was, so she raised her pistol and aimed above the door, cocked the hammer and fired. The flame of the pistol momentarily exposed the terrified visage of Elrod Lydon.

She started to pull back the hammer for a second shot when she heard a familiar, incredibly welcome voice.

"Lydon," Carl barked, "get on the floor or I'll blow your head off!"

Elrod turned. *It was him! The one he came to kill!* Without hesitation, he pulled his pistol and fired in the direction of the voice. The echo of his shot still hung in the air for a tick before a much larger blast obliterated it altogether. Lydon screamed as Carl's .44 ripped through his chest, destroying ribs, lung tissue, arteries and veins before nicking his thoracic spine and exiting his back as the powerful stench of gunpowder hung in the air, and Elrod dropped to the floor.

Carl waited for thirty seconds of silence, lit a match, found a nearby lamp and lit the wick, filling the hallway with light as he stepped to the lifeless body of Elrod Lydon. He took one long stride over the body and turned to Barbara's room as he slid his Colt back into its holster.

Before he entered her room, Carl said in a firm voice, "Barbara, it's me. You're safe. I'm coming in now."

Barbara was still huddled in the corner with the pistol in her hand when Carl stepped into the room, reached down and gently took the pistol from her shaking hands.

"Hopefully, you'll never need this again, my love," he said as he held out his hand to help her to her feet.

Barbara slowly came out of her trance, realizing that the terror was over and once she was steady, Carl enveloped her in his arms and she embraced him without shedding a tear.

Carl shouted for Tom and Emily to hear: "It's okay, Tom. He's dead!"

Emily heard the voice and rose to her feet, stepped out of the dark room and saw Tom standing in the hall with his pistol in his hand and realized that she still held hers in her hand as well.

She smiled at her husband and said, "I hope this isn't how you plan on settling family disagreements in the future."

He laughed and slipped his Colt into his holster, stepped forward and held his wife in a tight embrace.

Downstairs, Carl said to Barbara, "I believe that we need to go retrieve our daughter."

"Is she okay?" Barbara asked with a mother's concern on her face.

"She's fine. I checked on her before I came into the hallway."

As they entered the kitchen, Carl stopped Barbara with a gesture and then tiptoed down the stairs into the root cellar. He walked over to the barrel and said, "Bethany, I think hide and seek time is over."

Beth reached her hands up and out of the barrel. Carl lifted her from the barrel and held her tightly as he turned to leave the cold room.

"That wasn't as much fun as normal hide and seek, Hans."

"I don't imagine so, but it's all okay now. That man who tried to hurt your mama is dead."

By the time the two of them made it into the kitchen, Barbara had company.

"Hello, Luck," said Carl.

"Looks like you have something you may want to tell me, Carl. And it had better be good."

For the next half hour, Tom and Carl filled Luck in with the details of their mission to Cheyenne, finding Jameson and Lydon's brother, and the shootout at the lodging house.

After they'd finished, Luck said, "Well, Elrod is surely dead, and he certainly doesn't belong here. I'm pretty sure what you've said is accurate. I'll wire the sheriff in Cheyenne and tell him to hold those two until you and Tom can make it back there. I'll tell him it may take a couple of days to clear up this killing over here. That should keep him happy. For a while, anyway."

Tom and Carl followed Luck from the kitchen to the hallway and stopped when they reached Lydon's lifeless body.

"If you boys want to haul that carcass outta here, it'd be all right," said Luck, "I'll have someone come and pick it up shortly."

With that pronouncement, the sheriff took a long step over the body, reached the other side, leaned down and yanked the front of Lydon's shirt, rolling him flat on his back. There wasn't as much blood as Luck expected. Carl's .44 had penetrated his left side and went clear through to his chest, killing him almost instantly. Luck then reached down and picked up Lydon's weapon. He shook his head as he examined it.

"Another .32. Haven't any of these idiots ever thought of buying a real gun?"

With that, he stepped through the doorway and vanished into the night.

Carl and Tom carried the body out the front door and down the steps of the porch. They left it in the walkway where the mortician could find it and returned to the house.

"I think I've had enough adventure for the night," said Tom, "Besides, I think Emily's going to be in the mood to stay up and talk."

Tom and Emily went upstairs together as Carl continued toward Barbara's room and found her getting Beth ready for bed. Beth wasn't protesting but looked at Carl with a mixture of awe and fear.

As soon as she was under the comforter, Carl stepped over to her bed and sat down on the edge. He looked at those eyes of hers – like Barbara's in miniature – and said, "A lot of scary things happened tonight, Bethany. You had to experience things that no little girl should have to experience. Sometimes bad things happen to good people. Now, your mama is the best person I know, and this bad man was going to hurt her, and I couldn't let that happen. Do you understand?"

275

Beth nodded, and Carl continued, "I didn't want to shoot that man. I ordered him to stop what he was doing and lie down on the floor, but he didn't do that. Instead, he shot at me. Once he did that, my life and the lives of everyone I love were in danger. So, I did the only thing I could do and shot back at him. I've never shot at another person before, and I hope I never have to again, but if anyone ever threatens you or your mama again, I'll do it without hesitation. I love you and your mama too much."

Beth nodded as tears flowed into her pillow.

"I was afraid when I heard all the noise and the shooting. I was afraid that you were hurt, and the bad man would get me. But you made him stop. Thank you, Papa."

"You're welcome, sweetheart. Now you close those big blue eyes of yours and try to get some sleep, okay?"

She nodded, shut her eyes and rolled onto her side. Carl went to examine the front door and wasn't surprised that was a lot messier than the job Jameson had done when he broke into the Wilsons' room. The hinges were loose, and the closed bolt had splintered the door jamb. This wasn't going to be an easy fix.

Carl wondered why Lydon had spent so much time trying to smash in such a heavy door with a large glass window just four feet away.

"I guess passion overrules common sense sometimes," he muttered to himself.

By hammering at the front door, Lydon had given Tom and Carl time to get to the house and Emily and Barbara had time to get prepared. That crucial waste of time had made all the difference. Carl closed the door as well as he could and planned on fixing it in the morning.

Carl then returned to the kitchen and filled a pail with water and added some pine oil before taking the pail and a mop to the spot where Lydon had fallen. There wasn't much blood, but he knew it had to come up soon or it would soak into the wood. After a few minutes of heavy scrubbing there was no more evidence of the killing, other than the body on the front walk and he returned to the kitchen and emptied the bucket. On his way back to Barbara's room, he turned off the lamps in the hallway.

When he arrived in Barbara's room, she was already in her night dress. He leaned in and said, "I'll see you in the morning, Barbara. Are you okay?"

She nodded hesitantly.

As Carl left to go to his room, he heard her tremulous voice call after him.

"Carl. Please don't let me sleep alone tonight."

Carl knew that this was her voicing a need for protection, protection from the horrors in her memory. He entered the room, closing the door behind him.

Barbara slid under her blankets and comforter as Carl removed his boots, then turned down the lamp and joined her, staying on top of the covers as she snuggled in close, sighed, and was soon asleep. Carl knew his future as her husband was much more than as a provider and a lover but he was her protector as well, and he knew that he would play all three roles as best as he could.

CHAPTER 8

The next morning, Carl was up first and slipped out of Barbara's bed, picked up his boots, and then realized that he was still wearing his Colt. Luckily the leather loop was over the hammer, so it didn't fall out onto the floor. He slid the door open then closed it behind him without so much as the click of the latch, then used the downstairs washroom and went to the kitchen to make coffee. He didn't put on his boots yet, because he knew he'd have to go upstairs and change his clothes soon.

He had the coffee made and the water boiling for Beth's oatmeal when Barbara arrived and seemed like her normal self, smiling at him.

"Morning, ma'am. Glad to see your beautiful face," he said as he smiled back.

She took the cup of coffee he offered her, sat down and gripped the cup with both hands.

"Quite a night," she said softly.

"It certainly was, although I will say that I rather preferred the night before."

"I don't know if I can stay here anymore," she said.

"Barbara, you and Beth went through a terrible thing. So, did Emily. I'm sure Tom spent the night holding her just like I held you, but you have to know that it's over now, and it won't happen again. Jameson told me that Lydon wanted to kill me, so he'd have a clear path to you. I guess to his warped mind, he

278

figured by killing me you'd think he was a tough guy worthy of your attention. But you need to understand one thing: I'll always be nearby to protect you and Beth, whether it's in this house, in Omaha, or at the seaside. Okay?"

"Okay. But it may take me a while to get over this. Please be patient."

"Well, I think fifty years together will give us enough time, don't you think?"

She smiled as Tom and Emily made their way down the hallway.

"I've got to get breakfast going," Barbara said as she rose from the kitchen table.

For a brief second Carl thought of taking over cooking breakfast, so she could relax, but then realized that the daily routine would help her a lot more.

While Barbara busied herself frying bacon and eggs, Beth wandered into the kitchen and asked Carl whether he was going to make her oatmeal.

"For you, anything, Beth," he smiled as he began to make her oatmeal.

When everyone was seated and eating, Carl said, "The sheriff in Cheyenne is expecting me and Tom to show up there today to sign a formal complaint against the two would-be bombers. Luck told us that he'd notify his counterpart that we'd be delayed because of last night's incident. So, how about if Tom and I take care of that business tomorrow? Naturally, we wouldn't want to leave you ladies at home by yourselves, so we may have to drag you along and you'll naturally have to find something to keep you busy while we're taking care of the paperwork. I suppose you can go to the library for a few hours. Then again, they do have a few very nice stores that offer a wide variety of items that you may want to add to your collection of female things, but it's your choice. Library or shopping? What do you say?"

Emily spoke for the gentler sex when she replied, "I think we can find something to while away the hours in the stores."

Carl said, "That's settled then. We can catch the morning train to Cheyenne and the evening train back home. Barbara, you'll need to write a note for Beth letting the school know that she'll be playing hooky for a day."

Beth shouted gleefully, "I'm gonna ride on a train! I never got a ride on a train before. It'll be so much fun!"

"Not if you've spent as much time as I have inhaling the smoke from those stacks and sitting on those hard seats," said Tom, "But I think we'll survive this trip together."

After breakfast, Carl stopped by the hardware store and bought the supplies he needed to fix the door, and on his way back to the house, he stopped by the telegraph office and wired his bank in Kansas City for an additional two hundred dollars. With what he had left over from his previous trip, it should be plenty.

He spent the morning and well into early afternoon repairing the door and Barbara was pleased that he added a second security latch near the top of the door. When that was finished, he went over to the Western Union office and retrieved his cash.

———

The next morning saw everyone walking to the train depot, all except for Beth, who was skipping with excitement with an enormous grin spread across her face rather than walking. Carl was wearing his new vest and jacket.

They arrived at the depot and Tom noticed Carl reaching into his pocket to pay for tickets.

"Allow me," he said.

Tom pulled out a card from his wallet and after displaying it to the ticket agent said, "Five round trip tickets for Cheyenne, please."

The agent smiled, said, "Yes, sir" and forked over the tickets.

When the train arrived, Beth couldn't believe how big it was, even though she'd seen them hundreds of time before. But this one was bigger because she was going to be riding inside. She followed her mother onto the train, holding tightly onto her hand and took a seat by the window. When it started to move, she began rapidly chatting, commenting on anything and everything and didn't stop after the train left the station either. Soon the train was up to speed and she was amazed that anything could move that fast and pointed out everything she noticed whizzing by. Her excitement made the trip much more pleasant than it would have been without her.

The arrival at Cheyenne came too soon for Beth, but not soon enough for the ladies. After helping everyone down from the passenger car, Carl and Tom escorted them down the wide boulevard, and Carl directed them to Smith & Harrington. As they entered, Barbara was stunned at the variety before Carl pulled her aside. He reached into his pocket and pulled out five double eagles and dropped the coins onto her palm.

"Carl, this is a lot of money! I can't take this."

"Nonsense. You can, and you will, ma'am. You'll be needing a few day-to-day dresses, some shoes, maybe a new winter coat, and sundry other things. Beth will need the same. So, enjoy your time, Barbara. I need to buy a suit for our wedding while I'm here. Then I need to go with Tom to take care of the business with the sheriff."

He turned to Beth and bent down.

"Bethany," he whispered, "this is for you to spend as you like. Maybe you can convince your mama to take you to a toy store."

When handed her a five-dollar gold piece, her eyes grew wide and she stood there stunned. *She was rich!*

Carl stood up and announced, "Off with you, ladies. Tom and I have manly things to do."

The women needed no further inducement and hustled into the bowels of the store.

Carl said to Tom, "I need to buy a suit, but did you want to take care of the sheriff's business first?"

"We should," said Tom, "I received a telegram telling me to meet with some other Union Pacific executives this morning. They were on the train headed for Rock Creek on Wednesday with the governor, so this should be interesting. They want to know all about the incident with Jameson at the boarding house and the attempt to blow up the trestle. While I'm doing that, you can get fitted with your burial suit."

Carl snickered and replied, "Maybe it's because I know how lucky I am, but I sure don't look at it that way."

Tom laughed, smacked Carl on his right shoulder and they headed across the wide street and down a few doors to the sheriff's office, then Carl opened the door and let Tom precede him inside.

They were greeted by sight of three men with tin stars on their chests, one at the main desk and two seated in chairs nearby talking to each other but stopped and turned to look at them as Carl and Tom walked into the office.

The deputy sheriff at the desk looked up and asked, "What can we do for you gentlemen?"

Carl told him that they needed to sign complaints against the two prisoners that they were holding, and the deputy nodded and directed them to a nearby office. He handed them each a blank pad and a pencil and instructed them to write and then sign their statements and then return them to the front desk. It took about thirty minutes for Carl to finish. Tom took longer because he also included a lengthy account of the attempt on his life.

When they had completed their statements, they exited the small office, found the deputy, and handed him the sheets of paper.

He gave them a quick once-over and asked, "Are you going to be in town for a while? The sheriff is out at the moment and I'm sure he'll want to talk to you and to be honest, we would all love to hear the story ourselves."

"We can do that," Tom replied, "but right now, I need to go and talk to some of the Union Pacific officers that were on that train while my young friend here needs to buy himself a suit. We'll be back in a couple of hours."

"Good enough," the deputy said before Tom and Carl turned to leave.

They left the sheriff's office, and Carl found a men's clothing store called Hellman's, while Tom headed to the Metropolitan Hotel where he was to meet with the other Union Pacific executives. They agreed to meet at S.S. Ramsey's restaurant for lunch at noon, hopefully with their ladies who should mercifully be done with their shopping for the day.

Carl purchased a medium gray suit and decided to make a few other purchases at a different store. He left Hellman's, boxed suit tucked under his arm, and walked to Zenner's jewelry store, found Mister Jackson, and the man remembered him. This was a relatively easy purchase. He found a beautiful cameo brooch, paid for it and was back out on the street in ten minutes. He put the brooch in the pocket of his new jacket, then he crossed the street and walked a bit until he reached Underwood grocery store. He noticed that they had small carts available for customers to load with their purchases, took one and wandered the aisles. He bought two large tins of raisins, five pounds of brown sugar, two tins of cinnamon, and one of nutmeg. Then he added a large tin of cocoa. Without realizing it, he was indulging the demands of his own sweet tooth. At the counter, he asked if he could have everything crated and shipped to the depot, and the clerk was happy to oblige.

From a clock on the counter, he saw that it was 11:10, so it was time to collect the ladies, he thought, then left the grocery store and found his way back to Smith & Harrington where he waded his way to the ladies' section and it didn't take him long to find the women. They were chatting amiably with the same clerk who had helped him when he bought the dresses. What made him nervous, though, was that they were laughing, and it didn't take him long to figure out what the subject was. As he drew closer, he discovered that he was correct in his assumption as to the topic of their merriment.

When Barbara heard his boots on the hardwood floor, she looked over at him and she and Emily started giggling again. He was going to say something but thought it wiser to remain silent and let the hilarity die on its own, hoping it would expire sooner rather than later.

"Did you buy anything at all?" he asked.

"A few things," Barbara answered with a smile, then nodded toward the counter in the back that was stacked with boxes, big and small.

"Did you have enough to cover all that?" Carl asked. Barbara's face assumed a guilty appearance and she admitted to coming up a bit short.

Carl feigned displeasure and said, "Well, I suppose you'll have to put some of it back, then."

Before she could react, he produced another double eagle to cover the shortfall.

"You're worth it, ma'am," he said with a grin.

"I don't know what came over me," said Barbara, "There were just so many beautiful things."

"It's perfectly fine," he said. He turned to the desk clerk, "Can we add this box to those stacks and add them to the shipping crate?"

The clerk noticed the Hellman label on the box and nodded.

She replied, "We should be able to find room in one of the crates."

Carl wondered whether half of Cheyenne would be making its way to Pine Bluffs on board that train because that was only Barbara's purchases, and he assumed that Emily's had already been crated up for shipment.

Carl and the ladies went to meet Tom at the restaurant, Carl having never asked what they had found so hilarious in the store but was sure that it was his own earlier adventures in Woman Wear Wonderland that had them giggling.

Barbara and Emily chatted about their purchases as Carl took Beth's hand and led them to S.S. Ramsey's restaurant and didn't take long to find Tom waiting for them, and he asked Emily if she had found everything that she wanted. She said she had found more than she expected to buy as they took seats in the nice restaurant and Carl caught Tom's eyes and wiggled his eyebrows to give him an idea what to expect when they disembarked in Pine Bluffs.

After their sumptuous lunch, as they sipped their coffee, Beth destroyed a bowl of ice cream, sticking just to a single scoop of chocolate this time after her recent memories of the cherry strudel tummy ache.

After lunch, Tom and Carl headed for the sheriff's office after Carl had given Barbara another forty dollars to make it through the afternoon.

When they entered the office, they found the sheriff waiting for them at his desk.

"Afternoon, gentlemen. Have a seat," he said as the two men pulled up chairs, "I read your statements, and everything seems pretty solid. The judge stopped by and reviewed your statements. We're holding Jameson for the assault charge and the attempted bombing, but Lydon's bail was set a lot lower and he's out pending the trial scheduled for next Thursday. You'll both have to be in attendance, of course."

"*Lydon's out on bail*?" Carl said loudly in exasperation, "You can't be serious. That man's brother tried to kill me two nights ago. The brother was assisting the man you just let walk out of here."

"*His brother tried to kill you?*" asked the surprised sheriff, "No one bothered to tell me that! Is that the feller involved in the shooting down in Pine Bluffs? It was in the paper, but the paper said the dead guy was someone named Litton. I guess they spelled it wrong. Damn it!"

"That bastard broke into my fiancée's house and was looking to kill me. It was pitch black, but I knew he was there. I told him to get down on the floor, but he took a shot at me instead. I fired and killed him. I know his brother thought he was an idiot, but I still don't think he'll be all that happy with me for killing him."

"I reckon not. Damn! That changes the complexion of things. One of my deputies mentioned that you were in town to write the statement and that you would be here all day, too."

"Let's not forget that his intention in blowing up the trestle was to kill as many Union Pacific executives as possible," said Tom, "There are four of them at the Metropolitan Hotel right now. Lydon may not know that, but it's hardly a secret. He may not know that you shot his brother, either, Carl."

Carl said, "He'd know. Remember that Jameson told us that Elrod was going to come and kill me. If Lydon heard about the break-in and shooting at the boarding house, it's pretty simple to guess who got killed and who made him that way."

"Sheriff, I think I know where he might have gone," said Carl, "When did he get out of jail?"

287

"About forty minutes ago."

"Neither Tom nor I are armed. Can one of your deputies accompany us?"

"Hell, I'll come with you."

He motioned to one of his deputies and said, "Ed, come on, and grab a scatter gun!"

The deputy took the weapon from the rack and followed the three men into the street.

Together they trotted toward 17th Street, where Carl knew of a shop that might come in handy. As they rounded the corner, Carl pointed at P. Bergersen's gunsmith shop.

"He wasn't armed when he was released, so he'll need to get re-armed quickly. With any luck, he's still there."

As they ran toward the store, Lydon stepped out from the entrance. His head was down as he filled the .44 caliber chambers of a Smith and Wesson Model 3. He wasn't going to use a toy gun this time.

He heard the footsteps coming his way on the cobblestone and his head snapped up, spotted the two lawmen accompanied by the two bastards who had sabotaged his plans. He snapped the cylinder closed, then screamed, "You sons-of-bitches!", then raised the pistol at the oncoming lawmen, and cocked the hammer.

Even through his rage, he could see that the deputy with the shotgun presented the biggest threat, so he took aim and fired. The deputy was too slow to bring his weapon to bear before Lydon began firing while Carl and Tom, both unarmed, hit the cobblestoned street on their stomachs. The deputy took Lydon's first shot in the shoulder and it knocked him spinning to the roadway. As he whirled, the centrifugal force whipped the shotgun from his hand, and it struck the back of the sheriff as he was about to return fire.

The jolt from the bulky weapon sent his shot flying straight up in the air, as he tumbled to the paved roadway. Lydon's second shot hit the sheriff in his left ankle. Lydon fired twice more, the first screeching off the pavement between Carl and Tom, who rolled in its wake. The second of Lydon's bullets whistled just above Carl's head. The sheriff struggled to get upright with his shattered ankle into shooting position, but the shattered bones kept him on the ground. Carl scanned the cobblestones for the dropped shotgun, and found it sitting half under the wounded deputy, who was rolling on the street in agony.

Carl wormed to his left and caught the double barrels of the weapon in his hand as Lydon's fifth shot hit the street eight inches in front of his face, scattering chips of stone that flew into his face, but he still yanked the shotgun from under the deputy and quickly pulled it to his shoulder to aim at Lydon, the hammers already cocked.

Lydon had Carl in his sights and grinned as he squeezed the trigger. Even amid all the other noise in the street, Carl could hear the click as the hammer fell on an empty chamber and didn't wait to see if there was a live round in the next hole, as he squeezed the trigger, emptying both barrels into Lydon. He wasn't sure what type of shot was loaded into the gun, but it didn't matter. Lydon was blown off his feet by the blast as his chest turned into a bloody mess.

Tom scrambled to his feet, then he and Carl jogged over to Lydon to check his vitals, but not finding any before they quickly turned and trotted back to the lawmen and began to check their wounds. A crowd was assembling, and Carl heard one man tell another, "Go get Doc Ricker," and two men ran off to fetch the doctor.

Carl turned to a bystander and said, "Go into Bergersen's Gun Shop and see if everyone is okay in there. I don't think the shooter had enough money to buy that gun."

The man ran to the shop and a few seconds later he was waving for help, as he had found Bergersen prone on the floor with what looked like a head wound.

Carl bent over the sheriff and said, "Sorry I caused all this mess, Sheriff."

Through clenched teeth, the sheriff hissed, "Not your fault. We should have held the bastard."

Moments later, Dr. Ricker arrived with a second doctor in tow. Each doctor examined a patient and instructed the men around them to help carry the patients to their surgery the next street over, and four men quickly assisted the two lawmen away from the scene.

Before he was taken off, the sheriff ordered Lydon's body to be brought to the undertaker.

"Are you okay?" Carl asked Tom.

Tom nodded and said, "I should go back to the Metropolitan and explain what happened to the other Union Pacific men."

Carl pointed to two women and a young girl staring wide-eyed from the boardwalk and said, "I think we need to explain things to them before we talk to a bunch of train guys."

Tom blew out his breath as he and Carl walked sheepishly toward Emily, Barbara and Beth.

Beth wore a strained look on her face as she saw the blood oozing from the cuts on Carl's face, then Barbara took out a handkerchief to wipe the blood from his face.

"You need to get to the doctor's," she said with much more concern than blame as she dabbed at his face.

He replied, "I'll be back soon," and started walking to 16th Street, where they had taken the wounded lawmen.

After he arrived, Doctor Quinby didn't take long to remove the chips from his face, give them a good cleaning with alcohol, which stung like crazy and covering them with bandages. None of the cuts were deep or long enough to require stitches, so he left the doctor's office and headed back to meet everyone after only thirty minutes.

Carl met everyone at the restaurant where they had just eaten lunch to have some coffee while Carl added any new details to the story that Tom had already told them.

"So, please tell me that this is the last of it," Emily had finally begged Tom after Carl had finished with his part of the story, "No more shooting and scaring the life out of me."

"I don't think Carl and I will be involved in any more trouble," Tom replied, "but I don't think the problem itself has gone away just yet. I met with the U.P. executives who went on that train with the governor. They found out that the white miners, and even some of their women and children, had killed twenty-eight Chinese miners and wounded seventy-nine. They then burned Chinatown to the ground and kept the survivors from leaving. The white miners then demanded that all Chinese miners leave the area and that all white miners be granted amnesty, and threatened retaliation against anyone who objected to their demands."

You've got to give the governor credit though. No one else would dare go out there, but he stepped right out on that platform like he was standing on the bully pulpit and dared the crowd of angry miners to do anything about it. They didn't lift a finger, then he telegraphed President Cleveland and requested Federal troops to restore order. They're on their way and they'll get here in a couple of days. It's still a powder keg back there. The only innocents in this are the Chinese miners. They were willing to work hard for less money. The railroad took advantage of that by bringing in more and more of them, squeezing the Irish, German, and Welsh miners out of jobs. Makes me embarrassed to work for Union Pacific, to tell the honest truth."

Carl said, "It's not just Union Pacific, Tom. They're the same as any other giant company that views their employees as just another commodity, like railroad ties or box cars."

The men that run these companies never see the conditions that they force their workers to live in. Maybe if they spent some time watching track get laid or watching the miners cutting coal deep underground, they'd understand their workers and treat them better, but don't hold your breath. It's a cutthroat world out there, and the higher-ups know it. If they paid their workers more, some competitor would come in and undercut them, driving them out of business. You know this, Tom. All we can do is wait for the change that is coming."

"It has to come sooner rather than later or there will be a lot more violence," said Tom, "As for us, I'd just as soon return to Omaha and live a quiet life just doing my job and nothing more."

"You never did tell me what your job was, Tom," asked Carl, "Are you an engineer?"

"No," admitted Tom, a bit sheepishly, "I have a degree in history from the University of Michigan, and now I'm in charge of logistics."

"How the heck did you get to work for a railroad in the first place?" Carl asked.

Tom smiled and nodded in Emily's direction.

"My fault, I'm afraid," she said.

"Now that must be an interesting story," said Barbara.

"It is. My godmother was Mary Lucretia Creighton. She was married to Edward Creighton. If you haven't heard the name, Edward Creighton was one of the builders of the transcontinental telegraph line. Edward and his brother John were big investors in Union Pacific, despite owning their own railroad, the Omaha and Northwestern. When I married Tom, he was looking for a job and I asked my godmother if she knew anywhere Tom would fit in."

Initially, I thought it was odd that she recommended him to Union Pacific rather than their own line or to First National Bank in Omaha, which the Creightons also owned. But she thought the size of Union Pacific would give him more opportunity to advance himself based on his abilities rather than sponsorship. So, he started as a small department head and within five years, he'd made it all the way to vice president. My godmother was a very special lady. She dedicated her entire life to helping the poor and needy, and when she died, she bequeathed a huge sum of money to establish a college in Omaha. They named it after the brothers and it's the first Catholic college west of the Mississippi."

"She sounds like a great lady," said Carl, "and Tom, you must have done some outstanding work to move up so quickly."

"Enough about me," said Tom, embarrassed by the praise, "Where do we go from here? We still have four hours to kill before we head back to Pine Bluffs. We'll need to have dinner by six-thirty. Any suggestions?"

Beth spoke up for the first time.

"I need to go shopping, too," she said.

"Okay," said Carl as he smiled at her, "you and your mama and Aunt Emily go do your shopping and we'll have to head over to the sheriff's office to check on the sheriff and his deputy. We'll meet you back here at five."

With that they went their separate ways again. Carl and Tom wound up staying at the sheriff's office for nearly an hour telling the entire story to the deputies. Both officers were expected to recover, but the sheriff would take longer and would probably always walk with a limp. The deputies assured them that Mister Jameson would be spending a long time in Federal prison and he may even miss a meal or two every so often under their custody.

On their way back out to the boardwalk, Carl said to Tom, "I don't like getting caught without a weapon nearby. I still have those two Colt Navy pocket pistols. Why don't we head back to Bergersen's and pick up a pair of shoulder holsters to fit them?"

Less than an hour later, they were leaving the shop with their newly acquired shoulder holsters, and they hadn't stopped there. After telling Paul Bergeson, who was wearing a head bandage, why they needed the shoulder holsters, the gunsmith suggested that they abandon the old Colts and buy new Webley Bulldogs and shoulder holsters. When they saw the small pistols that used the same .44 cartridges as their big revolvers and repeaters, they didn't waste a second forking over the cash.

They arrived at S.S. Ramsey's a little early, so they sat at the counter nursing a cup of coffee until almost exactly five o'clock, when the ladies entered the restaurant carrying hat bags. Beth was squeezing the life out of a porcelain-faced doll and had a child-sized white purse draped over her arm.

After they had all placed their dinner orders, Barbara and Emily listed off their additional purchases, most notably hats as they men pretended to be interested.

"So, what do you gentlemen have in your bags?" Emily asked Tom.

"Nothing special. Just some, um, leather goods," said Tom.

"What kind of leather goods? A strop for your razor or something else perfectly innocent?" she asked with raised eyebrows.

She had him cornered now, and then went in for the kill as she kept her eyes on Tom, making him squirm.

"It was just something that Carl suggested," stammered Tom, in a desperate attempt to deflect her stare.

Carl felt the heat of the women's eyes then descend on him and knew it was best to make a confession and get it over with.

"Well, ladies, if you must know," he began, "I thought that we needed to be able to protect you better, so I figured we'd pick up a couple of shoulder holsters for our Colt Navy pocket pistols. That way, we won't have to carry those huge .44 pistols on our hips everywhere we go. And, as it turned out, we found some smaller pistols that used the same .44 cartridges, too. That way, we will never find ourselves on our stomachs in the street with nothing to defend ourselves."

Barbara glanced at Emily and shrugged.

"That sounds like a good idea, Carl," she said as she and Emily smiled.

Carl and Tom were shocked and looked at each other. They had won the women over, but then realized that perhaps, Emily and Barbara were just having a bit of fun at their expense. Either way, they were glad it was in the past.

The rest of the dinner went quietly, and Beth showed the men her new favorite doll. She had christened her Maggie.

Carl told her that it was a beautiful doll and he complimented her on spending her money wisely.

"Mama bought me Maggie," she said, "I bought something else."

Beth put Maggie aside and opened her new purse.

"This is what I bought," she said, pulling out a thin, rectangular box, handed it to Carl and said, "It's for you, Papa."

Carl took the proffered box and opened it. Inside was a dark brown wallet made of alligator skin.

"Why, Beth. This is fantastic. I don't even have a wallet. Did you know that?"

Before he could show the gift to the Wilsons, Barbara said, "There is something inside the wallet that we both wanted to give you."

He opened the wallet. On the left side was a cellophane window and behind the window was a tintype of Barbara and Bethany wearing warm smiles in front of a painted backdrop depicting a seaside scene.

He looked up at Barbara and Beth and said, "Thank you, both. This is the greatest gift that anyone could ever give me. I'll treasure it forever, just as I'll treasure you both. Forever."

He showed the wallet to Tom as Beth and Barbara smiled, knowing he was sincerely grateful for the gift and even Tom was impressed.

Tom said, "That's really a nice piece, Carl. I wish I had one like it."

The words were barely out of his mouth when Emily tapped him on the shoulder and handed him a similar box.

"I wanted you to have a picture of me before I get all fat with the baby," she said as he opened his gift.

He hugged her and thanked her for the wallet and the wonderful picture inside, which he proudly displayed to Carl.

After dinner, the two couples plus one strolled leisurely down the walkway to the depot. The sun had gone down, but the street remained well-lit by gas lighting. When they arrived at the station, they saw three crates awaiting them. Carl paid the station manager for the two crates from Smith & Harrington as his was already marked as paid.

"What's in the third one," asked Barbara.

"No dresses this time. I just picked up some things while you were shopping."

She decided not to press the issue. Besides, she'd find out in a couple of hours anyway.

The eastbound train arrived shortly, and everyone boarded for the short journey back to Pine Bluffs.

Beth demanded separate seats for her and Maggie, and after everyone was seated and the train began to move, Barbara turned to Carl.

"Carl," she said, "I feel a little guilty about something."

"You have nothing to feel guilty about, my love. The gift that you and Beth have given me is more than enough."

"No, it's not that. I spent a lot of money today on things I don't need," she said, "I think that I should have saved some of that money."

"I didn't mind your spending one penny."

"I know. But before you arrived, my finances weren't in order. I didn't know how much longer I'd make it and I ran up a debt over at Jensen's, and I should have saved the money and paid that off. It would have been the right thing to do."

"This is hard for me to fess up to," said Carl, "but your account was paid off almost two weeks ago. You have a positive balance now."

"*Two weeks ago?*" asked an astonished Barbara, "You'd only been here three days or so by then. Why would you do such a thing?"

Carl was uncomfortable as he replied.

"Remember I told you that I fell in love with you the first time I saw you? Well, it was obvious to me that you didn't have a lot of money. I didn't think that it was fair, either. You worked almost non-stop from sunrise to bedtime trying to make ends meet. The clincher was when Jameson made that remark about not having bacon for breakfast. That very day, I went over to Hank's and bought all that food. Then I asked him about your credit. He didn't want to talk about it, said it was private information. But I convinced him that my intentions were honorable, and he caved in. So, I gave him a hundred dollars to pay off your account and to leave you some cushion. You have to understand that even though I knew I loved you, I didn't know if you'd ever care for me in return. I thought there was a chance that I'd have to move on and never see you again. So, I did what I could then, without knowing what the future might bring. You have to understand, I didn't need the money but you needed less worry in your life."

"So why didn't you tell me before?" she asked quietly.

"I couldn't tell you when I did it. I was worried that you may have thought I was trying to buy your affection and that was the last thing I wanted. I wanted you to be able to take care of yourself and to take care of Beth. It was my wildest dream that I could get you to love me and that we could get married, but at the time, that's all it was, a dream. I wanted you to make those decisions by yourself and not because you felt a sense of obligation to me."

"Oh, Carl. How did I ever live without you?" she asked quietly as she squeezed his arm.

She leaned over and kissed him, then rested her head on his shoulder for the rest of the ride home.

After they returned to Pine Bluffs, they arranged for the crates to be brought to the house as they strolled across the dirt street encumbered with hat boxes and bags.

After they had set their hand-carried purchases down in the sitting room, their three crates arrived on the porch. The men then moved the two Smith & Harrington crates into the sitting room before Carl carried the third crate into the kitchen as Barbara still wondered about its contents.

For the next hour, the crates were unpacked, and the contents were praised and admired. It was getting late and Beth was yawning, so Barbara got her ready for bed, then after Beth was under her blanket, Barbara returned and sat down in one of the easy chairs.

"Do we get to see what's in your mystery crate now?" she asked Carl.

"Sure," he said, and rose to his feet.

Three curious adults followed Carl into the kitchen, and after a short bit of levering wood with the screwdriver, Carl lifted the top panel and laid it aside. He reached in and began removing assorted tins from the crate.

Barbara sat in disbelief as one sweet confection after another was set onto the counter.

"Carl, this is going to add so much to the menu."

"Well, a lot of it was for Beth's breakfast. She hasn't had real oatmeal until she's had it with brown sugar, cinnamon, and raisins on top, and I plan on making some hot cocoa for breakfast if anyone is interested."

"You know how to make cocoa?" asked Emily.

"You bet. I'll show you in the morning."

With that comment, it was universally decided that it was time to call it a night. Everyone said their goodnights then Carl, Tom, and Emily went upstairs then ten minutes later Carl returned to Barbara's room and once again slept in his britches.

The following morning, Carl was in the kitchen before anyone else in the house had stirred from their slumber. By the time

Barbara emerged from her room, a delightful cinnamon scent permeated the house and she was drawn to the kitchen where she saw Carl bustling about and noticed that he wasn't wearing her apron.

"So," she said, "taking over my job, are you? This from a man who said he could barely manage making bacon and eggs."

"I wanted to surprise you and I'll only be taking over cooking for the day. I couldn't do this every day. I'd go crazy."

"What's in the oven?" she asked.

"Cinnamon rolls. I'm almost done with the cocoa. Beth's oatmeal is next."

She shook her head in admiration for the man who she already considered her husband.

A minute later, Beth arrived so quickly, it was as if she just materialized from the ether.

"What smells so good?" she asked excitedly.

"The cinnamon rolls. You can have one after your oatmeal, if you want one."

"I do! I do!" she said as she bounced.

By the time Tom and Emily made their way into the kitchen, Beth's face was firmly suspended over her oatmeal, looking at the differently colored breakfast.

"It smells good, but what's in it, Papa?" she asked.

"Cinnamon and brown sugar, and those round things are raisins. Go ahead and try it. Have you ever known me to give you anything that tasted bad before?"

Beth took a tentative bite which included a raisin and it didn't take long for her to realize that this wasn't like any oatmeal she had ever eaten before and began shoveling whole scoops into her mouth.

Meanwhile, Carl poured four cups of cocoa and brought out the cinnamon rolls. The adults indulged their communal sweet tooth and did extensive damage to Carl's breakfast offering.

Beth managed part of a cinnamon roll in addition to her oatmeal and tasted the cocoa but was too full to drink very much. Carl offered to keep some warm for her to have later in the day.

———

On the tenth of September, both couples boarded the train to Cheyenne for Jameson's trial. Each of them would be called as a witness. Beth would stay with the Jensens until they returned.

When they arrived in Cheyenne, Carl and Tom stopped in at the sheriff's office to make sure that the trial was still on and were told that it was set to begin at ten o'clock, and that the defendant would appear before Judge Fremont.

They entered the large brick courthouse just as the trial was set to begin and took seats in the front row of the courtroom reserved for witnesses. Visitors and court appointees began to filter in before two deputies led a shackled John Jameson to the front row of seats.

The jurors were led single-file to their seats and, less than a minute later, the bailiff called the room to stand as Judge Fremont entered and the trial of John Jameson had begun.

The prosecutor's opening remarks vividly recalled the heinous crimes of the accused, including breaking into the

Wilsons' room as they peacefully slept, and shooting an unarmed man whose only thought was to protect his beloved wife. He then outlined the defendant's hideous plan to murder the governor of the territory and a number of railroad executives.

The defense attorney presented a picture of the defendant as a victim of circumstances. He noted that no one had ever seen the defendant with a gun, that no one could place him at the scene of the shooting, and that he and his murdered partner were out camping when they had been apprehended. They didn't even have the dynamite in their possession. He suggested that Tom and Carl had ridden up with the dynamite with the intention of framing his client.

To Carl and Tom, and they believed to everyone else in the courtroom, the defense attorney's arguments were bordering on silly.

The prosecutor began calling witnesses. Tom was his first witness and he told his story just as he had in the past as he knew it by heart. The defense attorney, on cross examination, pounded home the fact that Tom was unable to conclusively identify the shooter and after Emily's testimony, that point was reinforced when she also failed to identify Jameson and even had to admit it could have been the already murdered Elrod Lydon who had invaded the boarding house just recently with a handgun.

Carl's testimony was more challenging for the defense attorney. After he had related his version of events to the prosecutor, the defense attorney not only interrogated Carl about his independent detective work following the shooting but noted that Mister Jameson had not at any point shot anyone, whereas, Carl had shot and killed two men in the past two weeks alone without having any legal authority to do so. The attorney implied that Carl was a murderer and that his client was an innocent victim of Carl's hostility.

The prosecutor asked Carl questions about his reputation, about his background and his origins, and whether he had ever shot at another human being before the sorry events of the past two weeks, but Carl could already tell that the prosecutor felt he had lost points in the cross-examination.

Barbara's testimony was short and both attorneys treated her with kid gloves.

After the sheriff and his wounded deputy provided their testimony, three Union Pacific executives were summoned, but because they had little knowledge of the plot or the actions taken by Carl and Tom, they had little to contribute.

After ninety minutes, the defense rested its case without having called John Jameson, final arguments were made, and the jury went into deliberation.

Tom and Carl escorted Barbara and Emily to the restaurant before they waited around the courthouse after lunch, but the jury didn't return a verdict. Carl thought this was a bad sign but didn't remark upon the fact. A little after five o'clock, the judge adjourned for the day without a verdict having been reached, and as hard as it was for any of them to believe, they began to think that Jameson might get off without being found guilty.

The two couples took the eastbound train home and returned to the house, and Tom left instructions with the sheriff's office to wire him with the results of the trial as soon as they were received. They had done all they could.

On the return trip, as it had been all afternoon, the discussion had been about the trial and how their absolute conviction in the guilt of John Jameson still could have left enough doubt in the minds of just one or two jurors that could allow the man to walk out of the jail.

After they returned, Carl and Barbara went to the Jensens' and retrieved Beth, and even she sensed the somber mood that prevailed among the adults and was quiet in turn.

The following day, a messenger arrived with a telegram for Tom.

Tom opened the sheet and read:

T WILSON MATHIAS BOARDING HOUSE PINE BLUFFS WYOMING

JURY FOUND JAMESON NOT GUILTY OF ASSAULT
JURY HUNG ON ATTEMPTED MURDER FOR BOMBING
PROSECUTOR WILL NOT RETRY
JAMESON RELEASED TODAY

WILLIAM HENDRICKS DEPUTY SHERIFF CHEYENNE WYOMING

"Damn," he said. With that expletive, all gathered knew that the news hadn't been good. Tom handed the telegram to Carl, who read it and passed it to Barbara.

"Now what?" said Carl, "This seems like it'll never end."

"He'd be a fool to come here," said Tom, "He knows we're all here and he knows that we're armed. My guess is that he'll head back to Rock Creek. The Federal troops are there now, so I don't see that he has any options left. The mines aren't running, either. Union Pacific pulled a quick one on the Chinese miners after Chinatown was burned. They put them all on a train, promising them they'd take them to San Francisco.

Instead, U.P. took them east a few miles and then brought them back. When the Chinese asked for their two months' back wages, the U.P. refused to pay up. They asked for transportation to San Francisco, but this was also denied. The whole episode makes me sick."

"One thing we need to do is notify Luck of the situation," said Carl, "He can keep an eye out for Jameson. Another thing we can do is to make sure we stay armed. Barbara, do you and Emily want to keep the Pocket Navy pistols with you now that we have the Bulldogs?"

"I'd prefer that you kept them and just stayed close," said Barbara, remembering the terror that night when she had tried to shoot Elrod Lydon and not wishing to try and shoot anyone again.

Emily nodded in agreement.

"There are far worse sentences," said Carl, "than being forced to stay close to you, Barbara. In the meantime, I need to go see Luck."

Carl left the house, then trotted to the jail, found it empty and after some more searching, Carl found Luck at the saloon, having a beer.

"Good afternoon, Luck."

Luck turned and waved.

"Back again from Cheyenne?"

"Yup. I thought I'd let you know, they let Jameson out. He's free."

"How the hell did that happen?" asked a stunned sheriff.

"You can never guess with juries. Go figure. He had a good defense attorney, and no one actually saw him with a gun. No one could identify him as the shooter either. The trestle bombing matter was a hung jury, so the prosecutor figured he couldn't win this one and decided not to take him back to court."

"Well, that might cause some trouble hereabouts."

"Maybe so. I just thought I'd let you know so you could keep an eye out and pass the word along for the townsfolk to do the same. Tom and I will stay armed just to be on the safe side."

"I'll let everyone know. Stay safe out there, okay?"

"I'll try," said Carl before he left the saloon.

———

Over the next week, Carl spent his nights in Barbara's room and left the bedroom door open so he could hear any and all noises. As an added precaution, Carl hung bells from both the front and back doors.

On the seventeenth of September, Carl and Tom each received a large packet from the Union Pacific. The packet contained an effusive thank you from the president of the railroad for their actions in preventing the loss of a trestle and the train full of executives and the governor. Each received a bank draft for a thousand dollars. Barbara and Emily were duly impressed with both the draft and the contents of the letter.

On September 20th, after dinner was finished and all the dishes were cleaned, Beth was sentenced to her room for homework and the two couples adjourned to the sitting room and Carl could tell that something was weighing on Barbara's mind.

He waited until Tom and Emily had gone upstairs before he broached the subject.

"You seem a bit upset tonight, Barbara," he said.

"Are you forgetting what's happening tomorrow?" she asked.

"You mean the minor event of my parents' arrival at 8:15 in the morning?"

"I'm scared to death, Carl. I know you think it'll be okay, and it probably will, but I can't escape this feeling of dread and there's nothing I can do to make it go away."

He joined her on the couch and pulled her close.

"Well, you go on feeling the way you believe is necessary. I don't think I can change that. But in less than twelve hours, I assure you that you'll be as happy to know them as they will be to know you."

He gave her a soft kiss, then they rose to check on Beth, and found her already asleep in one of her new dresses, so Barbara pulled off her shoes and pulled the covers over her daughter and lowered the lamp light.

"This is happening a lot lately," Barbara said as she turned and smiled at Carl.

"You go ahead and get ready for bed," Carl said to Barbara, "I'm heading for the washroom and will be back in a few minutes."

He never admitted how much torture it was for him these past few days to lie there clothed so close to her. Then again, after recalling her unrestrained passion on that one glorious night, he wasn't sure it was any less difficult for her. In ten more days, it would no longer be an issue, but those ten days would pass slowly.

Everyone was up and about by seven the following morning. A hurried breakfast had been prepared and eaten, and Barbara whirled like a dervish cleaning as much as she could. At seven-thirty, she changed into one of her dresses and set about frantically brushing her hair into place.

Carl had just let her go to ease her worries, confident that in another hour, she'd be as happy as she usually was when they didn't have bullets hurtling at them.

Carl had on his slacks, vest, and jacket, left his Colt in his room, but still had his shoulder holster on under the jacket. Barbara didn't notice, and Carl was convinced that she was so wound up right now, she wouldn't notice if the building burned down. Beth was going to miss another day of school, so she was in a very good mood.

The whistle of the train greeted them as they left the house, so they picked up their pace and arrived at the depot before the train did. Carl could tell that Barbara was still very anxious, while Beth was just curious, so he took Barbara's hand and smiled at her as she looked up at him with a weak smile of her own.

The locomotive huffed, hissed and squealed to a stop before the platform and the few passengers whose destination was Pine Bluffs began to exit the rear passenger car.

When Carl's parents emerged, there was no doubt as to who they were as Carl had described them so vividly. Carl's mother was dwarfed by her husband and could probably fit in one of his trousers' legs.

Because there were only six people waiting on the platform for arrivals, it didn't take long for Gus and Bernadette to spot their son. Gus looked like he was ready to pop a button, but he deferred his upcoming bearhug to allow his diminutive wife to greet Carl first.

She trotted across the short space as Carl reached out and embraced his mother in a warm embrace, picking her feet off the wooden platform as he did.

"Mama, you haven't changed a bit. You're as beautiful as ever!" he exclaimed.

"You always did have a way of charming me, Carl. I hope that never changes," she replied with a warm smile.

She was still smiling as he put her back on her feet as Carl prepared himself for his father's crushing embrace.

"Son, you've gotten bigger! You should come and work with me at the smithy!" Gus roared as pulled his son into the expected vice-like hug.

"Papa, I'd love to, but I think I have some other plans in mind. One of which is breathing."

Gus laughed as he released Carl, allowing him to catch his breath.

Carl then reached out for Barbara and brought her forward.

"Papa and Mama, this is Barbara, who will soon to be your new daughter."

Barbara smiled, hearing Carl refer to her as a daughter and not a daughter-in-law.

Bernadette smiled at her, then turned to Carl and said, "My, oh, my son. You were quite wrong in your letter. You wrote that

310

she was pretty, but she is much more than pretty. She is stunning."

She turned to Barbara and extended her arms then two women held each other in a tight embrace, Barbara having to bend at her waist.

After Bernadette and Barbara separated, Bernadette said to her, "We are so happy to meet you, Barbara. You must be a wonderful person. My son told me in his letter that he knew you were the one for him from the first time he met you. It took me many years to convince him that such things were even possible and I'm glad you made this dream come true for him."

Before anyone else said anything, Carl picked up Beth and walked to his father.

"Papa, this is Beth. She's your new granddaughter."

Gus looked into the little girl's bright blue eyes and said, "I am a lucky man indeed to be blessed with such a perfect little girl for a granddaughter."

He then kissed her lightly on the forehead.

"Are you really my papa's papa?" she asked.

"Yes," he grinned, "and that small little lady near your mama is his mama."

"So now I have a grandpapa and grandmama, too?" she asked with wide eyes.

By then Bernadette had approached Beth and had gently run her fingers across the little girl's cheek.

"Hello, Beth. Your papa told us all about you, too, and you're even prettier than I could ever have imagined."

Beth smiled at her and said, "You're my grandmama!"

"Yes, dear. I most assuredly am."

Carl then introduced Tom and Emily to his parents, who greeted them both enthusiastically.

Carl set Beth back down and walked with his father back to the house while his mother hooked her arm through Barbara's, and they began chatting as they walked behind the men. Beth trotted along, glancing at one grandparent to the other and then back again.

As they came up the walk, Gus said, "This is a very nice house. Are you going to stay here?"

Carl replied, "For a little while, until I can get settled into my new job in Omaha."

"I didn't know you were moving to Omaha. You'll have to explain everything to me and mama later on," his father said in his deep voice.

"I have a lot to explain to you both, but for right now, I'm just happy that you're here."

They first entered the sitting room where they talked about the simple things, like the train ride from Texas and how the rest of the Ritter family, but never got around to the difficult things of the past two weeks.

Barbara had prepared a stew that didn't need anything more than reheating, so they all sat around just talked until it was time to eat, and then Bernadette insisted on helping, as did Emily.

As they ate, there was a considerable amount of storytelling, a fair amount of it at Carl's expense. He accepted the teasing with grace because he knew that everything was being told in good humor.

The afternoon and evening were spent in similar discussions and plans for the wedding and beyond. There had been hints about what had transpired, but Carl had asked that the stories be held back today. This night was for his parents and his future wife to get to know each other.

Beth was put to bed around nine o'clock, and the adults stayed up talking for another two hours. As the evening was winding down, Carl reached into his pocket for a small box.

"Mama, Barbara and I are going to be married soon," he said, "The reason this is happening is because of you. If you hadn't convinced me that Barbara was out there waiting for me, I would have never known the happiness that you and papa have shared for all these years. So, to thank you for that precious gift, I have a *petit* present for you."

He handed her the box. She opened it, revealing the beautiful cameo brooch, then lifted it from the box and smiled at him.

"My son, this is a beautiful gift, and I thank you. But it doesn't come close to the wonderful gift that you have given papa and me by adding such a wonderful daughter and granddaughter to our family."

There were hugs for everyone and a few handkerchiefs were passed from hand to hand.

Tom and Emily said their goodnights and went upstairs to their room, then Barbara said she'd show Gus and Bernadette to their room, while Carl went out to retrieve their luggage.

After his parents were safely ensconced in their room, Carl returned to see Barbara, who smiled at him, finally free of reservations or concerns. He sat on her bed beside her and she curled up under his arm.

"Carl, your parents are two of the loveliest people I've ever met."

"I know. It makes you wonder where I came from doesn't it?" he asked with a grin.

"No," she said, "It makes it perfectly obvious where you came from."

He held her tightly and whispered in her ear: "No more concerns anymore?"

"None at all," she whispered back, "I thought I couldn't be any happier than I was before, but now, somehow, I am."

"Wait until the end of the month," said Carl, "Then we'll see how happy you can really be."

She giggled as he made his way back out of the room.

"Good night, Barbara," he said, gazing into those bright blue eyes of hers.

He gave her a soft kiss, stood and left the room, closin the door behind him, then stepped down the hallway and climbed the stairs to his room.

When he reached the top of the stairs, he found his father waiting for him.

"Papa, can I do something for you?"

Gus waved him over and put his massive arm around his son's shoulders.

"You need any help, son?" he asked, "You know. Financially?"

"No, Papa," smiled Carl, "I've still got almost three thousand in my account in Kansas City and I received another thousand dollars a few days ago from Union Pacific as a reward for preventing an accident."

Gus smiled and patted his son's shoulder.

"I always knew you could handle your money."

Father and son parted as Carl went to his room, took off his coat and removed his shoulder holster, then removed his boots and went down the hall to the washroom. He returned after a few minutes, undressed, laid down in bed, and was fast asleep less than five minutes later.

———

Tuesday morning's sunrise found Bernadette and Barbara in the kitchen, chatting like old friends about things both trivial and vital as they prepared the morning meal.

Carl beat his father downstairs by a hair, and both Ritter men entered the kitchen and greeted their respective better halves before taking cups and filling them to the brim with coffee.

Carl thought it was time to bring up some of the dark events of the past few weeks.

"Papa, mama, I do have to tell you of some things that have happened recently that resulted in my having to kill a man. Two men, in fact. The troubles that caused the shootings are still going on, so you both need to know what's happened, so you won't be caught unaware."

Both parents stared at Carl, stunned by what he had said. Neither could see how the son they knew so well had come to be a killer of men. But at the same time, knowing him as they raised him, they knew that he must not have had any other choice.

Bernadette was the first to speak when she said, "Son, I have no doubt that you had your motives for doing what you did. After breakfast we can all sit down, and you can tell us what happened."

Carl nodded and said, "This may take some time. We'll need to have Tom and Emily there to fill in some blanks. Tom was the first one shot."

That piece of news surprised them both.

"That nice Mister Wilson was shot?" asked Gus.

"By a man who only wanted to kill him because he worked for the railroad."

"It sounds like you've got quite a tale to tell," said his father just as Beth arrived.

Emily and Tom arrived a few minutes later, and just a few minutes after that, they all were seated around the table.

They talked over breakfast and well past as the story took two hours to tell.

Once everyone finally finished the extensive tale, Gus said, "Son, I'm proud of you. You did what you needed to do in order to protect the ones you love. You could have done nothing less."

"Thanks, Papa. It means a lot coming from you."

"Now," Gus continued, "what do we do about this last one? The one who is still loose."

"We've notified the sheriff and he's got everyone on alert. We'll find out if he comes back into town. The sheriff's office in Cheyenne is on the lookout, too. Bear in mind that there can't be an official manhunt because Jameson was tried and found not guilty on one charge and the jury couldn't reach a decision on the second one. So, all we can do is watch out for him. Even if we *do* see him, we can't do a thing unless he does something first."

His father mulled over what he had just been told and agreed that it was a difficult situation at best.

"Do you have guns?" he asked.

"Yes, Tom and I each have three pistols and a Winchester. We carry at least one gun with us at all times, even to church."

"Doesn't that bother the church folk?"

"They don't know. Just like you didn't know. Until now."

Carl opened his jacket, revealing the shoulder holster and the Webley, then Tom showed his.

"Good," said Gus, "Until this man is either far away or dead, you need to be prepared."

"I think you and Mama understand by now what we're dealing with here. Barbara and I are planning on taking a week's honeymoon in Denver. Then we'll meet with Tom and Emily in Omaha to settle things there. Barbara will sell the house here and we'll buy one in Omaha. Then everyone will be safe."

Gus smiled at him and said, "You have become quite a man, son."

"Thank you, Papa. I had a good upbringing and a mother who showed me that some things were worth waiting for."

He was looking into the smiling eyes of his mother as he finished the statement. She may not have been crying, but there was enough moisture in her eyes that it wouldn't have taken much of an emotional nudge to unleash the waterworks.

The next day, Gus made some of his cherry strudel and Beth had to be practically restrained from eating it for dinner.

————

During the five days leading up to the wedding, Barbara and Bernadette began to seem more and more like daughter and mother and Emily and Tom began to feel like family as they were becoming more of a part of the wedding preparations.

The men talked men talk and did men things and around the house, they tackled small and troublesome repair jobs alike.

Tom received word that the Union Pacific had given an ultimatum to the miners, both white and Chinese, who were still refusing to work, that they either return to the mines immediately or none of them would ever be permitted to work for any Union Pacific controlled enterprise in the future. As incensed as they must have been, they had no choice but to return to the mines. Tom saw this for what it was, a temporary truce that could turn ugly in the future.

Sixteen mine workers had been arrested for the murder and mayhem on the 2nd of September, but because no positive identifications were made, the grand jury failed to issue a single indictment.

To replace the lost homes in Chinatown, the railroad had simply dropped off lumber and supplies to the Chinese miners. If they wanted new housing, they'd have to build it themselves.

Though there were those who sympathized with the plight of the Chinese miners, most felt powerless to improve the situation. Not even Tom could do much that would make a significant impact, so all they could do was hope that history wouldn't repeat itself in the future.

On the 26th, Carl received a telegram from Cheyenne and opened it in front of his assembled friends and family. As he read it, a look of exasperation crossed his face.

"Not now," he muttered as he handed the telegram to Tom.

C RITTER MATHIAS BOARDING HOUSE PINE BLUFFS WYOMING

POSSIBLE SIGHTING OF JAMESON FRIDAY
WITNESS CLAIMS SAW HIM BOARDING EASTBOUND TRAIN
NOT SURE OF SIGHTING
WITNESS GOING BY DESCRIPTION ONLY

WILLIAM HENDRICKS DEPUTY SHERIFF CHEYENNE WYOMING

"What do you make of that?" Tom asked.

"I'm not sure. If it's really him and he's coming here, I'm sure we would have spotted him already. Luck and his deputy have been watching that train like hawks. He couldn't have gotten past them unnoticed. If it was him, he could have been taking the train further east, and there's always the chance that it wasn't him at all."

Tom said, "Maybe. But if he was coming, he could have easily stepped off the train before the platform as it was slowing to a stop."

Carl replied, "True, but the odds are better that it wasn't even him in the first place. Why come here? He has no grudge like his partner did. Neither of the Lydon brothers meant anything to him, and he's free of prosecution. He can go anywhere. It makes no sense for him to come here."

Then he scratched his chin and continued.

"Tom, have you noticed a pattern to this whole trail of events? The problem is that there is no pattern. They don't seem to take the logical course at all. Look at Emerson Lydon. I can understand his being vengeful after finding out I killed his brother, but to walk out of jail a free man only to go assault a shop owner and go hunting for me in the streets of Cheyenne? That's beyond illogical. That's stupidity. Think about his brother, when he was trying to break into the house. He wasted time trying to smash down a stout door when a fragile window was six feet away. Then, when they were going to blow up the trestle, they built a campfire that could've been seen from a mile off. We found them sitting there practically waiting to be captured. Nothing this crowd has done has made a lick of sense. Why not come back here and cause mayhem?"

"I see where you're going with this, and I agree that they have done a lot of stupid things, but I still don't think Jameson will make an appearance in Pine Bluffs. All we can do is keep up our eyes wide open," Tom said.

With no sightings of Jameson over the weekend, everyone began to relax, believing the threat to be gone.

———

It was the evening before the wedding, and everything was set. Even though Carl and Barbara expected a small affair, word spread quickly, and half the town wanted to witness the happy event.

After the ceremony, there would be a reception at the hotel restaurant and Carl absolutely refused to allow Barbara, his mother, or Emily to do any of the cooking. He threatened to blow up the stove if they mentioned it.

The ladies demurred rather than allow the destruction of such a noble appliance.

———

The sun was long gone from the sky and Jameson was getting cold. He couldn't make a fire as one of the locals would be sure to see him, and he knew he couldn't risk that.

All of Krueger's plans had been foiled and the railroad had won. They had forced all the miners back to work, but at least the bastards didn't cut their pay again. But they hadn't gotten rid of the damned Chinks either and were probably bringing in more of them to replace what was left of the white miners. He was mighty tired of losing, and maybe he couldn't do anything about Rock Creek, but he could still get in some licks.

He looked down at what he considered his private 'arsenal'. There were four five-gallon cans of coal oil, which had been surprisingly easy to obtain. That idiot of a storekeeper kept the fuel away from his mercantile in a shack just fifty feet behind his store and it had taken him less than a minute to snap off the hasp. It was a much bigger task carrying the awkward containers all the way to his hideout in the trees behind the church. He'd had to make two trips and keeping the whole maneuver quiet had been the toughest part of all.

Next to the coal oil was the real headliner, the four sticks of dynamite and the fuse that he had planned on using for the trestle. He had to laugh at the stupidity of the judicial system. First, he got off scot free, then because the law said so, they had to give him back all his property, including his explosives, even though his defense attorney had argued that the explosives weren't even his. They had given him back his horse, but not the nice Appaloosa that Emerson had. He had blamed that damned sheriff for that. Too bad, too. That Appaloosa had been a mighty fine horse. His not-so-fine horse was tied almost a quarter mile away from him, near a small stream.

It was time to begin building his bomb. The quarter moon provided just enough light for him to be able to set up the coal oil and explosive combination. He had originally planned to wait until the wedding started and then sneak up behind the church and roll the dynamite with its fuse lit under the crawl space of the church, but in an inspired moment, he considered the added destruction of the coal oil. The heat of the explosion would set off fires on the splintering wood and it would fling flaming splinters for maybe a whole mile around and smiled at the thought. The whole damned town of Pine Bluffs, Wyoming would cease to exist by the first of October.

Then, amid all the confusion, he'd simply walk back to his horse and head south. He was through with mining anyway. He had retrieved the two pistols from the gully where Ritter had tossed them, too. They were dinged up a bit, but they'd do the trick. But the explosion was the main thing, and he wished he could stick around and watch it, but for practical reasons, he wanted to be nowhere near the place when it went off.

He lugged two of the coal oil cans to the back of the church, then, when he reached the crawl space, he turned them on their sides and rolled them into the black darkness under the church. Even on their sides they barely made it under the joists. He dropped onto his stomach and rolled the canisters in front of him as he slid under the low opening.

He found it downright creepy under the church, but when he was about twenty feet from the back edge, he stopped and positioned the coal oil, so the broad edge faced outward, then crawled his way back out. He then made a second trip under the church, positioned a second pair of cans in the same way, making a shallow U under the floor of the building, right under where the altar should be. Then, after taking a short breather, he measured out thirty feet of blasting cord and inserted the blasting cap into the dynamite.

Back under the church he went, situating the dynamite right in the center of the U shape of the kerosene. Trailing the fuse behind him, he made his exit from the dank darkness that lurked in the crawlspace, then tried to minimize the exposure of the fuse, curling it just before it snaked out from under the structure. He left about four feet exposed, and knew it was safe from discovery. No one would come behind the church because there was no reason to be back here. There wasn't even a privy.

The next morning, about ten minutes after the ceremony had started, all he'd have to do would be to sneak over, light the cord, and then run like hell. He should be able to reach a safe distance and hide behind a large tree trunk to protect him from the blast and the debris, but he couldn't wait to see the entire church disappear.

CHAPTER 9

At last the big day arrived. The weather was as good as could be expected for that part of the country and that time of year. There was a light frost in the morning, but the sun was bright, and the trees were full of rich autumnal colors that added to the festivities of the occasion.

Barbara opted to wear her favorite dress, the blue and cream silk dress purchased by her soon-to-be husband. She held a bouquet of flowers that she would carry down the aisle and had never been so excited in her life. Nothing could ruin this day for her. It was her day and despite it being her second wedding, she felt in her heart that this was her only one – the one that mattered because Carl was the only one that mattered.

By eight-thirty, the men were dressed and perched in the sitting room and Carl had a hard time keeping focused.

Carl looked at Tom and asked, "Are you armed?"

Tom shook his head and raised his eyebrows as if to ask, "You?"

Carl shook his head. This was not a day to be wearing guns, even those hidden in shoulder holsters.

An hour before the ceremony was to start, Carl said to Gus and Tom, "Do you want to start heading over to the church? We're supposed to be there before the womenfolk, you know."

They agreed, but before they started off, Tom asked, "You do have the rings, right?"

Carl nodded but checked his pocket to be sure.

It was a five-minute walk, and everything was quiet on this beautiful morning as the three well-dressed men strolled casually down the boardwalk of Pine Bluff's main and only street.

Together they entered the church and Carl and Tom scrutinized every last detail to make sure that the smoothest possible ceremony was about to take place.

"I hate to do this," Gus said to his son with sudden urgency, "but I have to pee."

"Go around the back, Papa," Carl grinned, "There's no outhouse, but only the Lord can see you out there."

Gus half ran and half walked his way out of the church and Tom made a casual remark on the joys of getting old. Some of the guests began filtering in, and Carl was surprised to see Fred Jenkins in a suit, or at least what was passably matched clothing. Fred stopped by the altar and told Carl how Hank Jensen had given him a job and was letting him stay in the stock room. He was really very pleased with everything and he thanked Carl as he shook his hand. With one last pump, he went to the back of the church and found a seat.

When Carl's father finally returned, he wore a puzzled expression on his face.

"What's on your mind, papa?"

"I'm new here so I don't know what's what around these parts. But when I was around the back of the church, it sure looked like a piece of fuse was lying there on the ground. I could be wrong, but I don't know. It looked suspicious."

"Show me," said Carl.

Tom joined them, and the three men set off.

———

Jameson had seen the old man relieve himself near the fuse but didn't think the old man had a clue what he'd seen, so he wasn't concerned about any impact on his plan as he waited in the trees for the ceremony to start, still giddy about the idea of the church being reduced to flying, flaming splinters in another half an hour.

———

Carl, Tom and Gus headed to the back of the church, and Carl immediately caught sight of the what had attracted his father's attention. Smack in the center of the wall, a four-foot length of fuse cord extended from under the church.

———

Jameson saw the three men studying the ground and knew he had a problem now and was torn between running away or trying to set off the dynamite using a different method. He had his two pistols, and all six cylinders were loaded on each gun, but he knew he wouldn't be able to reload. He'd have twelve chances to blow up the church, and he was more than fifty yards away.

He was still making his decision as he watched the three men.

———

Carl saw a board nearby and picked it up, so he could use it keep his new suit relatively clean. He knelt on the board and peered into the crawlspace and could make out silhouettes of what looked to be large cannisters, but little else. He decided to follow the cord with his fingertips. He reached back as far as he could without feeling a thing. He was in the process of pulling the cord when he felt a bullet smack the wall of the church eight inches to the right of his head as John Jameson decided that he'd at least drive those men away from the dynamite. The three men scattered, rounded the church, and flattened themselves against the wall to get out of the line of fire.

"Anyone see where that shot came from?" asked Carl.

Tom and Gus shook their heads.

"Do you think he's still out there?" asked Tom.

That question was answered by a second report then Tom and Carl looked at each other with the obvious question unasked. *What is this guy shooting at?*

Carl quickly glanced around the corner. He noticed the cloud of gunsmoke from the recent shots hanging back in the trees directly behind the church. Jameson was pacing his shots to make sure he hit his target, but they hadn't realized yet that his target wasn't them, but the dynamite.

"Jameson's still there," said Carl, "I can't believe they gave him the dynamite back. Wasn't it bad enough that he got off? They had to give him the damned dynamite?"

His comment was immediately followed by a third shot.

"Why the hell is he shooting? He could be away and gone already. His plan has fallen apart!" Tom exclaimed.

"Beats me. But the real question is that he seems to be shooting at the church and not us. That doesn't make any sense."

Tom's eyes flew wide and he said, "Yes it does! He can't expose himself to light the fuse, so he's trying to set off the dynamite with gunfire."

Carl looked at him and realized he was right. *But what should they do next?* Then he knew and started pulling off his shoes.

Before Tom or Gus could ask him what in God's good name he was doing, Carl turned to Gus and said, "Papa, I need you to get everyone out of the church and across the street. Tell them not to panic. Just get them out of that church calmly and quietly, but as quickly as possible, okay?"

Gus turned and ran to the front of the church. By now, Carl had removed his jacket and tie, which he handed to Tom.

"Tom," he said as he continued to disrobe, "I'm going to crawl under there and see if I can get that dynamite out of there before he can set it off, but I'm not ruining a new suit over this."

As Carl disrobed, the shots continued at a steady pace, one every forty seconds or so. Jameson seemed to be taking his time to aim, and they didn't know how many rounds he had available.

A quarter mile away in the boarding house, the women heard the gunfire.

"Sounds like target practice," Emily remarked, "Hear how there's spacing between the shots?"

"Maybe so," said Barbara, "but it still makes me nervous. Let's hurry it up a bit."

Back at the church, Carl was making his way under the crawlspace, moving as fast as he possibly could, and it only took him fifteen seconds to crawl the distance to the coal oil-dynamite combination. He could smell the kerosene, as one of the cans was leaking, maybe from a ricochet. Luckily, a fire hadn't broken out already, which would have set off the dynamite when the fuse was lit by the flames. Right now, his primary concern was the dynamite itself. He reached out with his right hand and, as his hand touched the bundle of sticks, a bullet buried itself in the dirt just to the right of his hand, spraying muck everywhere as a muffled report reverberated in the crawl space as Carl quickly snatched the dynamite and turned to make his crawling exit. It took almost twice as long to get out, but he soon stood in the sunlight in his filthy union suit, handed the dynamite to Tom and brushed off the dirt and cobwebs covering the front of his torso.

Tom turned to leave, and Carl caught his arm, "Wait, Tom!"

"For what? That idiot is still out there, and if you haven't noticed, he's armed, and we aren't."

"Yes, we are," said Carl as he held up the dynamite, "Tom, how fast is this fuse?"

Tom glanced at Carl's determined face, then replied, "I don't know. Let's test it."

Tom reached in his pocket for his trusty pocket knife and cut a six-inch piece of cord.

"Got a match?" he asked.

Carl produced a box of matches from the breast pocket of his discarded jacket.

Tom struck a match and lit the end of the cord then counted as soon as it began to smoke. It took six seconds to burn.

Carl borrowed Tom's knife and cut the cord at the four-inch mark.

"That's cutting it mighty close, partner," said Tom.

"I don't want it coming back at us. Now comes the hard part. I'm going to have to expose myself to his fire, but this won't take long, so I should be okay. What I need you to do, Tom, is light this thing. I'm going to stand at the edge of the wall and get ready to throw. When I say the word, you light it. As soon as you see the fuse catch yell 'Fire!' and plaster yourself against the wall."

"Got it."

Carl slid to the far corner of the church. He lifted the bundle of dynamite and cocked it behind his right shoulder. He was as ready as he'd ever be, then waited until Jameson took another shot and then he yelled over his shoulder, "Ready!"

He heard Tom yell, "Fire!", and he stepped out, an open target in his soiled but still red union suit.

He saw a flash in his direction and heard the report as he hurled the dynamite, then turned and ran for cover behind the church not caring where Jameson's last shot had gone. He scrambled around the corner and flattened himself against the wall.

John Jameson had been startled when he spotted Carl appear suddenly wearing his red union suit and had been laughing when he turned his pistol's sights in his direction, then lost his smile shortly before pulling the trigger when he spotted his own dynamite flying through the air in his direction leaving a smoking contrail behind it. He was cocking his hammer to try shooting at the arriving explosive but never got the chance.

As Carl and Tom had their backs pressed against the white boards of the church's outer wall, with a thunderous detonation, the dynamite went off before splinters, leaves and shards of wood rained from the heavens.

After the initial blast of debris, Carl peered out through the dust and smoke. To no one's surprise, there were no more gunshots as he and Tom stepped cautiously forward into the devastation that just minutes before had been a quiet copse of trees.

The entire episode from the discovery of the cord by Gus to the explosion had taken no longer than nine minutes. Gus came trotting toward them with Luck Emerson and they spotted Carl in his union suit walking with Tom toward the still smoking blast site.

"What the hell was that?" yelled Luck as he and Gus jogged up behind them.

Carl had seen the waste left behind by tornadoes, but this was different. What yawned before them was a twenty-foot crater, and ten feet to the right lip of the crater, they found John Jameson. He was impaled on a huge splinter jutting out against a large cottonwood, and oddly still held his revolver in his right hand. Why it hadn't been blasted fifty feet away was just one of those inexplicable quirks of physics. The men knew that Jameson deserved his fate, but the sight still sickened them.

Carl glanced over at his father and said, "Papa, this is one hell of a way to start a marriage."

"That much is true. I'd recommend getting yourself dressed, though, or you might see a second explosion."

After he had quickly dressed and used his handkerchief to wipe his face clean, he pulled out his watch. It was 9: 28, so he quickly turned to the three men who had returned from the explosion site and said, "Gentlemen, we can't disappoint the ladies. This will have to be cleaned up, but not now."

They all agreed, then walked back to the church. As they rushed down the aisle, Carl and Tom just waved down any inquisitive guests and took their respective places near the altar.

Barbara, Emily, Bernadette, and Beth had all heard the explosion that shook the town and each of them felt the cold chill of fear, wondering what had happened to the men in their lives. They plucked up their wedding accessories and hustled down the boardwalk, lifting their skirts as they ran. They could see a cloud of smoke still hanging over the church and it did little to assuage their sense of dread.

But by the time they arrived at the church, the guests were all in their seats, smiling as the bride and her entourage entered. The priest put out his hand to stop the womenfolk from walking down the aisle prematurely.

Barbara saw Carl smiling at her from near the altar with Tom standing next to him but was still shaken by the feeling and hearing blast, then seeing the smoke. She was almost startled when she felt a nudge at her elbow and turned to see Gus offering his arm to her.

She absent-mindedly placed her hand on his arm, as Beth, who didn't seem as disturbed as her mother, began walking down the aisle in front, spreading flowers as the organist began to play.

Barbara was still dazed and simply had difficulty focusing as she stepped down the aisle, but then she saw her future husband's warm smile, and she snapped her back into the present as she felt the warmth of his love reach across to her.

She reached out to take his hand and felt the rush of his touch as his father stepped away.

Her eyes were only for Carl as she listened to the priest start the ceremony.

Carl barely heard the words as he sank into her blue eyes, yet at the appropriate time, each of them exchanged their vows and placed the wedding bands on each other's fingers.

When Father Maher pronounced them man and wife, neither of them had to think twice about what came next, and they shared their first kiss as a legally married couple as if it was their first and their last.

After the kiss, they stood and stared into each other's eyes for what seemed like ages, before the magic moment was broken by the loud applause from the church full of guests.

Even as their faces were almost glowing as they returned down the aisle, Barbara still whispered to her new husband "You'll have to explain that explosion to me. Sooner rather than later, if you don't mind."

Carl whispered back, "Yes, Mrs. Ritter."

Barbara smiled knowing that he wasn't addressing his mother as they left the church, then walked down the stairs.

The explanation began as soon as they turned to greet their guest and Carl was sure that Tom and his father had to explain the matter to their wives at the same time. Later, they'd have to explain it all to the sheriff, but when the sheriff finally reached him, he had to keep it short before going to the restaurant for the reception.

"Luck, there are four cans of kerosene still under the church. I think that Jameson was planning on not only blowing up the church but starting a massive fire with the coal oil under there. He could have set the whole town afire."

Sheriff Luck pretty much summed up the day when he said, "Just couldn't have a traditional wedding, could you?"

Even Barbara laughed when Carl said that he didn't know because this was his first and his last wedding.

"Well, I'll take care of the kerosene and the rest. Just come by later with your father and Tom Wilson to make your statements."

"Thanks, Luck," Carl said, then took Barbara's arm, and followed his father, who was carrying Beth, and his mother as they headed for the hotel.

Tom and Emily walked behind them leading a long line of guests.

––––––

After the long reception luncheon, the wedding party returned to the boarding house. Beth had been told that the house would no longer accept tenants, and that now she would have her own room upstairs. Initially upset that her mama and papa might be angry with her, she hung her head until Carl explained that now that she was almost grown up, she needed her privacy. But if she had any bad dreams or was afraid for any reason at all, she could just pop on down and stay with them.

Barbara did warn her to knock three times first, that way they would know it was her and not some stranger.

Bethany was elated to be told she was almost a grownup and that she now had her very own secret knock to announce her arrival.

Tom and Emily were heading back to Omaha on the evening train and had to get their trunks to the depot. They had become more than good friends to Carl and Barbara, they become part of their extended family.

Carl and Barbara had already packed for their honeymoon to Denver and would be leaving on the morning train to Cheyenne, where they would stay one night at the Metropolitan Hotel. Carl had reserved the Bridal Suite without telling anyone, especially not his bride. The following day, they would take the train to Denver for a week, and after the honeymoon, they would return to Pine Bluffs for a few days to see if they could sell the boarding house and then make their way east to Omaha.

Tom had assured them that they had plenty of room in their house and that the newlyweds were more than welcome to stay with them while Carl was assigned his position and they began their house hunting process.

Carl didn't like to presume his employment, but Tom told Carl and Barbara that he would talk to the head of engineering, who was a good friend, and find a slot for him quickly. He knew that the man was always on the lookout for qualified engineers, so it wasn't like Tom would be calling in a favor. If anything, Tom said, he might win himself a recruiting bonus for finding Carl.

Barbara laughed and said that she expected a cut because she'd recruited Carl first.

Beth would be living with her grandpapa and grandmama while the newlyweds were gone, and Gus and Bernadette felt as though they had received the best wedding gift of all.

At 7:45, with sunset already past, all five Ritters and the two Wilsons headed for the depot. There was the usual assortment of pre-departure joking and light chit-chat, kisses and hugs, as appropriate, then Tom and Emily boarded the train.

Those remaining waved from the platform as the train pulled out from the station.

After watching the train fade away into the dark, they wandered back to the house, in no particular hurry to return. Two of the five assembled were wishing it was already a little later in the evening for a very special reason. It was their long-awaited official wedding night, after all.

When they entered the house, everyone headed for the sitting room. It had been an exhausting day that had begun with a beautiful morning followed by an explosive wedding and ending in a heart-wrenching farewell to good friends.

The couch was reserved for the three younger Ritters, with Beth sitting between the adults. He had the legal adoption papers in his pocket, having had them drawn up earlier. Now that he and Barbara were married, they just needed to have a judge sign the papers and Beth would legally become his daughter.

Gus, leaning back in his chair, said, "This has been one exhausting day and I am dog tired."

Bernadette smiled at her husband and said, "So am I. I can barely keep my eyes open."

"I'm not tired at all," chirped Beth, "Why is everyone so sleepy?"

Carl was trying to come up with an excuse when Barbara replied, "That's because you're younger than we are, sweetheart. When you get older, you'll see what we mean."

"Then how come grownups always stay up later than children?" she asked, putting the kibosh to that argument.

Carl decided to give it a shot when he said, "Because adults have to stay up to do work, so we can make money to buy things for our children."

Beth was mostly satisfied with his answer, then sprang from the couch as she said, "Okay."

Gus and Bernadette then led her upstairs to her new room, and as they reached the upper landing, Bernadette called back, "Don't stay up too late now."

After they disappeared, Carl smiled at Barbara and said, "Well, I guess we have our orders."

"Oh," said Barbara, "you need orders to perform your husbandly duties now?"

Carl stood, then suddenly scooped her off the ground as Barbara shrieked.

Carl was sure that his parents were coming up with some explanation for Beth after hearing her mother's startled cry as he carried his wife down the hallway.

"It isn't the traditional way of carrying a bride across the threshold," said Carl, "but it's the best I can do."

She whispered in his ear, "It'll do."

Carl closed the door and the new husband and wife spent the rest of the night and a few hours of the next morning being husband and wife.

———

Gus and Bernadette were up before the newlyweds, and when the new bride and groom arrived in the kitchen arm-in-arm, the aroma of something baking was already filling the house. Bernadette refused to let Barbara help in the kitchen, but she did allow her husband to help and he did so magnificently, conjuring up a breakfast for the ages. He even managed to churn up some of what was already Beth's favorite dessert – cherry strudel.

They didn't have long to chat, so after breakfast Carl lugged their travel trunk and two travel bags to the porch and was going to walk to the depot to have someone come and pick them up when a Union Pacific employee rolled up in a wagon.

He walked up to the porch, picked up the trunk, carried it to the wagon, and slid it onto the bed. When he returned, he asked, "Did you wish the bags to go as well, sir?"

"No," Carl replied, "We'll carry those. The trunk will be following us to Denver. How did you know I'd need to have a trunk picked up?"

"Mister Wilson told us you'd be taking the morning train and to stop by this morning and pick up your baggage."

"Oh. That explains it. Thank you."

Carl reached in his pocket and tipped the man a quarter.

He tipped his cap, hopped into the driver's seat, turned the horse and wagon around and drove back to the depot as Carl returned to the house to retrieve his bride.

Five minutes later, Gus, Bernadette, Carl, and Barbara made the short walk to the depot. Beth enjoying the trip more than usual because she wasn't walking. She had a higher-than-adult view atop her new grandfather's shoulders.

Carl stepped to the ticket window to buy the tickets and the ticket agent looked at him and asked, "Mister Ritter?"

Carl replied, "Yes."

The agent then slid two tickets across the small shelf, before handing him a card.

"Mister Wilson said to give you this when you arrived."

Carl looked at the card and shouldn't have been surprised to see that it was a Union Pacific employee card with his name on it and he turned and showed it to Barbara.

"I think Tom wants you to work for the Union Pacific," she said.

"It sure looks that way," he replied before slipping the card into his jacket pocket.

They said their good-byes to Gus and Bernadette, and Barbara started to say good-bye to Beth but began to cry.

She quickly recovered and hugged her little girl as she said, "We'll be back soon, sweetheart."

Carl understood her reaction, knowing it would be the first time in Barbara's life that she would be separated from her daughter for more than a day.

Beth looked at her wet-eyed mother and said, "It's okay, Mama. I know you and papa will be back soon. Besides, Grandpapa Gus said he's going to cook something special for me every day!"

Barbara smiled through her tears, dabbing her eyes with a handkerchief as Carl leaned over, hugged Beth, and gave her a kiss on the cheek.

"Good-by Papa," said Beth, "I'll miss you."

When the conductor began calling for them to board, Beth turned, took her grandparents' hands and began walking to the empty boarding house.

Barbara took a deep breath and said, "I knew that it would be hard. I'll be fine, now, but it was harder than I expected."

Carl said, "She'll be really excited to see you again when we return."

Barbara then smiled at him and replied, "She'll be excited to see both of her parents."

———

An hour and a half later, the train was pulling into Cheyenne, but the trunk continued on to Denver as Carl carried their bags from the depot. They dropped them at the hotel desk, telling them they would be checking in that afternoon.

ROCK CREEK

After spending the rest of the morning walking the streets of Cheyenne, they had lunch at an elegant restaurant, then left with their arms locked together to return to the Metropolitan.

Carl gave his name to the desk clerk and was handed a key, and the clerk smiled broadly at them and told him that a boy would bring up their bags shortly.

"He seemed awful cheerful," Barbara remarked as they climbed the carpeted stairs, firmly holding onto Carl's arm.

"I have a feeling," said Carl, as he held out the room key, "that this is the reason for his behavior."

"What's so special about that key?" Barbara asked.

"You'll see," he replied with a smile.

When they reached the room, Carl swung the door open wide and Barbara froze and understood what he meant.

"Oh, my!" she exclaimed quietly as they slowly passed into the room.

It was Carl's first sight of the room as well, and he was in awe of the sumptuous decorations and furnishings.

"This, my love, is the Bridal Suite," he said.

She turned and looked in his eyes. There was a delayed response of a couple of seconds, then Barbara burst into laughter, before saying, "No wonder the desk clerk was smiling so much."

The porter found them standing there laughing and gave them a curious look, but after Carl tipped him well, he vanished with a big smile on his face and couldn't have cared if they had started tickling each other.

After closing the door, Carl gathered Barbara into his arms, kissed her deeply, then said, "I think this is more what the porter expected to see, rather than us laughing."

After he let her go, Barbara inspected the huge suite, eventually reaching the second door in the room. Barbara tentatively opened it, half expecting it to be another room with other guests, but as the door swung wide, she gasped.

"Carl, look at this!"

Carl glanced inside and saw an enormous bathroom with ornate tiles and a large tub with two faucets.

Barbara walked over and switched them both on and after a few seconds, the one on the left turned hot. She closed both faucets and slowly turned to face Carl.

"Do you mind if I take a bath? Just to warn you, though, I may be in there for a while."

"You go right ahead," Carl replied, smiling at his beautiful wife.

He handed her the bag containing her clothes which she placed on the tile and as she began to close the door, she purred, "I'll make the wait worth your while."

Carl spent a tortured thirty minutes wondering if he'd survive long enough for the door to open, and when it finally did, Carl was rendered speechless. Barbara stood before him wearing a beautiful silk gown, almost the same color as the dress he had picked out for her, but unlike the dress, she was wearing nothing underneath and he could almost see all of Barbara as it clung to her curved figure.

"That's not the night dress you usually wear," he said breathlessly.

"Would you want me to change?" she asked coyly.

"No," he answered softly before walking to her and taking her in his arms and feeling the same Barbara that he could see beneath the silk.

"I love you, Mrs. Ritter," he whispered.

"I love you, Mister Ritter. Now take me to our enormous bed and make love to me."

He didn't carry Barbara to the bed, but he didn't recall how he did get her to the soft mattress. How it happened didn't matter, but what happened most certainly did matter.

———

After leaving Cheyenne, the week in Denver went as quickly as expected, although neither could recall much of the city. They returned to Pine Bluffs on the evening train on the 9th of October and Carl could see Gus and Bernadette with Beth standing between them waiting on the platform before the train stopped.

Barbara was first to get off the train, rushing to scoop up Beth while Carl stepped down carrying the two bags. Everyone was smiling from ear to ear, when they returned to the boarding house and then entered the sitting room. Just a minute later, Carl heard the trunk thump down on the porch, went out to tip the porter, then carried the trunk into the house, leaving it in the foyer before returning to the sitting room.

As soon as Carl entered, Gus quieted everyone down and said, "Mister and Mrs. Ritter, welcome home. I may have some good news for you."

Carl and Barbara looked at him expectantly as he said, "I believe we have found a buyer for your house, Barbara. A couple has just arrived to settle here and is looking for a home. I heard about them from the sheriff and contacted them right away. They came by two days ago and were very interested in your house. I think they are going to offer you eight hundred dollars, but I told them that the decision was up to you."

"I paid six hundred and fifty dollars for it seven years ago," said Barbara, "so I think that would be fair. I'll talk to them about it tomorrow."

"One thing I forgot to mention about the gentleman is that he came here because he heard that the town had a vacant barber shop that he could buy at a good price. He's a barber himself."

That had its expected effect on both Carl and Barbara as they both broke into laughter. Talk about irony!

———

Three days later the deal was finalized for eight hundred dollars, then they took the bank draft and put it in an envelope with Carl's draft from the Union Pacific and would deposit them after they set up a joint account in Omaha. Then they could transfer the balance of Carl's Kansas City account as well.

———

Two days later, they were on the train platform again to bid a cheerful farewell to Carl's parents, who promised to come and visit them in Omaha soon, and just as it had been when the

Wilsons departed, there was a sadness when they left, but there was still a lot to do, so it didn't last long.

They had freighters come the next day to pack the items that they would be taking with them, but most of the furnishings stayed. They'd buy what they needed in Omaha.

The day after everything had been packed everything, Carl, Barbara and Beth boarded the evening train going east toward their new home and Carl had telegraphed Tom and Emily to let them know of their pending arrival.

———

The train pulled into the massive Omaha Union Pacific station at 10:15 in the morning and Tom and Emily were waiting on the platform to greet them after their long train trip.

After their normal greeting, Tom wasted no time, saying, "The head of engineering is anxious to meet you and expects you to be on the job next Monday."

"Hold up a bit there, Tom," said Carl, "I'll need to talk salary, job duties, and all that stuff, and I need some time to do some house hunting and to settle in before I can go to work."

"I know," laughed Tom, "I'm just letting you know how excited they were to have you join them. You know, if you do choose to work with us, I really do get a recruiting bonus."

"Then let's get this ball rolling," Carl said as he took Beth's right hand and Barbara took her left.

The conversation was animated as Tom led them to a waiting carriage. After boarding, Tom asked, "Out of curiosity, what did you do with Jules?"

"I gave him to Ethan," said Carl with a tinge of guilt, "I couldn't bring myself to sell him. I knew that Ethan would take care of him as well as I did, so that was my best option."

The carriage arrived at a beautiful brick home with gas lighting outside the walkway. Tom and Emily escorted them up the four brick steps to the magnificent oak porch, took out a key and unlocked the door.

Carl and Barbara were mesmerized by the intricate woodwork, the rich carpeting, and the glimmering hardwood flooring. There were gas lamps throughout the house, illuminating the beautifully furnished rooms.

Beth wandered wide-eyed through each room.

"Wow!" Carl exclaimed, "You have an incredible home, Tom."

Emily had a grin on her face as Tom smiled and said, "No, Carl, this is your home, not mine."

Carl was speechless as he turned to Barbara, who wasn't doing any better, then looked back to Tom.

Finally, Carl stammered, *"How...what...how?"*

Tom, his smile growing even bigger, explained, "It's a wedding gift from your mother and father. I happened to know that one of our senior vice presidents was retiring and moving to Baltimore. Your parents had told me to keep an eye out for a nice house for you, so when I heard he was leaving, I asked if he'd be willing to sell. I've been in this house many times, as we live three houses down across the street, and knew it was a wonderful place. He was happy to sell it without having to go through the pain of using agents, so I got it for a great price. So, welcome home."

He handed them the key, and Carl accepted it with a shaking hand. He still couldn't come up with anything to say, but Barbara crossed over to Emily and hugged her. Both women were smiling and crying at the same time, knowing that they'd be neighbors for a long time.

Tom leaned over to Carl and whispered, "You'd better get used to the tears when Barbara gets pregnant. It happens all the time with Emily now."

Carl shook Tom's hand, saying, "Thanks, Tom. No friend could do anything more. You've made me and Barbara very happy."

Tom turned to Emily and said, "Emily, let's go home and let them explore their new home."

Then he turned back to Carl and continued, "We'll be back in a few hours to bring you over to our house for dinner. There's plenty in the pantry for your lunch."

With the Ritters still speechless, the Wilsons stepped through the front door with a wave.

After they'd gone, Barbara, Carl and Beth set about exploring their new home, finding every room a revelation. The house had steam heat with a coal furnace, and just like the bridal suite, it had running hot and cold water. It even had water closets in the three bathrooms. Three!

The kitchen was enormous, and Barbara noted that the previous owner had left a complete set of beautiful china and as she opened the drawers, she found two sets of flatware. There was glassware and cooking utensils as well and none looked as though they had been used even once.

Beth was exploring the upstairs and claimed one bedroom as her own.

Barbara was in heaven. Just three months ago she had been a single mother raising her daughter and struggling to make ends meet. She had been alone, so very alone. Now, she had a husband she loved deeply, a husband who loved her and Beth as much as she did. They had beautiful clothes and now this gorgeous house. She was overwhelmed as she stood in the kitchen and clenched her hands in front of her face. Through her misty eyes she focused on the diamond and sapphire ring on her finger next to her wedding band and began to cry. The tears were running down her face, trickling down onto her dress and she made no effort to stop them or to wipe them away. Never in her life could she imagine such happiness.

Then she felt two strong hands on her shoulders, turned slowly and let her eyes find her husband's.

This was what life should be. It was all it could be and so much more and as Carl's eyes smiled at her, Barbara knew that she'd never know another day without love.

EPILOGUE

Cape Cod, Massachusetts

Carl stretched out on his makeshift couch in the sand and watched Barbara guiding little Tommy as he toddled along the beach waiting for the cold Atlantic water to nip at his toes. Beth was already sitting in the shallow edge of the ocean, then turned and saw him looking at her and waved. She had fallen in love with the ocean.

The previous evening the Ritters and Wilsons had dined on lobster and clams, and Beth had not been impressed, so she settled on a hot dog, which she devoured with a passion.

But it was the ocean they had come to see, and they were not disappointed. The clean smell of the breeze and the rhythmic shush of the waves breaking on the sand enchanted adult and child alike.

Tom and Emily laid in hammocks nearby, their small daughter Rebecca playing in the sand. This was the first vacation Carl and his family had enjoyed in three years but had insisted on this one because he knew that he needed to fulfill his promise to Beth.

Tom leaned over to Carl and said, "So, Carl, I hear you're planning on opening your own engineering firm."

"I've been thinking along those lines. I feel that I need to diversify my designs. I'd hate to spend the rest of my days working on bridges and trestles."

"Well, when you do, let me know. I may want to join you. I know I'm not an engineer, but I can handle the logistics and business side."

"You know that you'll be the first one I tell when I make the decision, after Barbara and the children, of course. And if it looks promising, you'll be the first one I'll bring on board."

Barbara brought Tommy with her and sat down next to Carl.

"Are you two talking business again?" she asked.

"Not really. Tom was asking whether I was going to start my own engineering firm."

"I'll always support you," she said with a smile, "no matter what decision you make."

He looked across at her. She was still just as beautiful that first day he had seen her standing in the aisle at Jensen's. He reached over and took her hand, the sun glimmering off her engagement ring.

"You know," he said to her, "one of the advantages of being your own boss is that you don't have to wait three years between vacations. In fact, I'd like to take another one next year. I'm thinking about visiting the Grand Canyon and there's a sunset there that I'd like to share with you."

ROCK CREEK

1	Rock Creek	12/26/2016
2	North of Denton	01/02/2017
3	Fort Selden	01/07/2017
4	Scotts Bluff	01/14/2017
5	South of Denver	01/22/2017
6	Miles City	01/28/2017
7	Hopewell	02/04/2017
8	Nueva Luz	02/12/2017
9	The Witch of Dakota	02/19/2017
10	Baker City	03/13/2017
11	The Gun Smith	03/21/2017
12	Gus	03/24/2017
13	Wilmore	04/06/2017
14	Mister Thor	04/20/2017
15	Nora	04/26/2017
16	Max	05/09/2017
17	Hunting Pearl	05/14/2017
18	Bessie	05/25/2017
19	The Last Four	05/29/2017
20	Zack	06/12/2017
21	Finding Bucky	06/21/2017
22	The Debt	06/30/2017
23	The Scalawags	07/11/2017
24	The Stampede	07/20/2017
25	The Wake of the Bertrand	07/31/2017
26	Cole	08/09/2017
27	Luke	09/05/2017
28	The Eclipse	09/21/2017
29	A.J. Smith	10/03/2017
30	Slow John	11/05/2017
31	The Second Star	11/15/2017
32	Tate	12/03/2017

33	Virgil's Herd	12/14/2017
34	Marsh's Valley	01/01/2018
35	Alex Paine	01/18/2018
36	Ben Gray	02/05/2018
37	War Adams	03/05/2018
38	Mac's Cabin	03/21/2018
39	Will Scott	04/13/2018
40	Sheriff Joe	04/22/2018
41	Chance	05/17/2018
42	Doc Holt	06/17/2018
43	Ted Shepard	07/13/2018
44	Haven	07/30/2018
45	Sam's County	08/15/2018
46	Matt Dunne	09/10/2018
47	Conn Jackson	10/05/2018
48	Gabe Owens	10/27/2018
49	Abandoned	11/19/2018
50	Retribution	12/21/2018
51	Inevitable	02/04/2019
52	Scandal in Topeka	03/18/2019
53	Return to Hardeman County	04/10/2019
54	Deception	06/02/2019
55	The Silver Widows	06/27/2019
56	Hitch	08/21/2019
57	Dylan's Journey	09/10/2019
58	Bryn's War	11/06/2019
59	Huw's Legacy	11/30/2019
60	Lynn's Search	12/22/2019

Made in the USA
Coppell, TX
07 December 2020